ALL IN

TROPHY DOMS NEW YORK #1

KATE HAWTHORNE

ALL IN

KATE HAWTHORNE

All In
Trophy Doms New York #1
by Kate Hawthorne

Copyright © 2024
Kate Hawthorne

Edited by | Jordan Buchanan

Cover Design | Amai Designs

DEDICATION

For everyone who knew five millionaires would never be enough.

CHAPTER 1
KALE

MY TWIN BROTHER, BOSTON, AND I WERE ON 5TH AVENUE IN FRONT of the French Consulate talking about how many carrots our parents had sent with their last unwanted CSA shipment when I caught the first gust of a fall breeze in New York. Shivering, I gave a little wiggle of my shoulders and tossed the long end of my scarf around my neck to keep my throat warm.

"It's cold," Boston groaned.

I threw a sidelong glance at him, dressed down from work with a pair of dark gray slacks and a pale pink button-up. He had on a tie, the knot loosened, and if he'd started with a jacket, I couldn't tell you where it was now.

"And you made fun of me for this." I smacked him in the face with the ends of my cashmere scarf, also a present from our parents, but I'd lost track of when it had arrived at my brownstone. Maybe the winter before? Or spring? I didn't have the best sense of time because I was always busy and days bled into each other with no real separation or distinction.

"It was eighty earlier today," he said.

"And it's October."

He folded his arms in front of his chest and tipped his head back, most likely cursing the height of the buildings around us, the French flag whipping around in the breeze above us.

"Anyway." I was warm. "You were saying about the carrots."

"Like a hundred carrots, Kale." He threw his arms up, quickly returning them to his chest after another gust blew past us. "What am I supposed to do with that many carrots?"

"Maybe if you ate them, you could stop wearing your glasses."

He glared at me, pushing the thick black-rimmed frames up his nose. "You know that's not even a real thing, right?"

"Isn't it?"

"Beta-carotene is good for your eyes, but it was some WWII propaganda that got out of control," he said.

"Well." I wrapped my scarf a little tighter around my neck. "Stew or something."

"Do I strike you as the stew type? When was the last time you had stew?"

"I'm not a fan. I don't even like soup."

Boston snorted, rolling his eyes. "Gazpacho is soup."

"I don't know how to help you," I told him, "My box had pumpkins. Enough to start my own patch."

Boston let out a hearty laugh at that. "What are you going to do with them?"

"Donate them, probably."

"You could make a pie," he suggested.

"I could make a thousand pies with the volume of pumpkins currently sitting in my pantry."

Our parents were hippies in the best sense of the word. And the life my brother and I had built for ourselves couldn't have been any more different than what our parents had chosen. The money came from our paternal line, with roots and bank deposits settled deep in the city since the first high-rise buildings had gone up.

Our father had bucked tradition, though. And after finding himself in California for undergrad, he'd met our mom. She was a free spirit from the Bay Area with a degree in agriculture and a wild dream to chase. She was older than him by almost ten years and, as they told the story, it was love at first sight. Our grandparents had not been her number one fans, but dad had stars in his eyes and there was no stopping him.

Boston and I were both born in California, but farm life never appealed to us. Dad had always made sure we knew there were other opportunities available, even if they weren't things our parents wanted for themselves. When it was time to start Junior High, Boston and I both hitched a ride—that's a figure of speech, we actually flew first class on grandpa's dime—to a New York boys' school and never looked back.

I mean, we did look back. We visited our parents at least once a year since there was no way in hell they'd ever come to New York, and they made sure we always received care packages with whatever the commune had decided to provide. Hence the carrots and the pumpkins, and the scarf.

After high school, I'd gone to California for college because I was nothing if not rebellious, and I liked to keep my grandparents guessing as to where I'd end up. Boston stayed on the

East Coast, but I'd known long before I graduated that the beach life L.A. offered was not for me. I longed for the massive concrete and glass towers of the city, for the winter, and for the sense of home I'd always found with my grandparents. Even though California had brought me one of my closest friends, Beamer, by the time I earned my diploma, I was ready to go *home*.

My grandparents set me up with a brownstone on Madison Ave, got me a job, and I'd been ready to go. They'd offered me a cushion so soft it fluffed all the rebellion right out of me, at least it had.

I couldn't tell you how Beamer and I met Brooks and Alex, but it was probably at a hotel bar, and as they say...

The rest was history.

I apparently had a little bit of rebellion left in me after all, though, and it earned me a membership at New York's most exclusive sex and kink club—The Black Door. Grandma and Grandpa didn't know about that one, of course.

Neither did Boston.

My journey into kink had been unexpected, but welcome, and I sometimes wondered how it had taken me so long to find it. Boston and I had been sort of late bloomers coming into boarding school because life on a farm in northern California was obviously nothing like the sturdy brick walls we found ourselves in after the move. But those boys and their old money worked fast. I'd known before our first winter break that I liked telling people what to do and, even better, there were people who liked to be told.

Admittedly, I'd come into dominance almost as a bully. But there hadn't been another way to adapt to the abrupt changes in our lives. While Boston and I had both welcomed boarding school and a life in the city, it was different and we were surrounded by boys who'd spent their entire childhoods prepping for something we'd only just been thrown into. I was a fast learner, though. And before I knew it, William would carry my books to class and Tim was doing my homework, and none of it had come from a place of fear.

It was reverence.

Boston thought I was being mean, but it couldn't have been any further from the truth. Back then, I didn't have a name for how I was or how I treated people...how they *wanted* me to treat them. It was simply a part of my personality and I'd always been a take-or-leave-it kind of guy. I carried that with me into adulthood, and my friends either adapted or they left.

Just like my partners.

"Did you want to get a hot dog?" Boston asked.

My eyes went wide at the sound of his voice because I'd gotten so lost in my head, I'd forgotten he was there. We'd walked well past the consulate and his building was to our right and a shortcut into Central Park on the left.

"I don't think I've ever had a hot dog in my whole life," I said.

"No stew and no hot dogs?" Boston scoffed at me.

I gestured behind me, toward Columbus Circle at the far corner of the park. "Per Se is right there. There's hundreds of fine dining establishments in this city and you want to pop across the street for a fucking hot dog?

"Or a gyro." He grinned at me, head bobbling from side to side.

I wanted to smack him in the mouth, but I loved him too much.

"You must have had a hot dog," he said.

I shook my head.

"You're missing out."

"If you say so." I crooked my finger into the scarf looped around my neck and loosened it a smidge. "But no, I'm not interested in sharing street food with you tonight. If you want to have a decent meal, I'd be happy to oblige."

"The gyro is decent."

"You're a heathen."

"You're classist," he countered.

I sighed, shaking my head and giving Boston a dismissive wave.

"Enjoy your processed meat trimmings, Boston."

"Enjoy your pumpkins!" he hollered.

I flipped him off before letting my arm fall and tucking my hand into the pocket of my pea coat. Fall was definitely coming on quickly, and as the sun dipped down below the skyscrapers of the city, all the warmth of the day fell toward dusk. As I headed away from Boston's apartment and toward my own home, my phone vibrated against my chest. Reaching into the interior pocket of my coat, I pulled it out to find a decent volume of unread text messages, the most recent being from Beamer.

It was a photo of him on the beach, his blond hair almost the same color as the sand. He looked relaxed and happy, and I couldn't help but think about how funny it was...the way California life suited some, but not others. It had only been a matter of months since he'd moved across the country with his husband, Dalton, and I honestly missed him terribly.

Dalton and I had not gotten off on the right foot, and I wouldn't say Beamer and Dalton had left with us on the right foot yet either. We'd reached some tepid kind of truce, which was all Beamer had hoped for and pretty much all I was able to offer. Because I couldn't help the way I was, or if I could, I didn't want to. I would never apologize for being controlling and protective. It was as much a part of my personality as my unbridled ambition or my gross mistrust of people who said calculus was simple.

I snapped a picture of myself, scarf and pea coat in clear view, and sent it back to Beamer. He responded with a cry laughing emoji. I told him I missed him, and he said the same. That was enough of that, because if I thought too long about it, I would get emotional over it, and I tolerated having feelings about as much as I tolerated collegiate math.

I also had an unread message from Ford, which riled an entirely different kind of feeling inside of me.

Ford: Black Door?
Me: It's a Wednesday
Ford: BLACK DOOR?
Me: I need to eat first.
Ford: Brooks and I will meet you.
Me: I wanted to enjoy my meal.
Ford: I meant at The Black Door, but now you make me want to find you and ruin your dinner.

I turned off friend finder and sent him a middle finger emoji.

Thinking of the duality that existed for Boston, eating what had to be fake meat that cost pennies to make on the elevator ride up to his multi-million dollar apartment was enough to send me right into a small Italian restaurant that didn't have a name over the door. The restaurant was small and modern, with those flower vases that only held a single stem flower in the center of every white cloth-covered table. There was a small bar against the back wall, with mirror-backed shelves of decent enough looking alcohol that I decided I'd be able to find a passable meal and a strong enough martini.

"Can I eat at the bar?" I asked the bartender as I settled onto one of the low-backed leather stools.

"If you like," he answered.

I bit the tip of my tongue to swallow back the first condescending thought that popped into my mind at his answer. Instead I forced a smile and unwound my scarf from my neck. Shrugging out of my coat, I laid both garments on the chair beside me, averting my gaze when he slid a paper menu in front of me.

"Do you have Nolet?"

"We do."

"Martini, then," I said, giving the menu a fast glance. "Please and thank you. Also the caponata."

"Wet?" he asked, bottle of Nolet already in hand.

"Dry."

"Shaken?"

I arched a brow, my lips quirking up in the corner against my will. "Thrown."

The bartender locked his stare onto mine, eyes nearly as green as the bottle of gin in his hand.

"Coming right up," he murmured, eyes still searching me out through the dark fan of his lashes. His chin was tucked against his chest, a clear sign that he knew I was reading correctly.

My cock stirred—the eye contact, the posture, *and* the commentary clearly a challenge. I licked my lips, waiting for him to get started and hoping that Ford and Brooks would be okay on their own for a while because dinner was shaping up to be far more engaging than I'd initially expected.

CHAPTER 2

CHRISTIAN

I ALWAYS IMAGINED SNEAKING OUT WAS SOMETHING MEANT FOR children and rebellious teenagers, but I was well into my twenties and I hadn't been able to give it up yet. It was the curse of living with my parents and their security detail, I justified to myself every time I managed to give the lot of them the slip. It was also the byproduct of being a prince, but I was the third spare, which made me eleventh in line at the rate my older siblings were popping out kids of their own, and I didn't really see the need to keep such a tight rein on me.

My parents, of course, disagreed.

That was how I found myself at a ballet in New York City in the middle of October, when I should have been home hooking up with my best friend, Parrish. Parrish and I had practically grown up together, always under my father's foot since Parrish's father was my father's most trusted advisor. We'd gone to the same boarding schools, played the same sports, and both returned home after University.

Unfortunately, I was royalty and Parrish wasn't, which meant he was allowed to get his own apartment—in the city, no less—while I was forced to stay home. In hindsight, I prob-ably would have been able to venture out more, but I'd been pushing boundaries my entire life, resulting in the leash getting drawn tighter on me than my siblings or their children.

Home was a sprawling castle estate and I had my own set of apartments that didn't even share a foundation, let alone a wall with my parents or any of my older siblings, but the secu-rity that came with being a royal was heavy-handed and far reaching. When Parrish and I were away at school together, we'd both perfected sneaking out of windows and climbing down trellises, skills I still employed at least once a week when we were home.

But I was in New York with my oldest brother, his wife, and their three children because I'd gotten caught on a cell phone camera with a cock in my mouth at a bar outside the city, and that hadn't gone over well. At all. Parrish's father, of course, managed to get the pictures scrubbed from the inter-net, but it had admittedly been a close call. It was careless of me, but we'd had an argument over my desire to move in with Parrish and tensions were higher than high by the time my parents dismissed me back to my apartments. The problem was every time they restricted me, it caused me to act out *worse* the next time. We'd found ourselves in an annoying cycle of tight restraints followed by more brash escapes, ad nauseam.

To be fair, though, living in a castle wasn't all shit. Neither was being a prince, but it made having a social life insuffer-ably hard sometimes. There were about a thousand things Parrish had done that I'd only dreamed of, and about a hundred more I'd never even dared to imagine. And it wasn't like I lived under lock and key. I had my own car and I had the liberty to come and go mostly as I pleased, but always with security, and always after having my itinerary reviewed and cleared.

There was no spontaneity in being a prince, and that was beyond miserable. It was privileged to complain about the consistency of my life—I knew that. But I yearned for new experiences and new people. Parrish kept me stocked up with stories and pictures of his escapades, but as the divide between us deepened, I understood it was only a matter of time until our friendship was fully severed.

"Christian," my brother Philip whispered at me, his hand raised to shield his mouth.

I lifted my eyebrows, angling my head toward him while doing my best to keep my eyes on the performance. "Hmn?"

"You're not paying attention. People are watching."

I made a show of slowly and dramatically turning my head away from the stage, swiveling it a full ninety degrees to look him head on. "Aren't I?"

"You're a million miles away," he said.

"How would you know?" I asked under my breath. "Unless *you're* not watching the show either?"

Philip muttered something at me, and I stood up, quickly buttoning my jacket. One of my knees cracked, and I gave my brother a dismissive wave.

"Going to piss, you bothersome asshole," I said.

He rolled his eyes and turned his attention back to the stage, even though I could tell by the glaze on his eyes he wasn't paying attention either. There wasn't anything wrong with ballet, or opera, or stage performance at all. It was just... we'd both seen them all. I'm certain that was an overstatement to some degree, but the sentiment rang true. To me, ballet was ballet, whether it was American or Russian or in any other country that felt like holding women to such an insane physical form was reasonable.

We didn't have a professional ballet company in our country.

Slipping out of the box, I stumbled right over Philip's head of security, who was standing far too close to the door of our box for anyone's comfort.

"Your Royal Highness."

"Bathroom," I said, a curt answer to his unspoken question.

He pointed to one of the other men standing guard, and my shoulders deflated at the assignment. Niko was new to the detail, and he was beyond diligent about our level of care. Part of me wondered if he'd been assigned specifically to keep an eye on me while we were abroad, but I also didn't want to take credit where it wasn't due.

"Did you want to come hold it for me, Niko?"

He pursed his lips. "No, thank you, Sir."

I brushed past him and down a flight of red velvet-carpeted stairs until I reached the mezzanine...and the bar. I did have to take a piss, I also needed to get away from Philip, and more urgently, ditch Niko, but first...

He was right on my tail, so I detoured to the bar and gave a little wave to the bartender, calling him over with the crook of my pointer finger.

"French 75," I ordered, turning to Niko. "You'll hold *that* for me at least, won't you?"

Before he could answer one way or the other, I slipped into the bathroom, letting out a tired breath when I saw an older man sitting just inside the door beside the impressive array of towels, mouthwash, and other various toiletries.

"A hundred dollars if you lock the door until I'm finished in here," I offered.

The corner of his mouth quirked and he angled his head toward the tip jar, which was overstuffed with far beyond a hundred dollars already.

"I'll double that," I tried, pointing at the jar.

He flipped the lock on the door and I braced myself against the counter. Letting my chin drop toward my chest, I tried to come up with a plan of attack. Or, rather, a plan for escape. The thing I hated the most about New York was the obscene lack of windows that actually opened because everything was built so close together. Not to mention how tall all the buildings were, so even if there had been a window that opened, escape would have been treacherous at best.

"Is there another way out of here besides that door?" I asked.

There had to be, if for no other reason that places like this tended to do everything they could to keep the help separate from their paying guests.

"There's an employee door, sir," he answered, gesturing over his shoulder to a cutout in the wall that I wouldn't have even noticed if he hadn't shown it to me.

Looking up at my reflection in the mirror, I picked at the edge of my royal order with my fingernail. I couldn't ditch all the ridiculous pageantry of my outfit without bringing hell down after the fact, which I did try to avoid, but it would make blending into a city of millions that much harder. I'd just have to make it out quick enough to get a decent head start before Niko realized he was babysitting a drink and not me. I loosened the knot on my bow tie and popped the top button of my shirt undone. Hopefully that would be enough to blend me in to put some distance between us.

The attendant watched me curiously, his eyes barely even widening when I fished my money clip out of my pants. The money—and my access to it—had been another knockdown, drag-out fight with my father, but one of few that I actually won. There was no need, he'd said, for me to have American dollars on the trip, as I wasn't meant to be without security or my brother at any given time. I assured him I had no plans on sleeping in bed between Philip and Liz, nor their three children, and thankfully my mother had calmed him down and brought him around to reason.

I had tucked ten hundred dollar bills while getting ready for the ballet, and I pulled out five of them. Making sure the attendant saw them all, I dropped the fold in the tip jar and pointed at the hidden door behind him.

"How do I get out of here?"

"Down and to the left there's a freight elevator. You can take it to the lobby or the garage."

"Where does the lobby let out?" I asked.

"The office."

"And the garage?"

"The garage," he confirmed. "But the code to get down is one-nine-three-two."

Returning my money clip to its home, I unpinned my royal order and folded it in on itself before tucking it into the inside pocket of my jacket.

"Down to the left," I repeated. "One-nine-three-two to the garage."

"You'll be right off Fifth Avenue."

"Your Royal Highness?" Niko's voice echoed through the closed bathroom door, the knob rattling against its lock, but not giving so much as a budge. "Is everything all right?"

"Quite, Niko," I called out. "Are you still holding that drink for me?"

"Please open the door, sir."

"I'm about to."

The attendant stepped out of the way, and I kept my word, opening the hidden door that led me into a brightly lit and industrial-looking hallway. It was more like a tunnel, but much like trellises and towers, tunnels I could do.

"*Thank you*," I mouthed, holding my hands together like a prayer before slipping into the hallway and pulling the door closed behind me. I heard Niko's frustration mount as the door refused to open, and then I was off in a sprint for the elevator.

He'd caught on a lot sooner than I'd expected because, while he was attentive, he was also one for protocol, which meant he hated to speak first and interfere. I stabbed the down button on the elevator panel, imagining the frustrated look that would flash across his face as soon as he realized I'd given him the slip.

I rubbed the pad of my thumb against my first and second fingertips, a nervous habit, but a quiet one, while I waited for the ancient elevator to reach my level. The car sounded like it was going to groan itself to death as it settled on the floor, and I wondered how everyone on the stage and in the audience didn't hear the grinding gears.

The door slid open, and three men stepped out, one of them dressed like the bathroom attendant and the other two like the theater's own security. I was quick to look down and cover my face, side-stepping past them into the elevator and madly pressing the button for the garage. The light wouldn't keep, and I remembered the code, which I quickly entered before giving the garage button one more try.

One of the guard's radios crackled to life, a calm woman's voice coming out of the speaker.

"We have a situation," she said.

God, this elevator was slow. The doors closed at a snail's pace, and I looked up just in time to lock eyes with the guard holding the radio.

"What's going on?" he asked.

He registered my clothes first, and I was thankful I'd taken the time to hide away my royal order, or he would've caught on to who I was far faster than he did. Out of instinct, I patted my pocket to check that it hadn't fallen out. There was maybe six inches left for the doors to close.

"Prince Christian is missing."

The guard's eyes flashed, and I gave him a quick smile as the doors finally slid closed. I knew it was going to be all downhill from there, and I would be lucky to make it out of the garage considering how slow the elevator moved. But when it reached the garage and opened up to emptiness, I knew I'd gotten lucky. I wasn't arrogant enough to think it would last, though, so I didn't hesitate to dart out as soon as the door opening was wide enough to accommodate my frame.

My footsteps echoed off the walls as I sprinted for the pedestrian exit onto Fifth Avenue. I heard Niko's voice from somewhere behind me, but I wasn't going to stop and double-check to make sure it was him. I did make a note that he was faster and more resourceful than I'd originally given him credit for, because it took me what felt like a year to get to the garage and he'd managed it in half the time.

"Christian!" He shouted my given name, which meant I was very much in trouble, but I shoved the heavy metal door open and sucked in a disgusting breath of city sewer air that tasted enough like freedom that I wasn't ready to give up.

The sidewalk was bustling with people going in every direction, and my first instinct was to go right, so instead I spun left and took off down the street, a wide and satisfied smile on my face.

THE BARTENDER TOLD ME HIS NAME WAS AXEL. IT WAS ADMITTEDLY A name I couldn't imagine myself moaning in *any* circumstance, but I played a few scenarios out in my head to see if I could make it work.

That's right, Axel, breathe through your nose. Just like that, Axel. You swallow cum like you were made for it, Axel. Sssh, sssh. Quiet down and take my cock, Axel.

Half turned off, but not ready to give up, I finished my caponata and took the last swallow of my second drink of the night. I was feeling loose enough to call him "baby" so I could take him to bed without having to use his name, but he wasn't off work until two, and Brooks and Ford hadn't stopped texting me since I sat down in the first place.

"Can I get my check?" I asked, sliding my glass toward his side of the bar.

His waxed eyebrows knit together for a flash, and then settled back in place. "Sure," he said.

"You didn't misread the situation," I assured him, pulling my credit card out of my wallet and dropping it down on the bar beside my drink. "I just have annoying friends and previous obligations."

His expression softened—marginally—and he turned around to run my card. Axel was definitely attractive enough to be baby for a night, and he shimmied his hips side to side like he was dancing to a song I couldn't hear. He knew what he was doing. He knew *I* knew what he was doing, and worse...he knew it was working.

He turned around, pert ass hugged by the tight black pants he wore, and he pushed my card and the receipt back to me with a pen.

"Do you sleep well?"

"Not often." I tipped him fifty percent and left him my phone number.

"I'll call you when I get off?" he asked.

I climbed off the stool and shrugged into my coat, winding the scarf around my neck while Axel focused steadily on my hands. The scarf smelled like dust and honey, and it reminded me of home in a sharp and unexpected way. Clearing my throat, I tucked the ends of the cashmere behind the lapels of my coat.

"Call me when you *want* to get off," I corrected.

His cheeks immediately darkened to a gorgeous peony shade of pink, and I smiled at him, turning to go. I texted Brooks and Ford to let them know I was on the way, but no sooner had I stepped onto the sidewalk that I found myself slammed against the wall. My breath left my lungs in a rush and my phone fell out of my hand, crashing onto the sidewalk after bouncing off my foot.

"What the fuck?" I shoved away my attacker, and he stumbled back, eyes wide and face flushed.

"Sorry," he said quickly. His voice was laced with a hint of an accent I couldn't quite make out, and he was dressed, or half-dressed rather, in a well-tailored tuxedo. He smelled like sweet champagne and spicy cologne, and he looked just as decadent. The man was admittedly so attractive I could prob-ably still call him Axel during sex and not lose my hard-on.

"Watch where you're going, maybe?" I suggested.

My phone was on the ground at my feet, screen up. Thankfully it survived the impact with nothing more than a hairline crack across the top right corner. I bent over and snatched the device, only for something bright and blue to catch my eye on the ground beside it. I reached for the scrap of fabric, when the man muttered something under his breath in a language I didn't understand.

There was shouting from down the street, and he bent over, slamming his shiny black shoe on top of the blue bundle, narrowly missing my finger.

"What is your fucking problem?" I asked.

He grabbed my shoulders and spun us both, pressing his back against the wall and my chest against his front.

"I'm sorry," he said again.

And then he kissed me.

I opened my mouth to protest, but he slid his tongue into my mouth and any argument I'd had about why I shouldn't be making out on the sidewalk with a man who'd just mowed me down disappeared like a morning fog. His hands relaxed around my arms and slid inward, dragging their way under my coat and over my chest. He pressed one of his knees up between my legs, groaning when he made contact with my cock and balls.

Loud and angry footsteps raced past behind us, and the

stranger kept kissing me until the street had fallen back into its usual hum of conversation and traffic. It was long enough for me to get my wits back, and I took his face into my hands, changing the angle of my mouth so I could deepen the kiss. He tasted like gin, or maybe that was me, and as soon as I shifted his head back so I could *really* kiss him, he once again shoved me.

This time, I stumbled back toward the street instead of toward the building, a little caught off-guard by the whole ordeal. I think most men would have—or should have—cried assault at the whole thing, but I'd never been most men. I was always down for a bit of fun, and kissing strangers was one of the tamest things I managed to do on troublesome nights.

The space gave me time to really take him in, from the sharp angle of his clavicle, exposed through the unbuttoned top of his shirt, to the slim taper of his hips further down. He bent to pick up the blue fabric that he'd stepped on, not even bothering to dust it off or unfold it before tucking it into the interior pocket on his jacket.

"Sorry," he said for a third time.

"You say that a lot."

"Thanks for the help."

The ache between my legs was a reminder that the only thing I'd done was make a problem for myself, and maybe I could go back inside and convince Axel to take a five minute break before I went to The Black Door so I didn't walk into a kink club guns a blazing, so to speak.

"Is that what that was?" I glanced in the direction the other men had run. "Are you being chased?"

"Collected, more like."

"Did you need help?"

I had no idea why I asked him that. I didn't know him from Adam—or Axel—and I definitely wasn't in the business of helping strangers in the city. Especially when I was half-hard and turned on beyond all comprehension. I wasn't a good man. I was selfish and I was sex-driven, and whatever had just happened shouldn't have been more than an annoying interference between me and my goal for the night.

"I don't need *help*." He said the word like it was acid in his mouth, that soft accent thickening with his anger.

"Duly noted." I slid my phone into my pocket and adjusted my scarf, which he'd brushed aside to touch my chest, and my pants, which were tenting and growing tight. Also because of him. "Best of luck, then. I'm running late and I have some-where to be."

Pivoting on the ball of my foot, I turned in the direction the men had come from and headed off toward The Black Door. It was a short walk, no more than four blocks, and I planned to count the steps the whole way to calm myself down before I got there. But I'd only made it one step when a hand wrapped around the back of my arm, just above my elbow.

"I may need help," the man said. "I'm a little out of my element here."

I stopped and he stepped up beside me. The color had dulled on his cheeks, but he still breathed heavily.

How far had he been running for?

"In the city?" I asked.

"In America."

"I thought I heard an accent."

"I don't have an accent," he snapped, mouth angling down into a miserable frown.

"And you don't need help." I repeated his comment from earlier. His argument about whether or not he had an accent —he did—only served to make my cock *harder*, which was the last thing I wanted. At least, in that very moment. Normally, I was a strong advocate for hard cocks and bratty attitudes. I found them to be a stellar pairing.

"I said I might."

"And I told you I'm late," I told him. "So unless you want your help to look like disguising yourself as a man who likes to be told what to do, you're unfortunately on your own."

I took another step, and he matched me, keeping pace as I walked toward the corner.

"Where?"

"Where what?"

"Where would I do that?" he asked.

I stopped to regard him. To honestly regard him for the first time, beyond taking in his appearance and his clothes. It was clear as day he came from money, the attitude spoke to that. He wasn't from here either, which should have been appealing. The whole encounter was something out of a movie, and I didn't quite trust it. Instead of answering him, I kept walking and he kept pace beside me.

"I wasn't hardly being serious," I said to him.

He made a frustrated noise, but kept walking, his whiskey-colored eyes scanning the crowd in front of us and behind us as we rounded the corner. He was on alert and this wasn't the first time he'd been on the run. I could tell a man who knew what he was doing, in anything, and this man knew how to evade whoever was chasing him. The taste of him on my tongue was still proof enough of that.

"What is your name?" he asked.

"Kale," I answered.

"I'm Christian," he offered, unprompted.

"You're trouble," I said.

He huffed out a laugh, mouth angling into a smile before falling back into a relatively straight line. As straight as his mouth could be, considering how plump his lips were. His mouth was shiny under the city lights, and I found myself wondering if he could still taste me the way I could taste him.

"Not that it matters, but why are those men after you?"

We'd reached another corner and we didn't have the right of way, but traffic was clear, so I stepped into the street just the same. Christian lingered back, but ran to catch up to me before I was halfway across. The street was less clear for him, and he narrowly managed to avoid getting pancaked by a taxi. Back on the sidewalk, I made another turn and he still followed after.

"I have places I'm supposed to be," he answered.

"And I assume none of those places is kissing a stranger in front of an Italian restaurant or walking to a sex club with him when you're done?"

His steps faltered, but he was quick to regain his composure. "A sex club?"

"Where else would you pretend to be a man who does what he's told?"

"Literally everywhere," he muttered.

By the time I had my answer, we were one building away from the unmarked entrance to my favorite place in the world. Lit by a single bulb over the aptly painted black door, there was no way to know what lay inside the walls unless you were already in the know.

My phone buzzed in my pocket, and I was relieved to find

out it still worked. I knew the message was from Ford without having to check it, and I threw a glance toward the door that marked my end destination for the night.

"I can't just take you in there," I said apologetically. "There are rules and expectations and secrets."

"I can keep a secret," Christian said.

"I'm sure you can, but you don't strike me as the type to follow rules."

A muffled shout from a few blocks down drew both of our attention. It was two of the men who'd been chasing after Christian in front of the restaurant. They ran, coming to a stop and looking around helplessly. They'd lost him, but I didn't think that would hold forever. The city blocks all looked the same, and the lot of them would run themselves in circles until they crashed back into each other. I didn't know why Christian was trying so hard to get away from them. I hadn't thought to ask and I didn't really think it mattered. He didn't seem the violent type, and if he were a thief, he would have grabbed my phone, not the blue ribbon that had fallen from his pocket. But with the scent of home in my nostrils, I did know what it was like to need to get away.

He rubbed both of his temples, again mumbling in a language I couldn't quite place, then he let out a long and tired sigh. Christian looked over his shoulder, and the two men after him split up. One turned back in the direction they'd come and the other headed straight for us. He hadn't seen Christian yet because he meandered more than jogged.

"If you get me in, I'll follow the rules," he said, letting his hands fall to his sides.

"It's non-negotiable," I told him. "If you don't, not only will I make sure you get thrown out, but I'll make it my mission to personally hand-deliver you to those men who are after you."

"You have a mean streak." He smiled when he said it, which did nothing to help the burning weight that had taken up residence in my balls.

"Yeah," I said, even though it was meant as a warning. "You have no idea."

CHAPTER 4

CHRISTIAN

Kale curled his fingers around my arm and ushered me into a nondescript building with an otherwise indistinct black door. He'd called it a sex club, and it was giving speakeasy, but either way, as the door latched closed behind us, I breathed a sigh of relief at avoiding Niko. Even if only temporarily. Inside the quiet foyer space, a man sat behind a desk, and he greeted Kale with a curt nod. "Mr. Sheffield."

"I have an unexpected guest," Kale said, tilting his head in my direction. "I hope that won't be an issue."

"Not for you, sir," the man behind the desk said before turning his attention toward me. "I'll just need to see some identification."

"I'd rather not."

"You're not even inside and you're already not listening?" Kale tutted his tongue against the roof of his mouth and something flared hot and sharp in my chest. "You can go, Christian."

"It's not that." I rolled my eyes and checked my pockets for my passport, which I wasn't even sure I had on me.

"I told you compliance was non-negotiable."

"You sound like my father." My fingers grazed over the well-worn pages of my passport, and I dropped it down on the desk, alongside the blue royal order ribbon.

The attendant's nostrils briefly flared, and he took the book and flipped it open. His jaw clenched and he was quick to flip it closed, sliding both items back in my direction. I tucked them both back into my jacket and raised a brow.

"Everything in order?"

"Quite. I want to also assure you that at The Black Door, we take the utmost care around confidentiality and privacy."

"I'd assume as much," I said.

"Mr. Sheffield," he said, turning to me next, "Yo—"

"Are we good, then?" I cut him off, not interested in the slightest about outing my royal title to Kale, or anyone for that matter. He'd seen the royal order at least half a dozen times since I'd run into him on the street, and if he hadn't bothered to put it together or ask questions to get the information, I wasn't going to press him on it. And judging by the very excitable and eager way he'd kissed me back on the sidewalk without so much as a hello-how-are-you, I didn't pin Kale as the kind of man who cared about names and titles so much as he cared about gag reflexes and stamina.

He cared about good listeners, though.

Unfortunately for him, I wasn't one of those.

"Jesus, you have a mouth on you," Kale muttered, exhaling at me, frustration clear on his face. His stare flickered over my shoulder toward the door and I knew he was *very* close to taking me outside and finding a way to deposit me right into Niko's waiting hands.

"I wish you were wrong about that, but you're not," I said

with playful shrug. "Sure you can find a way to shut me up, though. If you think real hard about it."

The corner of his tongue darted out of his mouth and he licked the corner of his lip, eyes narrowing in thought as he gave me a slow appraisal.

"Alright," he decided, gesturing toward the wall behind him that looked just like a wall and definitely not a secret door. It opened, and I was suddenly desperate to know why this city was so fascinated with hidden doors.

"Be my guest, then."

I tipped my head in thanks to the attendant, who knew when to stop talking, and I followed Kale through the opening in the wall and into a space that speared the opposite of a kinky sex club.

"This looks like a place rich men with too much time go to smoke cigars and get off," I said after taking a perfunctory glance around.

The room was narrow, like most of the residences in the city were, with lots of exposed brick and some well-placed frosted glass panels. There were clusters of overstuffed wing-backs and leather seats with small tables nestled between them, almost every seat taken by a man or a woman who looked like they knew exactly who they were and what they wanted. It was a sexy sight to behold—all that power and confidence in one place. To me, it felt like the antithesis of home, which was filled with so much posturing and pretend. Everyone in this room dripped with authenticity and—to varying degrees—arousal.

"There's no smoking inside," Kale said. "Did you want a drink?"

I scoffed. "I want to know what you were thinking, bringing me here."

He sucked his tongue across the front of his teeth, mouth pulled down into a frown. "I'm not sure," he said.

"That feels like a lie."

Kale huffed, then pointed toward the back wall of the room. "Drink first?"

"If you must."

I followed him through the room, navigating between the clusters of the tables and the random couples grinding against each other on a makeshift dance floor. The air smelled like wood and sweat, but not gym sweat.

The air smelled like sex.

When we reached the bar, I knew better than to look down and check on the state of my dick. I was undoubtedly well on my way to being hard if I wasn't hard already, and while I could fathom a guess as to what Kale had intended by bringing me here, I'd long ago learned not to make assumptions.

"You drink champagne?" he asked when we reached the bar.

"How did you know?"

Again his tongue in the corner of his mouth. "I could taste it on you," he murmured.

"French 75," I said.

The corner of his lip quirked, and all I could think about was kissing him again. I studied him in profile, the ridiculous swoop of his hair against his thin and angular features. Kale wasn't broad or stocky by any sense of the word. Instead he was tall, well over six feet, and slender enough that I worried if the only thing he ate was the lettuce he'd assumedly been named after. His cheekbones were slightly hollow, only accentuated by the light brown scruff that had started to grow in around them and along his jaw. Kale was also dressed well, from that thick wool pea coat and impossibly soft scarf down to the shined tips of his shoes. Beyond that, I could tell during our kiss that his pants fit him well because he filled them out enough where it mattered the most.

He turned, catching me mid perusal, eyes sparkling and clearly taking my stare as flattery. Passing me my drink, he didn't say a word, so I took the chance to repeat the question I'd already asked him, "What were you thinking?"

He sipped what looked like an Old Fashioned, studying me from beneath the dark fan of his lashes.

"I wasn't thinking at all," he said. "At least not with my brain."

I chuckled, tilting the rim of my glass against his. "I'll take that as a compliment."

"It was meant as one."

"So what did your smaller brain have to say about the situation?" I asked, glancing down at his cock before looking back into his eyes.

He held my stare as he answered, "That I should get you on your knees someplace dark and quiet so I don't miss out on how good you'd sound choking on my cock."

"What reaction does that line normally get you?"

"Someplace quiet and dark." Kale smirked, and I was quick to see the power and authority that lingered just beneath the surface of his demeanor. He was a rich man, of that I was sure. But he was also dominant and probably a little arrogant. He had a dry sense of humor and was sharp as a whip with the conversation, yet I couldn't help but wonder what all of that humor and wit hid.

"Do you often ask strangers to swallow your cum?"

"I don't care if they spit," he said, that teasing grin on his face growing wider.

I took a sip of my drink, finding it fresh and cold, just as I liked it.

"Do you often run into strangers on the street and kiss them to the point of distraction?" he asked.

"Distracted you, did I?"

"Coy isn't cute on you," he murmured.

"What is cute on me, then?"

His eyes widened infinitesimally, and that curious tongue of his traced its way across the bottom of his teeth. "I could think of a few things," he said.

"Well, we're amongst friends, Mr. Sheffield. Don't hold back."

I made a mental note to look him up when I got back to my hotel, and I would have Niko run a background check on him. Or I'd have Niko run a background check when he was done being mad at me for giving him the slip in the middle of the ballet.

"You across my lap, for one." He shuffled closer, lowering his voice. I could smell him again, like honey and citrus in the air around us. "Out of these pants with your ass in the air."

"What would you do with my ass in the air?" I whispered.

He curled his finger over the waistband of my pants, tugging at me and closing the rest of the space between us. My shoes scuffed against his and I was close enough to feel the hot rod of his erection branding my thigh through the wool of both our slacks.

"Spank it."

Kale tilted his head to the side, and I gave him no reaction to work from. If he believed anything he'd thought about doing to me was in any way going to shock and awe me, he was in for a sore disappointment.

"Is that all? That sounds rather…anti-climactic."

I made a show of licking my lips before taking another sip of my drink. If Kale wanted to play a game of innuendo, I was more than willing to oblige him.

"You've clearly never been spanked well if you think it wouldn't be enough to get you there."

"I've been spanked plenty, Kale."

"I preferred Mr. Sheffield," he murmured, leaning in just enough that I could smell the whiskey on his breath now mixed with the citrus and champagne in the space between us.

"I'm sure."

"What if I told you to call me that?" His voice was barely above a whisper, but somehow louder than a thunderclap. My pulse thrummed in my ears, and my vision narrowed in so precisely on the dark brown pools of his eyes that I had to brace myself against the bar so I didn't fall over.

"Well." I swallowed. "I did promise that I would be a good listener."

"Kiss me," he said.

He demanded.

I set my drink on the bar so I had free use of both of my hands, then I grabbed him by the lapels of his coat and crashed our mouths together. He managed to get his drink out of the way before our chests collided, and then one of his hands was firm against the back of my head, the other resolute around my waist. I was thankful for the dual support because standing wasn't any easier and breathing was about ten times harder.

Opening my mouth wider, Kale's tongue dipped into my mouth, swirling against mine like he was chasing after the taste of himself from the first kiss on the sidewalk. I tested his hold against me, pressing my head back into his hand, only for him to spread his fingers through my hair to keep our mouths sealed tightly together. I moaned, cock pulsing against my leg for how badly the move made me want him.

I'd spent my whole life fighting against authority and bucking against those who tried to control me, and now here was this man, this absolute stranger who talked about taking me over his knee and making me come from spanking alone? The whole idea was preposterous. Not just the orgasm, but him in general, my reaction to him.

I wasn't a blushing virgin, but my name and my status made it hard to find discerning partners. It was one thing to risk a blow job at a bar, another entirely to suggest that someone tie me up or hold me down. Pictures of that would be near impossible to come back from. Blindfolds had always been absolutely off the table, as were gags. Even as much as I liked to fight the limitations of what my family would allow me to get away with, there was only so much I could allow before things might go too far.

But that didn't mean I didn't want to.

That I didn't dream about it sometimes.

The freedom of it all.

Kale broke the kiss with a gasping breath, the brown of his eyes nearly obscured by the black depths of his pupils. His hands were still on me, against my waist and my head, and thank God for that because my knees felt like jello.

"You're extraordinarily sexy when you're obedient," he murmured, smiling against my mouth.

I'd been called a lot of things in my life, but extraordinary in *any* way had never been one of them. I found myself leaning into him, chasing after him. After more of the way his mouth and hands and words made me feel, after an end to the desperate ache between my legs and in my chest.

Kale may have tried to pretend he didn't have a nefarious intent in bringing me to a godforsaken kinky sex club to hide me from Niko, but I didn't believe that for a second. I wanted to see what he was like when he got his way, but more than that, I wanted to see how far he'd go to get it.

"Be that as it may…" I licked my lips and smiled, tasting him as I pulled my tongue back into my mouth. "I think I'm much more fun when I'm not."

NOT FOR THE FIRST TIME, I WONDERED IF I'D MET MY MATCH WITH Christian. With the taste of him still fresh and warm on my lips, I tried to catch a steadying breath and screw my head on straight. I had to start with the facts.

What were the facts?

Christian was on the run from someone, but he wasn't a criminal.

He wasn't from here.

He wouldn't be here for long.

I *really* liked when he called me Mr. Sheffield.

And if he fucked anywhere near as good as he kissed, I'd be ruined forever.

The last one was the problem because I desperately wanted to fuck him, but I didn't want to spend the rest of my life chasing after the same high and comparing every man who came after to the idea of him.

"What do you want?" I asked, finger still curled over the edge of his belt.

"Besides you?"

I huffed a breath out my nose. "Besides me."

"A place to hide for the night."

"And then?" I asked.

"Unfortunately, I can't run forever." He licked his lips and gave me an apologetic smile, almost completely counter to the attitude he'd carried up to that point.

"So, just for the night?"

Christian dragged his stare over my face and down my chest and back. "I don't have much of a choice," he said softly.

"Who are you hiding from?" I finally asked the question that I should have asked him back in front of the restaurant. "Why are those men chasing after you?"

"They're just doing their jobs."

"They aren't going to arrest me for aiding and abetting, are they?"

Christian chuckled, shaking his head. "Even if they could, I wouldn't let them."

"You have that kind of power over them?"

"I imagine so," he said.

"And yet you're still trying to hide from them?"

"It's complicated." Christian gave me a weak smile, then palmed my cock with his hand. The move was so unexpected I startled, nearly falling into him when the heat of his fingers registered in my brain.

"I'm not a fan of...complicated." I almost moaned at him, the way he cradled my dick in his hand good enough to erase any other thought I'd ever had that didn't involve getting both of us out of our clothes immediately.

"I assure you it's not anywhere near as bad as it sounds," he promised. "I've ditched them for the night and tomorrow

I'll deal with the fallout. You won't have to. So, what do you say?"

It was rare that I found myself on the answering end of a proposition. I didn't hate it. In fact, it did wonders for my self-esteem, but I needed to shift the balance of control back into my court. Through our conversation, I'd learned that Christian, wherever he was from, was a powerful man with a lot of pull over those around him. I should have asked where he was from. I knew there were more detailed and important answers to be had, but I didn't see the point. He'd be gone in the morning and none of the technicalities or specifics would matter.

With that thought in the front of my head, I knew there was no point in worrying about anything else. The only thing that mattered was getting us both out of the club and back to my place. I opened my mouth to tell him as much, but a warm body against my back had the words dead in my throat.

"There you are," Ford said, clapping his hand against my shoulder. "I was starting to think you'd forgotten about us."

"Not for lack of trying," I said to him with a smile.

Brooks and Ford were two of my best friends, and normally I loved spending a night at the club with them, but my fingers were still clutching Christian's belt and I was itching to get the damn strip of leather off of him. I wondered if he would let me spank him with it. God, thinking about the sound of leather cracking against his skin was enough to have my eyes rolling toward the back of my head.

He sensed my distraction and curled the fingers of one hand around my wrist and reached for his drink with the other.

"You didn't tell me you were meeting friends here," Christian said conversationally, raising his glass and taking a drink.

For his part, he looked utterly unaffected by the intrusion of my friends. Neither of them would know that Christian and I had been ready to get out of there and get into bed. He was good at pretending, at playing a part. I watched his eyes sparkle as he studied Ford and Brooks, sizing them up. It had been so long since I'd looked at either of them with new eyes, I wondered what he saw in them...in me.

But I nipped that in the bud because it was a dangerous train of thought to ride. The only thing Christian saw in me was a break from whatever he was running from. He saw me as a fun stop for the night, and that hadn't ever been a problem for me before, so why was the idea of it so annoying to me now?

"Yeah, Kale. You didn't tell me you were meeting friends here." Ford grinned and turned to face Christian. "I'm Ford and this is my friend Brooks."

"I'd shake your hand, but mine seem to be full," Christian said, tightening his grip around my wrist and yanking me impossibly closer. He took another drink from his glass and smiled at them.

"I believe you have us at a disadvantage," Brooks said, voice softer than Ford's had been. "I don't think I've seen you here before."

"You most certainly haven't," Christian responded.

"You do look familiar."

"Do I?" He poured the rest of his drink down his throat and smacked his lips with a satisfied groan. "I'm not from here."

"Where is your accent from?" Ford asked. "I can't place it."

"Not here."

I chuckled, almost impressed at Christian's evasive skills. Behind me, the tension rolled off Ford in waves, and it was impossible to not laugh at how frustrated the whole exchange was making him. With a flash of a memory and a frown, I wondered if this was how our other friend Beamer had felt when we'd all met his husband for the first time. We'd admittedly been less than kind. I'd been the worst offender, but it came from a place of protection and love. I cared fiercely for my friends and I didn't want to just hand them off to a stranger, and Beamer's whole affair with his husband, Dalton, had been...very out of character for him. Or so I'd thought. I was still bitter about losing him to California, but as I listened to Ford and Brooks try to hit Christian with twenty questions that didn't matter, I appreciated how much my own behavior had irritated Beamer. I'd have to apologize to him.

Again.

"Christian and I were just getting ready to leave," I said, mirroring his earlier action and finishing off my drink.

"But you just got here," Ford said.

"And I've accomplished my goal for the night." I gestured to Christian's tight grip around my wrist. "So there's no point in staying."

"You're no fun."

"That's yet to be seen," Christian said with a smile. "It's been lovely meeting the two of you, but..."

"This feels suspicious," Brooks observed, his tone still softer and less accusatory than Ford.

"It's all above board," I lied. It could have been the most upside down thing I'd ever done, but for some reason I trusted Christian when he said I'd get out of this whole thing alive. I still didn't think fucking him was going to be good for my mental health, but I'd never been good with the word no.

"We're going to discuss this tomorrow."

"We'll discuss whether we're going to discuss it." I set my empty glass on the bar beside Christian's and regretfully pulled my finger out of his pants. He relaxed his grip around my wrist, fingers spreading out and dancing down my palm like he was going to thread them through mine and hold my hand, but he stopped at the last second, taking his hand and tucking it into the pocket of his slacks.

"Gentlemen." Christian gestured with his pointer finger away from his forehead, a symbolic tip of the cap that had Brooks breathing out a laugh and Ford muttering a curse.

"I can't wait to hear about the rest of your night," I told them both, stepping away from the bar. Christian followed after me, and I gave Ford what I hoped was enough of a conciliatory look that it would earn me enough good will to get away with the whole thing. I wasn't the only friend who cared too hard for his friends. The whole group of us was probably a little too involved in each other's social lives than was healthy, but it worked for us and I didn't see a need to change anything.

Christian followed me back through the lounge and right to the exit. We both stepped onto the street without so much as a second look around, and I imagined the men who'd been after him had long given up their search.

"Do we need to watch our backs?" I asked, glancing both ways down the street anyway.

"I think the time for that has come and gone," he said, checking for himself. "Now the question remains, where are you taking me, Mr. Sheffield?"

"I would have taken you there." I angled my head back to the entrance of the club. "But not with an audience."

"Do your friends like to watch?"

"They like to play with my food," I said. It was the truth, and a very important part of the foundation of our friendship. Up until Beamer announced he had a secret husband a few months before, I hadn't thought any of us had secrets from each other. That had turned out to not be true, but beyond his infidelity—to us—we were open books. We shared locations, kinks, and more often than not, men.

"Sounds like fun for another time," Christian mused.

"Thought this was for one night?"

He hummed, a contemplative sound that vibrated through my bones with the promise of a thousand dirty nights that were just out of reach.

"I can take you to my place or I can get us a room."

I didn't make a habit of taking men back to my house, and I had no idea why I'd even put the offer on the table, but the words were already out of my mouth and I didn't see a way to take them back without looking like a huge prick. And I was one, but I still had plans for the night and they really involved Christian not thinking I was as much of a piece of shit as I was.

"There is something to be said about the bedding at a nice hotel," Christian said thoughtfully, tapping his fingertips against his chin.

"I should be insulted you think The Plaza has a higher thread count than the bed I sleep in every night."

"Too bad I don't have two nights to compare for myself."

Christian smiled at me, and suddenly the only thing that mattered was getting to The Plaza and kissing him again.

"It's half a mile," I told him, starting south without waiting for him to answer. "Hope you don't mind walking."

"You Americans are always walking everywhere," he grumbled, falling into step beside me.

"New Yorkers are walking everywhere," I corrected.

"Have you lived here your whole life?"

"No. I'm from California."

"Ah." Christian nodded, glancing up at the tops of the buildings we walked by. "The land of sun and palm trees."

"Have you been?" I asked, with a laugh. "There's much more farmland in California than people realize, I think."

"Are you a farm boy, Mr. Sheffield?"

The way he addressed me once again went straight to my dick.

"I might have been," I told him, "in another life. But here we are in the middle of New York City, on the verge of defacing every surface in the room of one of the nicest hotels in the city instead."

I came to a stop in front or the hotel steps, the stately white brick and marble building reaching for the sky in front of us.

"Well, when you put it like that." Christian grinned at me again, mouth quirked up in the corner as he pressed one hand against his stomach and held the other out in invitation. "Lead the way."

CHAPTER 6
CHRISTIAN

THE PLAZA WAS RIGHT NEXT DOOR TO THE RITZ-CARLTON, WHICH meant I was quite literally under Niko's nose—which sent a thrill straight up my spine. I tried to not look too obviously over my shoulder while Kale busied himself getting a room, and it wasn't until we were together in the elevator heading up to the twelfth floor that I let myself breathe a sigh of relief.

The room was smaller than mine at The Ritz, but it was partitioned off with a bedroom and a separate seating area, both boasting an ostentatious amount of gold plating. It was rich in that American way they all loved so much. There was a comfortable enough-looking couch, which I promptly took a seat on, kicking my feet up onto the marble coffee table and crossing my legs at the ankles. Kale shrugged out of his coat and unwound the scarf from around his neck, tossing them both onto a chair, which was also gold-plated.

"What does your house look like?" I asked.

He turned toward me, curious expression on his face.

"You could have seen it for yourself," he murmured,

popping open the buttons of his collared shirt, one by one, until it was fully open and putting his slender and smooth chest on display.

I licked my lips, dropping my feet onto the floor and leaning closer. I yanked my undone bowtie from around my neck and threw it on the table, then wiggled out of my jacket and let it fall to the plush carpeting. Kale took a step toward me, I stood up, and then he was on me, fingers working madly at the hidden buttons on my own shirt until he was able to properly divest me of it.

"Describe it to me," I managed to get the words out between kisses, but then his mouth was on my jaw, my chin, my throat. I toed out of my shoes, stumbling backward and crashing into one of the Queen Anne chairs opposite the couch. I landed hard on the back of my thigh and Kale's slight weight on top of me took us both straight over the arm and to the floor.

"Has more character than this place," he whispered against my skin, teeth nipping across my Adam's apple as he kissed his way down my throat and toward my chest. His hands went down, working at my belt and my pants. I lifted off the ground and shimmied out of them, groaning when he returned his attention to the erection that was currently trying to drill a hole out of my underwear.

"Tell me more." I set to work on his belt, using my elbows to push up off the floor. Taking him along, we ended up seated, and then it was my turn to explore the sharp angles of his cheeks and jaw with my mouth while we both busied ourselves getting him out of his shoes and pants.

"Wide-planked floors," he said, "lots of fireplaces. Oh, fuck."

I smiled against his ear. "I've never seen one of those."

He scoffed and levered his weight, pushing me down again onto my back. So, he liked to be on top. That was interesting. I hadn't thought for one second Kale was a missionary man, but I'd been surprised before.

"What's your favorite part of it?" I asked.

He reached inside my underwear and curled his fist around my cock. I could have died. I wasn't sure I hadn't, because his grip was so sure and so hot, and the sounds that left my mouth couldn't have sounded terribly different from a death rattle. My breath abraded my throat as I gasped, moaning rather surprisingly into his kiss.

"The garden."

"Why?" I croaked.

"It's peaceful," he whispered. "It's mine."

"Are you a possessive man, Mr. Sheffield?"

Kale hummed and gave a long, slow stroke up my cock. "Don't ask questions you know the answer to."

He dragged his thumb through the embarrassingly wet slit of my cock, and I loosed an equally embarrassingly high-pitched moan.

"Are you going to fuck me on the floor, Mr. Sheffield?" I asked, biting the inside of my cheek so I didn't fly into another galaxy as a side effect of my uncontrollable horniness. The adrenaline from the night was finally catching up with me, the rush of excitement and arousal churning together and growing into something that threatened to burst right out of my bones and swallow us both whole. "Or do I get to test out the thread count?"

"Why not both?" he asked.

"I have delicate sensibilities," I warned. "And even more delicate skin. I don't think I could survive the rug burn."

He hummed against my neck, licking a hot stripe up the underside of my jaw. "Are you worried I'm going to fuck you too rough, princess?"

If I had been ten years younger, I would have come on the spot.

"I don't think there's such a thing."

I shoved him off of me and stepped out of my underwear, kicking it toward where we'd discarded the rest of our clothes. I headed into the bedroom, barely having time to take in the ornate white and gold headboard before Kale was behind me, naked and burning hot. His body pressed against mine and he sank his teeth into the curve of my neck.

"I want you like this," he said, reaching around and taking my cock into his hand. He gave another tight and slow stroke up my length, then stepped back and climbed onto the bed.

Kale arranged himself against the headboard, pillows and bedding floating around him like a cloak. He looked like a king, and in his own right, I supposed he was. He carried himself with all the power and authority a king should wield, even if only in theory. I stood at the foot of the bed to take him in, the length of his limbs and the golden glint of the highlights in his hair. The chandelier above the bed was another overdone touch, but the sight in front of me was anything but.

"Unless you're going to magic a condom out of thin air," I said regretfully, "we have a problem."

He groaned, frustration at the delay flashing across his face. He already had his dick in his hand and it was impressively thick, if not an inch or so shorter than mine.

"The inside pocket of my coat," he said, angling his chin toward the lounge we'd entered into.

"Do you happen to carry lube with you too?"

"I'm a boy scout, Christian. Same pocket."

I laughed, heading out to rifle through the pockets of his pea coat until I found the one with a three-fold strip of condoms and a travel size bottle of lube. I tore one of the condoms off and left the rest, taking the supplies into the bedroom where I found Kale with his head thrown back and his mouth half open. He jerked his cock like he had all the time in the world, and he looked like a work of art.

Even though he was slim, the lines and curves of his muscles were visible, pulled taut from the barely restrained tension that coursed through his body. I had the thought of teasing him about not following through with taking me over his lap and spanking an orgasm out of me like he'd promised, but it was hard enough to breathe, let alone speak. I'd save the barb for the glorious haze of an orgasm afterglow.

"How do you want me?" I managed to ask, my voice scratchy and cracked.

I tossed the lube and the condom toward him and he made quick work of both, rolling the latex down his length and slathering himself and his fingers in lube.

"Come here and ride my fucking hand, princess. Get yourself ready for this cock."

I let out a nervous laugh and crawled onto the bed.

"I knew you'd be a talker," I said, climbing onto his lap and straddling him. The position made me taller than him, and he looked up at me with his head tilted back, looking every bit as regal and royal as anyone ever had before or ever would again. With one hand steady against my hip, he teased his slippery fingers up the crack of my ass. His hard and wet cock dragged against mine and I shivered, concerned for the very first time that I was going to finish the night before it even got started.

He teased his way around my hole and then slid one finger in all the way to the knuckle. I rocked against him, already needy for more than just one. I circled my hips like I could somehow turn his finger into his cock by willpower alone, and when I let out a tremulous breath, his nostrils flared, fingers tightening around my waist.

"Lift up," he said gently. "I told you to ride my hand, not grind on it."

"Ask me nicely," I teased, even as my hips began to rise.

"Do as you're told, Christian."

His finger slid out of me and then two were there, stretching against my rim as I sank back down around him.

"Yes, Sir," I rasped, half sarcastic but also entirely serious.

He grunted an approving sound that went straight to my cock and I wanted to hear it again from his mouth, so I did as he'd told me. I started to ride him, and then I was working myself on his hand so hard my dick slapped against my chest, rigid and sticky, and...ready.

"I wish you could see yourself," he said, cheeks flushed, the only splash of color in the entire room. "Turn around."

I was already half gone with lust, but Kale's fingers withdrew and I hated the absence. With a less than graceful shift, I turned so my back was to his chest, and came face to face with the sight of myself in a full-length mirror against the far wall of the room. Beneath me, Kale adjusted himself and then the swollen head of his cock slid across my already well-prepped hole. I bit my lip, and he reached around to take my cock into his hand.

"Just like that, princess," he whispered into my ear as I sank down his impressive thickness. The stretch of him hurt, sending shivers up my spine and gooseflesh down my arms. "Start with the tip. There you go. Just a couple inches to start."

His dirty talk was instruction, and I started to ride the top third of his cock, taking him almost to the tip and back down, a little more with every slide of my body. He touched as much of my cock as I took of his and it wasn't long until the tip was nowhere near enough for me. Gritting my teeth, I bore down and slipped more of him into my body. He rewarded me with a kiss against the side of my neck and a longer stroke up my own shaft.

I rode him like that for a while, getting used to the thick swell in the middle of his shaft, fighting against the uncontrollable shivers that hadn't stopped radiating up my spine since he first pushed into me. Right when I was ready to take the rest of him, Kale's other hand came up and around my throat. Not hard and not insistent, just like...like that was where it belonged.

"Is this okay?" he asked.

"You didn't strike me as the kind of man to ask permission, either."

"I ask once," he said, flexing his fingers.

"It's more than okay," I answered, leaning into his touch as I sank the rest of the way down his length. He let out a surprised gasp as my ass landed against his hips, and he gripped my cock so tightly I thought for a moment he was ready to tear it off.

I was still focused on the sight of myself in the mirror, the way his cock disappeared into me and the way my cock was half-obscured by the curl of his fist. My nipples were hard and pink, jutting out and begging for some contact of their own. Without thinking, without asking, I reached up and took them between my fingers, giving a soft twist.

"Fuck." Kale's cock thickened inside of me.

His chin was against my shoulder, and we both watched the sight of us in the reflection of the mirror.

"Do it again," he said.

I did, twisting harder.

He stretched his thumb up under my jaw, pushing my head toward the ceiling, and then he pressed hard, dragging it over my chin and turning my face to the side. I took his thumb into my mouth, sucking and licking at it madly, desperate for something to be in my mouth. His hips thrust up off the bed, and then his mouth was against mine, his thumb sandwiched between our lips. The kiss was awkward and sideways, but he kissed me until his thumb was back digging into my chin and I was moving on top of him, chasing after an orgasm for the both of us.

The only sound in the room was the rough pant of our breaths and the wet slap of our skin. His fingers danced up my cock like it was an instrument he'd been playing his entire life, his mouth against my ear whispering secrets and promises that neither of us had any place entertaining.

"I'm close," I blurted, needing him to stop talking before I fell in love with him.

That was stupid. It was careless. He was a man I'd met on accident who helped me lose my security for a night. A man who wasn't threatened by my defiance. If anything, he was turned on by it. But these moments, in this hotel room, they were all we would ever have. Maybe I could manage a bit of rug burn after all.

"Take what you need, Christian." He bit my earlobe, humming a sound so low and deep it vibrated through my bones. For as much as I loved it when he called me "princess" —the irony not lost—I didn't hate the sound of my name in his mouth either. It was so rare that I heard it used, it was just as special as any kind of endearment.

With one hand on my right nipple still, the left hand behind me and half around his waist for balance, I bounced hard on his lap. Over and over, the head of his cock stabbing past my prostate every time I took him back inside of me. Even with his sweaty hands, Kale's hold on me tightened, and as I sank back around his full length, he held me down, rutting up off the bed to get even deeper into me.

Kale whispered my name as he came. Sounding like a prayer and a promise, it was enough to send jets of cum out of my cock. My orgasm painted my stomach and his hands, and I forced myself to watch in the mirror. I didn't even recognize myself, from the disheveled look of my hair to the dark flush that speckled most of my upper body. My balls were so high, I could see the place his cock disappeared into my ass, which pushed another spurt of cum into his hand.

"Holy shit," he cursed softly into my hair, his hands still against my skin.

I echoed the sentiment silently, leaning back against him and trying to catch my breath. My heart echoed loudly in my ears, mixing with the gentle praise Kale continued to whisper against my skin. I waited until he looked away from our reflection to close my eyes, tears prickling the backs of my eyelids.

I was fine, I told myself.

It was just hormones and arousal and adrenaline all working together and skewing my emotions, because I was

Prince Christian Henry Davenport-Spencer of the Chance Islands, and I was many things, but I was not a man who *cried* after sex.

"I hope you have more in you," Kale said, and I blinked my eyes open quickly, catching the heat in his eyes, once again staring me down in the mirror. "Because I believe this gorgeous ass of yours still has a date with my hand."

Seeing stars, I lifted Christian off of me. I was running on pure instinct and muscle memory because that orgasm had drained every ounce of sense and life right out of me. Christian's cock had throbbed so hot and heavy in my hand, the muscles of his channel gripping me tighter than I would have thought biologically possible, and the sounds he made when he came…I was a man possessed, and there was no way I was going to let this man out of my life without making good on my earlier promise.

Our clothes were in the lounge, and it took me almost a minute to find the strength in my legs to carry me there. My thigh muscles quaked with every step, but it was the pure determination borne from watching the glorious shake of Christian's ass as he preceded me out of the bedroom that kept me going. I'd had enough forethought to bring the lube with me, and Christian bent over to strip another condom off the three he'd found earlier in the pocket of my coat. He passed it to me without a word, studying me with a half-dazed look gracing his face.

"Are you with me?" I asked, sitting down on the couch and patting my lap.

His nostrils flared and he swayed on his feet, but nodded before coming toward me.

When he hesitated, I set the condom and lube down on the arm of the couch and asked him, "Do you want this?"

"I do," he whispered, licking his lips. Christian's eyes darted from my cock, which was still surprisingly hard, to the couch and then up to my face and back again. "I've just..."

He trailed off and I wrapped my fingers around my cock, giving it a stroke that sent a spark of fire up my spine. His attention narrowed in on the movement, mouth hanging open with the rest of the sentence dead somewhere in the back of his throat.

"You just?"

"No one has ever..."

"Told you what to do before?"

He scoffed at that, a tremor going through his whole body that somehow served to bring him back into the room with me.

"Spanked me," he said, lips pursed.

"Do you want to be spanked?"

Christian traced his tongue across the front of his teeth and I kept stroking my cock, sending prayers out into the universe that I hadn't somehow grossly misjudged the brat in front of me.

"I want *you* to spank me," he finally said, and I was careful to register the difference from the answer I'd expected and the one that he'd given.

"Then come here and get over my lap," I said, voice raspier than I'd intended. "Let me get my hands on you."

Christian shuffled to the couch and awkwardly arranged himself over the top of my lap. I was by no stretch of the imagination a large man. All of my friends dwarfed me when it came to muscle, but I was tall and strong enough to move a man into position. So, I did. Christian's breath rushed out of his lungs in a surprised huff, and I made sure his thickening cock was tucked securely between my thighs. I kept mine out, pressed hard against my stomach and his ribcage.

Tracing my fingers down the length of his arms, I stretched him out across the couch so he was mostly on the cushions. I bore as much of his weight as I could manage, stroking the opposite way up his arm and then over his back. When I reached the swell of his ass, I kneaded the soft flesh until he grunted, then worked my way down the backs of his thighs to the ditch of his knees.

Touching Christian was as much torment for me as I imagined it to be for him. He writhed against my lap, restrained and controlled, but still using his body to make sure I understood what he wanted from me. He wanted to fuck. He wanted to come. And, luckily, I wanted to make him come. But I was dedicated to keeping my word and figuring out how to do it without actually fucking him. Crossing my legs at the ankles to bring my thighs closer together, I reached for the lube and drizzled a few drops on my fingers, then I pressed them right into his asshole. Christian startled and jumped, but my muscles held him down by his cock. With a pained whine, he settled back onto my legs, arching into my hand.

"If you tell me to stop, I'll stop," I told him.

He managed a nod, fingers scrabbling against the couch and I hadn't even started in on him yet. His skin burned beneath my touch, his cock like a branding iron between my legs.

"Use your words, princess," I warned.

"I understand," he whispered, turning his head to the side and pressing his cheek against the couch cushion. "Mr. Sheffield."

"You're trouble."

"Punish me, then." Even through the haze from earlier, hints of the brat I'd met on the street still peeked out, and I wondered if it was intentional or reflexive. Something about his hesitance from the start of this whole little scene had me wondering if he'd ever done something like this before. The thought of him just naturally being this way with no one to bring him to heel suddenly felt like a real possibility and one of the greatest losses of the modern world. Christian would be beautiful when he was broken, but one night in a hotel room as strangers was not enough space or time to get him there. No matter how much he didn't even know he needed it.

Before I could talk myself out of it, I spanked him. Quick to draw my hand away from his skin so he could feel the whole sting of the impact, my cock leaked against my stomach when the red outline of my palm and fingers was almost immediately visible. He cursed under his breath, eyes going wide before slamming shut.

"Are you good?" I asked, stroking my fingertips over the imprint of my hand.

"Stop asking," he grunted, lips twisted defiantly. "I thought you said you were going to make me come like this."

"That wouldn't be much of a punishment," I said, taking my hands off of him completely. "And you can't have it both ways."

Christian muttered something, again in a language I couldn't decipher, then he squared himself up, at least as much as a man could while bent over another man's lap. "Punish me."

"Have you been very bad?" I asked.

"I've broken some rules," he murmured, licking his lips. I wondered if it was a nervous habit, but before I could ask, he spoke again, "I've acted out."

I spanked him again. Instead of grunting, he moaned, so I gave him another. His dick jerked between my legs, and I made a note to leave a more than decent tip for the house-keeping crew.

"By running away?"

Spank.

Spank.

Spank.

"I don't like being told I can't do something," he whispered.

"That's bad news for you," I said, spanking him four more times in quick succession, alternating which side of his ass I hit. "Because that's the kind of thing that makes me. Really. Fucking. Hard."

I punctuated the last few words of the sentence with sharper slaps, this time a little lower against the soft spot where his ass met his thighs. Christian cried out and turned himself face first into the couch, shouting as I landed another hard slap against him.

"You're going to need to keep it down, though," I warned. "Don't want the neighbors to call security."

At that suggestion, he tensed, and I knew I'd said the wrong thing. It was too close to the reality we were both currently pretending didn't exist. There were men after him, and I doubted they meant him any harm, but he was running from them nonetheless. Breaking rules and acting out.

"I can't help it," he whined, rolling his head back and forth against the couch. "I don't want you to stop, but I can't keep it inside."

Empathy unfurled in my chest, and I knew exactly what he was feeling. There was a point sometimes, in these games I liked to play, when something inside got knocked loose. It might be as small as a pebble in a giant wall, but it would start a chain reaction that let out larger rocks and then bricks and boulders, and then everything kept behind that wall would tumble out after. It was an overwhelming thing, and some-times a scary one, but there was no point in fighting it.

Like most things in life, you had to just let it happen.

"Do I need to gag you, Christian?" I asked.

His ass was pink and red, with little dots of white poking up across the places where I'd hit him the most frequently. He wasn't anywhere near bruised yet, but I wanted to get him there.

"I've never..."

The closest thing to me besides the condom and lube was his discarded jacket on the floor, strip of blue ribbon sticking out from the inside pocket. Without thinking, I reached down and snatched it between my fingertips and balled it up in my fist.

"Open your mouth," I said.

He rolled his head to the side, eyes going wide when he saw what I had in my hand. I shoved the ball of material into his mouth and he looked at me a little scared and a little frenzied, but I teased his asshole with a lube-slicked finger and he settled down like a trained pony.

"Say stop," I demanded.

"Sthop." The word was garbled around the gag, but I could still hear him. He could hear himself too, and his lashes softly fluttered closed.

"Are you good?" I asked him again. I'd ask him a thousand times to make sure. I needed to be certain and I needed it to be good for him. More than good. The best he'd ever had, more like.

"I'm good," he managed, but he was already floating somewhere in space. I'd seen the look in his eyes when we fucked in the bedroom and it was almost poetic how easy it was to take him out of himself. He was a fucking sight to behold, and I wanted my fill before having to turn him back over to the obligations he'd been running so hard to escape.

"I'll make you better," I promised, and then I hit him again.

The next shout was muffled around the gag, and I had no intention of letting up until I'd spanked him absolutely mindless. It turned out Christian was just as stubborn as I was, because my hand ached from how many strikes I'd landed against his skin and the cherry red started to purple before I really heard the kind of noises I'd been after.

Against my stomach, my cock dripped a steady stream of precum on my belly, every time Christian's body jostled against mine it created enough friction to edge me closer to what was shaping up to be a technically hands-free orgasm. My thighs quivered from how hard I squeezed them around his cock, his hips pumping frenetically while he fucked the gap between my legs. His cries turned to moans, and then it was like a switch flipped and he turned *on*. The lower half of his body pumped hard against me, chasing after the orgasm I'd promised, and with every slap of my skin against his, I could feel him getting closer.

Christian's skin was burning hot, the color of a fiery sunset that I hadn't seen since I was a kid back in California. He moaned and gasped, panted. I pressed one of my hands against the back of his head, pushing his face into the cushions to further muffle the sound of him. There was no more controlling it, of that I was certain, and I felt his orgasm before I heard it.

A hot spurt of cum streaked across the inside of my leg and then he let out a desperately broken cry that shattered my heart and made me hard all at the same time. Jet after jet of cum poured out of his cock, against the couch and my legs, and his cry turned hoarse, voice cracking. The steady movement of his body against mine slowed and his wail turned once again into a whimper.

Keeping a steady hold on the back of his head, I closed my eyes long enough to enjoy the way his hair felt like silk against my hand. I threaded my fingers through the strands, and with the aching hand I'd used to spank him, I stroked the exposed head of my cock. I was closer to the edge than I'd thought, and it only took the slightest pressure against the crown of my dick to send cum flying out of me.

Gritting my teeth and bearing down through it, I fisted his hair and yanked his head to the side because, for some reason I couldn't make sense of, it was important for me that he see me come. I needed him to know that it was because of him every bone in my body had shattered and collapsed under the beauty of the surrender he'd given me.

My body shuddered, the release tearing through me long after I'd stopped coming, and with a shaking exhale, I forced myself to let go of how tightly I held his hair. He whimpered again, hand flailing behind him until he made contact with my arm. He smacked me and made an unhappy sound until I once again fisted the soft and silky hairs at the back of his head. That earned me a pleased noise and, with my free hand, I traced my way over the bruises that now colored the backs of his thighs and his ass.

"You needed that, didn't you?" I asked quietly.

He nodded, and I pulled the makeshift gag out of his mouth. It was creased and matted, soaking wet with his spit.

"Words."

"Yes," he croaked, voice as wet with tears as the rest of his face was. "Yes. Thank you."

"It's going to hurt to sit tomorrow," I warned him, pressing my fingertip down into the heart of one particularly dark bruise in the center of his left ass cheek.

"Thank you," he gasped. "So I won't forget."

"What aren't you going to forget?"

If he'd asked me the same question, my answer would have come quickly and simply. It wasn't more than three letters, a single word.

"What it's like to be free," he whispered.

Gently he angled his head back against my hand, and I released the hold I had on him. Smoothing the hair back into place, I helped him into a seated position, and then tucked him against my side. He curled into me like it was something we'd done a thousand times before, not just once.

"Are you hungry?" I asked.

"I could eat," he murmured against my skin.

"Can I take you into the shower first? Get you cleaned up?"

He leaned back and looked up at me, face damp and splotchy but eyes as clear as they'd been the first time I saw him.

"Will you fuck me again in there?"

"Can you take it?"

"I will," he vowed.

Something about the sincerity and the necessity of his tone brokered no argument from me. I helped him to his feet, waiting until he was steady enough to walk, then I grabbed the condom and lube and joined him upright. My own knees threatened to knock together for how unsteady my legs still were, but Christian had made it clear my duty to him was far from over.

And at the end of the day, that was what it meant to be a Dominant, wasn't it? It was a sense of duty, responsibility... obligation. But one that I willingly took on because it was moments like this that made me feel like I was doing good with my life. When I looked back at how it hurt my parents when I decided to leave California for New York, and how I'd hurt my best friend by being a prick to the man he loved...I couldn't be *that* bad of a person if I had moments like *this*.

Right?

I stopped at the small desk against the opposite wall and called in an order for room service, then walked Christian to the bathroom. He leaned shakily against the wall while I fussed with the water, then took my hand with ease when it was ready. Under the spray, I washed his body and his hair. I was gentle with the bruises on his backside, and I made sure to rinse all of the soap out of his ass before I put on the condom and got as much lube on it as I could manage.

I took Christian slowly against the wall, brushing his wet hair out of his face and hooking one of his legs around my waist. He kept his eyes trained on me and I called him a princess. I called him *my* princess. When he came, one valiant spurt of cum landed on his stomach, the rest dribbling down the length of his cock, making a mess between our freshly clean bodies.

It was going to take me ages to come, and I needed to get food and water in us both, so I kissed him gently, licking into his mouth and apologizing for falling short as I pinched my fingers around the condom and withdrew. He whined, but I swallowed it into my mouth and I rinsed the cum from our stomachs and his cock.

Something about the shower felt safe and sacred, but nothing good could last forever. With a shocking amount of reluctance, I turned off the spray and reached out for a towel. I made sure he was dry before I bothered with myself, then fetched the matching robes and slippers from the closet. Christian was quiet and pliable, but eager to be tended, his hands roaming over the top of my head and the side of my face as I tightened the belt around his middle.

"Are you good?" I asked him, an echo so constant and vital I could feel it in my pulse points as I said the words.

"Better than," he said with a small smile. "Just like you promised."

Pride swelled in my chest, and I kissed him again. My cock was tired, so far from being erect, but I would have used my fingers to tuck myself inside of him if it meant I could have continued on like that. In a very not creepy way, I wanted to unzip his skin and crawl inside of him. I wanted to consume him, in a near obsessive way. I'd known from the start that he was going to be too much for me, and still...

And still...

A knock on the door brought me back to the room, back to the reality that he was a separate being from me that I would have to take care of for only another few hours before we went our separate ways.

"Food," he murmured, a lazy and sated smile on his face. His lips were swollen from our kiss, and I wanted to kiss him again. Again. Again.

"Get into bed and I'll bring it in," I said, but he shook his head and followed me to the door.

"I'll help."

"What if I want to do this for you?"

"Too bad, Mr. Sheffield." Christian kissed the top of my shoulder, letting out a soft exhale of breath. There was the brat. There was my spoiled princess of a man.

"Alright."

I opened the door and didn't find a hotel employee on the other side, but a rather bedraggled-looking man in a suit with his finger pressed against a small black ear piece. Christian cursed and I turned, ready to ask him what was going on, but the question died in my throat. I was a smart man. I knew the answer.

"Your Royal Highness," the man said, looking utterly unimpressed at his own use of the title or my confusion over hearing it.

Turning my head slightly to the side, I caught Christian's profile in my peripheral. His fingers darted out, hooking against mine, even if the hold was obscured by the long sleeves of our robes.

"Your what?" I whispered the question, and Christian's face turned from one of perfect pleasure to apology.

"Not quite a princess," he said with a self-deprecating laugh, "but I am a prince."

CHAPTER 8
CHRISTIAN

KALE'S MOUTH FELL OPEN, AND I SAW THE MOMENT WHEN realization dawned. He snapped his mouth closed and inhaled a sharp breath, and I could hear all the things he wanted to say to me caught behind the seal of his lips. He blinked slowly and exhaled, stare flickering toward the balled-up and spit-soaked royal order on the hotel couch, then back to me. His cheeks went dark and then he looked down at our bare feet.

"A prince?" he asked softly, sounding as betrayed as I imagined he felt.

"I'll be with your shortly, Niko," I said, slamming the door closed in my guard's face before he could protest. Only after the bolt latched, did Kale look back up at my face.

"You should have told me."

"What difference would it have made?" I asked with a helpless shrug. I didn't want to be callous toward whatever emotions *he* was feeling in that moment, but I was having plenty of my own and Niko's arrival made it impossible to feel any of them in the ways that I wanted.

Whatever had happened between Kale and me over the

past few hours was beyond anything I'd ever experienced in my life. There weren't words for the way he made me feel. And whatever he'd spanked out of me on the couch? I'd spend years trying to dissect all of that. From the first crack of his hand against my ass, something had shifted. It wasn't like something coming loose, but more like something falling into place. With every strike he delivered, I started to understand myself with a new startling level of clarity. I didn't just like what we did together. I needed it.

Somehow, he'd known that about me. And when he shoved that stupid royal order into my mouth and pressed me down into the couch so I could scream my way into becoming...? It was the greatest gift anyone had ever given me, and he didn't even know. He couldn't know. And now Niko was here, ruining it like he ruined the rest of my life, always on Phillip's orders or at my father's command. Always someone making demands of me without caring how it made me feel. Was that why when Kale issued his instructions, it had been different? He cared how I felt, how I reacted. I could tell because he kept asking me if I was good. Kept telling me we could stop. He had given me a choice to let him lead, and that was everything.

"What difference would it have made, Kale?" I asked him again, snatching the ribbon from the couch and shoving it back into the inside pocket of my coat.

My mind was at war with my heart and both of them battled my libido. With every step I took, I was reminded of Kale. From the ache between my ass cheeks to the tenderness in my cock every time it dragged limply across the luxuriously plush robe and the burn against my ass and the backs of my thighs—every move made me think of him.

He sat down on the edge of the couch and I gathered my clothes, less one sock, and when I'd gotten everything together, he still hadn't answered me. Dropping the pile of garments onto the coffee table, I went to him, trailing my finger over his exposed knee. He tilted his head to the side and looked up at me, expression now unreadable.

"Would it have made a difference?" I asked, voice softer than before.

He stretched his fingers toward mine, twining our hands together. It was hilarious, I thought, that he had been inside of me with his mouth and his cock and his hands, but he hadn't held my hand until this very moment. We'd come close at the door, but I'd put that on the list as another thing that Niko had ruined for me.

Ever so slowly, Kale shook his head. He pulled me onto his lap and I came without complaint, straddling him and resting my hands on top of his shoulders.

"Would it have mattered?" He'd been so insistent up until that point that I use my words, and what I needed more than anything we'd just done together was for him to do the same.

"No," he whispered, shaking his head like he was more certain of the answer.

Relief washed over me and I fell forward, pressing my forehead against his. There was that damn burn against my eyelids again, and after our last time on the couch, I wouldn't have thought there were any tears left inside of me to let out. Leave it to this insufferable man to find them and draw them out at his whim.

Kale settled his hands on my waist, taking a deep breath but otherwise remaining quiet and still.

"What are you thinking?" I asked.

He chuckled. "You don't want to know."

"I wouldn't have asked if I didn't," I assured him.

"I was thinking about how I fucked a prince tonight," he said, wry smile flickering across his face. "How I spanked him until he cried and then fucked him again."

I swallowed, shivering. "You did."

He flexed his fingers against my waist, then trailed them inward, loosening the sloppy knot he'd only just tied on the belt of the robe. It came apart quickly for him, as I imagine most things and people would, and then his hands were on my skin. Dancing up my ribs and over my chest and around my back, Kale's fingertips mapped my skin with his hands, every exhale out of his mouth trembling between us. Even though he was touching me softly, reverently, he wasn't tentative. He still stroked his fingers across my flesh like he had any right to it and, fuck, how I wanted him to have a right to it.

"Tell me something about my prince," he whispered, stare trained on the places he touched me instead of my face.

"I'm the spare for a spare for a spare," I said with a disgusted scoff in the back of my throat. "There's no place in line for the throne for me, just all the limitations and restraints as if there were."

"Third place, then?"

"More like eleventh, because of the kids."

He hummed, moving his hands away from my stomach and down to the tops of my thighs. It was impossible to not moan at his touch, to spread my legs wider and sink down deeper onto his lap. He wasn't hard, but he was burning and that somehow meant more.

"What were you running from tonight?"

I put the tip of my nose against his, nudging him until he looked up at me. When he did, I pressed our mouths together. He didn't close his eyes and neither did I, but I parted my lips and committed the feel of his tongue against mine to memory. He broke the kiss far sooner than I would have, but between the two of us, I was not the one in charge.

"Use your words," he again demanded of me.

"All of it."

"Do you hate it?"

His thumbs were so close to my cock and his touch felt electric, leaving a trail of goosebumps in his wake.

"Most of the time," I admitted.

"If we'd met under different circumstances, would this still have been for just one night?"

"It's all I have," I said. "It's the only time that was mine."

Kale tilted his head to the other side, still close enough to my mouth that I could taste him. "And you shared it with me?"

"I gave it to you."

He slanted our mouths together, hands snaking around to my back. He splayed his fingers wide like he was trying to cover as much surface as possible with the limited resources he had. After all, no matter how much he'd rocked my world, he was just one mortal man. But I arched into him, leaning into the kiss with a whimper so soft he swallowed it down before I even heard it.

"Do you have to go right now?" he asked.

"I can leave Niko outside for a while."

"Can you leave him outside until the morning?"

Another knock at the door felt like the answer was no.

Kale's entire body went tense, and he gave me a little push as though he had to shove me away to keep from touching me.

"Room service, Mr. Sheffield," someone called out from the other side of the door.

I barked out a sharp laugh, and Kale slumped against the back of the couch, scrubbing his hands down his face with a frustrated grumble.

"I forgot about the food." He lifted me off of him and stood.

"Let me." I held up my hand for him to stop, and he sighed, nodding.

I imagined the entire night must have been quite the whirlwind for him, the last ten minutes probably even more so. I waited until I was sure Kale would stay on the couch, then I re-tied my robe and went to the door. Out in the hallway, I found Niko, who looked as stern and annoyed as he ever did, and a bumbling old man with a room service cart between him and the door. There were four silver domed trays on top with a bottle of champagne in a bucket of ice. Two glasses. Niko eyed the spread, but didn't say a word.

"You can take that inside," I said to the employee, stepping out of the way so he could come in with the cart. I think he could sense the tension, because he moved as quick as he could, running out of the room with the cart and not so much as a look back. I glanced at Kale on the couch, stare fixated on the carpet beneath his feet.

"Are you good?" I asked, a repeat of his refrain to me.

"Just thinking."

"I'm not leaving right now, but I need to speak with Niko alone."

He nodded, and I stepped into the hallway.

"Are you quite finished, sir?" Niko asked, tone laced with frustration.

"Nowhere near it, but I appreciate your detective skills if you were able to find me so quickly."

"The city has lots of cameras," he said.

It was the only explanation he offered, but enough to remind me that there was nowhere I could go that was out of the reach of my father...or the crown.

"Do I get points for being right under your nose?"

"It was ballsy," he said, "I'll give you that."

"Is Phillip mad?"

"Fuming."

"Has he called our father over it?" I scratched my chin, just below my lip. The skin there was tender, abraded from the scruff on Kale's chin.

"Not yet."

Another unanticipated wash of relief that I knew I didn't deserve, but would take just the same.

"Let me have the rest of the night then," I said, not quite begging, even though I didn't find myself above it in that moment. "You know where I am and you know how to find me if I slip off again."

"*Don't* slip off again."

"Is that an okay?" I arched a brow.

He checked his watch and frowned. "Don't leave this room."

I grinned, knowing I was going to get my way. "I wasn't planning on it."

"I'll be back for you at eight," he said, pressing some buttons on his watch. An alarm, I gathered.

"Bring me clean clothes. My tux is a bit soiled."

"You're incorrigible," he muttered, shaking his head and stalking off down the hallway toward the elevators.

Slipping back into the room, Kale stood as soon as the door closed. When I flipped the deadbolt latch closed, his brow knit together in confusion. "Are you leaving?"

I went to the desk where the food and champagne had been laid out. Taking both of the glasses and the bottle in hand, I turned to Kale and raised them both in the air. Triumphant.

"I have until the morning," I said, a little breathless with the promise of what we could do with those ten hours. "If you still want me."

The confusion on his face morphed into elation, and a wide, cocksure smile spread across his face. *There* he was. There was the man who'd pushed me so far out of myself I didn't even think it was possible to return to life before him. The man who'd called me "princess" because he wanted to spoil me with his dick, not because it was in the same realm as my actual title.

"Use your words, Mr. Sheffield," I teased, using my thumb to untie the bow I'd made on the robe when I went to barter for my freedom with Niko. The soft terrycloth fell open, and Kale licked his lips, humming thoughtfully at the sight of me.

"I think I'll want you for the rest of my life, princess," he said, sitting back down on the couch and popping loose the knot on his robe too. He spread the material open, putting himself on display for my perusal. "Now get your ass back on my lap where it belongs. We don't have much time."

THE NEXT MORNING, CHRISTIAN SNUCK OUT OF THE ROOM WHILE I was still half-unconscious. Calling it sleep would have been a disservice to the absolute lack of coherence I'd fucked us both into before the sun came up, and the fact he was able to draw himself out of it without waking me was just a testament to how good he was at sneaking out and around.

My phone vibrating against the white marble-topped nightstand was what finally woke me up, and when I opened my eyes to get my phone, I knew Christian had already left. The air felt quiet and settled, which wasn't possible if he were still in bed beside me. Christian was chaos personified, a mouthy brat who'd never been told no, even though he was in desperate need of the denial.

I snatched my phone and dropped it onto his cold and empty pillow to dull the noise, sucking in a deep breath that didn't make me feel nearly as whole and alive as a single thing I'd done the night before had. But among the things we'd done together after he'd bought us a longer interlude, discussing the future state of our encounters hadn't been one of them. It wasn't something he brought up, and I was never the type, but I made sure he was bruised and sore enough to remember me even after time had stretched between us.

I'd met more men than I could count in my life, and I'd fucked just as many of them, but there was something so special about Christian. I couldn't think about it, though, because then I would start to lament his departure and there was nothing good to come from that. It didn't matter that I'd never had a man more beautiful than him spread across my lap. With all his abstinence and his need tangled up like a yarn ball that only grew bigger and messier with every day that went on. There wasn't a future in that kind of living, but I also knew not many people were patient enough to untangle and rewind it back together. I wasn't even sure if *I* was a patient enough man for that task, but as my sleepy eyes landed on the hotel notepad arranged neatly between the discarded and torn condom wrappers, I wondered if I could be.

My phone vibrated another message and I ignored it in favor of the notepad and what turned out to be Christian's sharp lined handwriting scrawled across the page. He'd pressed so hard with the pen that his words transferred at least three sheets down, and I tore all four pages off the pad, raising them far enough above my face that I could read the note he'd left before sneaking off with the sunrise.

Mr. Sheffield,

Thank you for showing me the best things this city had to offer. I wish we had more time, but I don't think they'll ever let me back across the border after the obscenities we committed together.

Yours, Princess Christian

I read the note at least ten times before cursing myself and kicking the blankets down to the foot of the bed. There was a hickey on the inside of my thigh as dark purple as the night sky, and when I pressed my finger against it I could recall the sharp pinch of Christian's teeth against my skin when he'd turned from sucking to biting.

"Idiot," I told myself, trading the note for my cell phone, which had an unnecessary number of messages from Ford and Brooks in what was apparently a new group chat they'd started so they could harass me more easily than one on one.

Ford added you to the group.
Ford added Brooks to the group.
Ford added Alex to the group.

Ford: Who was the stranger?
Brooks: He was way too attractive for you.
Alex: Who are you two talking to?
Brooks: Kale.
Ford: Who showed up late to the club last night WITH A MAN and they left before we even had a chance to meet him.
Ford: A half-dressed man.
Brooks: He was dressed, to be fair.
Ford: Looking like Kale had already stripped him half-naked before coming inside.
Alex: I still don't understand what's happening.
Ford: He's not answering my messages.
Alex: He's probably muted you. I'm about to.
Brooks: You're no fun now that Beamer is gone.

Alex: I fucked men before him and I'll fuck men after him. Don't you worry about that.

Ford: We aren't here to talk about the past. We're here because Kale has gone missing with a stranger.

Brooks: Wouldn't be the first time.

Alex: It's kind of what he does.

Ford: This felt different.

Ford: Sheffield, you have until 8am to reply or I'm putting out an APB.

It was 7:45.

Me: I'm alive and in one piece. Yet to be taken for a ransom or whatever else you're concerned about.

Ford: I was obviously worried for your virtue.

Me: And yet I was the one fully dressed last night.

Ford: Meet me for breakfast.

Alex: Not me. I'm going back to bed. You're ridiculous.

Brooks: I'll take the cliffs notes too.

Me: Where?

Ford: Palm's Supper Club

Me: Fine. Half an hour.

Ford: It'll take me longer than that.

Me: Half an hour or you can get the Cliffs Notes too.

I dropped my phone on top of the note from Christian, throwing my legs out of bed with as much energy as I could muster. Shaking off the aches from the gymnastics of the night before, I showered, pressing again at the bruise in the fold of my thigh. If I closed my eyes, I could still see the wicked gleam in Christian's as he'd sank his teeth into me, and I could even hear the pleased noises he made when I flung him onto his back to spank him in punishment for it.

He'd needed the things we did the night before as much as I ever needed it myself, but in a very different and somehow far more visceral way. I was sure Christian was new enough to kink that some of the things I wanted to do to him would have been daunting, but the zeal with which he approached what he did have an awareness of was a sight in and of itself. His body knew what he needed, even if his brain didn't possess the words or the names for it. Christian was eager to be himself, blustering and bold, but against someone who wasn't intimidated by his demeanor. He needed someone who wouldn't back down, but who would see the facade for what it was—a mask. Not to say he wasn't blustering and bold. He was all of those things and more. He was also arrogant and sarcastic, intelligent, and so desperate to be handled properly. I imagined it was because of his rank and status that no one ever dared.

I could have spent the entire rest of my day in the shower overthinking about Christian and what he needed and what I wanted to give him, but I was the one who'd given Ford the timeline and the last thing I planned to do was give him more ammunition to poke and prod at me. Of our small friend group, he was the one most likely to come up behind me with some snappy commentary, but I was far more aggressive with the verbal barbs than he ever had been. Alex was far softer in his approach, and Brooks was another story entirely.

After carefully folding the note and the extra pages from Christian, I tucked them into the inside pocket of my pea coat. I didn't need to look out the window to guess the weather.

New York in the fall was predictable, and I wound my scarf around my neck as I checked the room to make sure I hadn't left anything behind. My roaming gaze landed on a bright shock of blue on the floor near the couch, the bundle of ribbon which turned out to be Christian's royal order. The bulk of the material was hidden, only the edge in view, and even then only because I'd done a full sweep with the intent to find anything I might have lost.

I imagined his parents would be none too happy about the loss, but it was very much my gain. The ribbon was cool and damp, undoubtedly from the fact I'd had it shoved into Christian's mouth to serve as a makeshift gag the night before. Unbelievable that I hadn't realized what it was, and even more so that he'd let me get away with the act. But, then again, I supposed he didn't care much for his position in life or else he wouldn't be so anxious to always get away from it.

Carefully, I folded the ribbon and slipped it into my pocket, alongside Christian's goodbye note. He'd signed it *Princess,* which stirred up no less than five very unexpected and unwelcome feelings spread between the center of my chest and the pit of my stomach. I knew I'd never meet another man like him ever again, and I couldn't quite decide if that was a good thing or a bad one.

After checking out of the hotel, the clock on my phone confirmed if I wanted to beat Ford to breakfast, I would have to take a cab. The drive was fast and the car was far too hot, but I managed to get to the door of the restaurant just as Ford strode around the corner, hands tucked into the pockets of a camel-colored coat. He also had a scarf around his neck, and I recognized the cashmere pattern was the one my parents had sent for him the Christmas before. When he saw me, he rolled his eyes, then brushed past me inside the welcome warmth of the restaurant.

"I win," he said, unwinding the scarf and shrugging out of his coat.

"I'm right here," I said.

He smirked, pulling at the ends of my own scarf like I wasn't divesting myself of my outerwear fast enough for his liking.

"I got inside first."

"You're insufferable."

"Thank you." He grinned at me, then turned toward the hostess. "Table for two, please."

I trudged after the two of them, coat and scarf folded neatly over my arm. When we reached the table, Ford was leaning in a little close to the hostess and she gazed up at him with stars in her eyes.

"Don't fall for it," I warned her, and my words seemed to break her out of the trance Ford had put her into.

Her face flushed and she stepped back, almost like she'd snapped out of some kind of hypnosis. Ford sighed and ordered us both drinks before taking his seat and giving me the finger.

"You take the fun out of everything," he complained.

"I rather think I put fun into it, but..."

"Is that what you're calling your dick these days?"

"I've never had to give it a nickname," I assured him, reaching behind me to adjust my coat on the back of my chair. For good measure, I checked the pocket to make sure the papers and the ribbon were still safe inside.

"What do you partners call it then?" he asked.

"They're generally unable to form sentences if I'm doing it right, Ford. Did you need another how-to lesson?"

"Tell me about Christian," he said instead, ignoring the taunt.

"I didn't think he told you his name."

"He didn't, but you used it."

A waitress, who looked far more unflappable than the hostess, arrived with our drinks and a stern look for Ford, which had me laughing under my breath. Ford was one of my very best friends, but the man had never met a person he didn't want to sleep with. It was the thrill of the chase for him, though. He wasn't quite a one and done, but once the novelty wore off, he was on to the next. I didn't think he was afraid of relationships, but he was very much afraid of stagnancy and boredom.

"Tell me about your night," I said.

"Brooks and I had quite a good time at The Black Door," he answered conversationally, stirring his Bloody Mary with the celery stalk garnish. "But the pickings were slim so I rang up a man who'd tried to get me into bed a couple weeks ago."

"What's his name?" I asked, already knowing how this story was going to go.

"Stefan," he answered, jaw tight, even as his mouth twitched at the corner. He avoided my stare and I exhaled loudly, shoulders sagging.

"Stefan?" I repeated. "My assistant?"

"He's quite good with his hands, Kale. I see why you hired him."

"Can you please stop sleeping with my assistants?" I

scrubbed a hand down my face with a tired groan. "You make it impossible to keep people on staff and I do need someone to stay on board for more than three months."

"We were hardly sleeping." He grinned. "Tell me about Christian."

"He was just in town for a stint," I mumbled, realizing I didn't know how long he was in the city for or when he'd be leaving, but judging from the stern look on Niko's face the night before, I'd wager Christian was already on a plane back to wherever he came from... and I realized I didn't know where that was either. "It was a one-time thing."

"He's from out of town?"

"Out of the country."

"I couldn't place his accent," Ford said, clearly fishing.

"Neither could I."

"Didn't you ask?" Ford arched a brow at me.

"His country of origin didn't seem relevant to our itinerary."

I swallowed down bile, something about the words and the lie diminishing the weight of what Christian and I had done the night before. We both knew it was only what it was, what it could be. There hadn't been phone numbers exchanged or any kind of promises, but to say that anything about him didn't matter to me felt like a gross misstatement.

"And now?" Ford asked.

"Now he's gone back to wherever he was from and I'm here having breakfast with you." I reached for my drink, hoping the spicy tomato and vodka would wash down the sour acidity in the back of my throat. "Just like everyone else before him, Ford. He wasn't any different, so I don't know what you expect me to say."

Ford cleared his throat and leaned back in his chair, the guarded look on his face making it clear he didn't believe a word that came out of my mouth.

I reached down and checked the inside pocket of my coat again, not believing them either.

THEY DIDN'T EVEN GIVE ME TIME TO CHANGE.

As soon as I stepped foot outside The Plaza, Niko's hand was around my arm and he ushered me directly into the back seat of a waiting limousine. He apparently took the spare hours he'd given me with Kale as an opportunity to get my bags together and update my itinerary. Or that might have been Phillip's doing. I wasn't certain and I didn't see the point in asking.

The drive to the airport was longer than it needed to be because New York had never met a toll bridge or a traffic jam it didn't like, but the crawling miles and the stark silence gave me the chance to close my eyes and daydream about the night Kale and I had spent together. Every shift of my weight against the smooth leather seat sent the most thrilling ache through my body, and even for as spent as my cock was, it still found the energy and the blood to sit heavy and plump against my thigh.

I pushed the button beside the wet bar to unroll the privacy partition between the back seat and the front. Niko's shoulders straightened at the noise, but he didn't turn around.

"Niko, how much trouble would you say I'm in this time?" I asked.

He sighed heavily. "I hope it was worth it."

"It was."

He nodded, and I rolled the partition back up between us.

The night with Kale had been more than worth it, but I knew Niko didn't want the details. He'd been sent to do one thing Kale had managed to do without even trying. Make me listen. Do as I'm told. Bring me to heel. If you had told me yesterday morning that my night would have ended on another man's lap with his handprints speckled across my backside, I would have laughed you out of the country. There were a thousand ways I knew of to be sexually adventurous, and until last night, taking instructions from a man I barely knew—because apparently being told what to do *in the right tone of voice* made my cock hard enough to cut steel—wasn't one of them.

And yet.

Pulling myself out of bed had been an absolute nightmare, but I knew if Kale woke up, it would have only been worse. He'd taken Niko's arrival and the discovery of my rank better than expected. If anything, the reveal had made him rougher with me, more dominant. He'd taken me back onto his lap after Niko left, put my cock into his fist, and brought me so close to the edge I thought we'd teleported to the top of the Empire State Building. Everything was cold and hot and sensitive and numb, and by the time he let me come, I was very near tears. If he'd denied me after that, I would have seriously debated abdicating, but he called me princess again and it sounded like heaven on his tongue.

"You're being foolish," I warned myself as the limo pulled to a stop alongside the curb at the private terminal at whatever airport they'd decided to rush me out of.

There was no good to come from letting myself think about Kale Sheffield for even a second longer than I already had. For one, I didn't think about the men I had sex with. That wasn't the goal of any coupling I'd ever stepped into, and it surely hadn't been the goal with Kale. I'd needed someone to hide me long enough to lose Niko and his team, which Kale had helped me with. The kiss...the rest of it...that hadn't been part of the plan. And two, I didn't think my father would ever let me come back to America after my most recent escape act, so there was no point in fantasizing about a man there was really no chance of having a repeat with. Besides, when I thought about Kale and what it was like to kiss him, to have him inside of me, something tightened behind my sternum that made it hard to breathe. I fancied breathing, and if the only way to keep on with that was to stop thinking about Kale, then I'd have to stop.

Eventually.

Somehow.

"The plane is waiting, Sir," Niko said as he pulled open the back door of the limo. I stepped directly onto the tarmac and checked my pockets. I'd never owned a cell phone, but I did still have my passport, so that felt like a win. If I'd been in extremely serious trouble, Niko would have snatched it from me before he'd tossed me in the back of the car.

"I'm sure it's being paid to wait," I assured him. "I wouldn't worry about it too much."

I yanked the loose bowtie from around my neck and shoved it into my pocket. My empty pocket. Because my royal order was not there where I'd left it.

I pinched the bridge of my nose and groaned.

It *was* in my pocket until Kale shoved it in my mouth to shut me up while my naked ass was in the air.

"It's not all that bad," Niko said softly beside me, not realizing that my very small oversight might in fact make it *that* bad. "You'll make it out alive."

"I appreciate the vote of confidence," I muttered, letting my hand fall. He didn't need to know the cause of my frustration or my concern. If I told him, I could probably get him to hold the flight, go back into the city, track down Kale, get the order, and circle all the way back to the airport, but...I didn't think the delay would do me any favors either. I'd just have to get a new one. It wasn't like my father didn't have a whole stack of them in a closet somewhere. It was the optics of the whole thing, that was all.

"Are you tagging along?" I asked when I was halfway up the stairs and he was still on the asphalt.

Niko shook his head. "Phillip doesn't think you stand a chance of sneaking off at thirty thousand feet."

"I thought he brought you on special for me." I crossed my arms in front of my chest and pretended to pout. It was a move I'd have done without thinking two days prior, but somehow it felt far too fake to hold up. I dropped my arms, shoving my hands into my pockets and leaning against the handrail of the stairs.

"I work at the pleasure of the crown, Your Royal Highness." Niko tilted his chin toward his chest, a bow. "Have a safe trip home."

"Right."

I finished climbing the stairs, fighting back the very ridiculous and childish feeling of having my toys taken away from me. Not that Niko was a toy, but his comment was a cold reminder that nothing in my life was ever truly mine. The things I had were because my father or my older brother decided they were for me. And maybe that was another slice of the appeal around Kale. He was foreign and he was so far out of their grasp that he was the first thing that felt truly to be my own. It was better to leave him behind, I thought, collapsing down into an overstuffed cream leather seat. Because as long as he was in America, in my memories, they couldn't have him.

They couldn't *take* him.

I scowled through the pre-flight checks, waiting until we were at cruising altitude to pick up the inflight phone and call Parrish.

"Good God," he groaned upon answering. "What do you want?"

"Did I wake you?"

"From a nap." He yawned. "What time is it there?"

"It wasn't even seven when we went wheels up." I thumped my head against the back of the seat and made a clapping motion with my free hand until the attendant slid a flute of champagne between my waiting fingers. "So if I'm still in American airspace, it's before seven."

"I thought you weren't due home for another four days."

"I got in a bit of trouble," I admitted.

The champagne was sweet and cold, but it did nothing to dull the ache in the back of my head or the one between my legs.

"What did you do?" he asked.

"I was very bored at the ballet," I started to explain, even as Parrish cut me off with a laugh. His amusement at the situation softened my displeasure enough for me to smile at his reaction.

"And then what?" he prompted.

"I bribed a bathroom attendant to let me out through the utility hallways. I met a man and kissed him on the sidewalk, then followed him to a sex club, and after that a hotel."

"Must have been a terribly boring ballet," Parrish muttered.

"I'm not sure which of my offenses Phillip found most egregious, but as soon as I left the hotel, I was in the back of a car on the way to the airport."

"And now you're on your way home, four days ahead of schedule."

"As it goes," I confirmed, clearing my throat. "I need you to do me a favor, though."

"Of course you do."

"I just need a phone."

"You're on one," he said.

"Yes, unfortunately I cannot take this one in my pocket back home with me. It kind of has to stay with the plane."

"Is your father still on the no cell phone thing with you?" Parrish asked.

"Even if he wasn't, he would be by the time I got home."

The "cell phone thing" had been a point of contention for years. But much like I didn't have keys or a job or live in a property that wasn't owned by my family, a cell phone was also on the no-fly list...so to speak. I knew it was because my father couldn't even begin to fathom the mischief I would get myself into if I had direct access to the world, but what he didn't know was I already did.

Emailing and using encrypted text apps on my computer were not my preferred methods of communication, but they were the ways I most often had to manage. Parrish had been used to it for years, which I was thankful for. And even though I very much viewed my home life as a prison, I knew I was privileged beyond measure. There was no door that wasn't open to me, even if it wasn't mine. I simply had to show up somewhere and people would be falling over themselves to attend me.

Maybe another reason Kale was so appealing because, even though he had been very big on the tending part of the night, I never once got the impression any of it came from a place of obligation. Kale was with me because he wanted to be, of that I was sure.

"Why a phone?" Parrish asked. "Someone you need to call?"

I didn't even have Kale's phone number, and I didn't know what I would say to him if I found it. But I wanted the phone just in case. I wasn't used to justifying myself to people, least of all Parrish, but I was too tired to snap at him over the comment.

"I think I may have some time to serve," I told him. "I'm just trying to get my affairs in order."

"Tell me about the sex club," he said, ignoring my request for a phone completely.

I toed off my shoes and stretched out my legs, taking another sip of the champagne. I knew the bottle had been meant for my brother, so I took a larger swallow, a smile creeping across my mouth as I drank down the contents of the flute and raised the glass for a refill.

"What do you want to know?"

"What did you do there?" he asked.

"Had a drink and left."

"That feels bland, even for you."

I thought about Kale's friends and found myself wondering what kind of story he would spin about our night together once they both pinned him down to ask their twenty questions. Neither of them had been overtly overbearing, but they wouldn't take no for an answer. And neither would Kale.

"It was too public," I said. "We went to a hotel and—"

Parrish cut me off again, "What hotel?"

"The Plaza."

"Suite?" he asked.

I sighed. "Yes."

"Go on."

"Do you think I'm out here fucking men who can't afford me, you asshole?" I chuckled, shaking my head at the insinuation.

"Tell me about the hotel."

"It's gaudy," I said. "White marble and gold everywhere, like what they imagine a European palace would look like."

It was probably true that Phillip's apartments may have resembled the interior design choices at the hotel, but my own quarters couldn't have been further away from that aesthetic. I'd always favored bright colors and modern lines, much to the dismay of quite literally everyone around me.

"I meant what you did at the hotel," he corrected.

I dragged my tongue up and down the inside of my cheek, some of my flesh still tender and swollen for how voraciously

Kale had kissed me the night before. If I closed my eyes, I could still feel his hands on me, heavy and strong against my bare ass, the insides of my thighs, the insides of *me*.

Letting out a trembling breath, I tried to clear my head, but found no reprieve. Even though I could never escape reliving the best few hours of my life, I didn't want to share them with anyone else. I'd tell Parrish anything and everything about anyone else, but not this. Not about Kale. Even though Parrish wasn't part of the family or anything like that, I didn't want to share Kale with him. I needed Kale and the things we'd done together to be just for me

"Nothing worth mentioning," I lied. "Ask me something else."

CHAPTER 11
KALE

A WEEK AFTER THE MOST UNFORGETTABLE NIGHT OF MY LIFE, Christian emailed me. I had just finished dinner with Boston and I was half a block away from meeting Ford for drinks when my phone pinged like a doorbell in my pocket. I normally made a habit of keeping my phone on silent, but I had a new sender alert in my work email that would switch to sound if the email was from a new contact. Generally, the alarm would draw my attention to client requirements and communication from opposing counsel on new cases, but this time it was Christian's name in the sender field.

Or rather, his title.

New message received: HRH Christian Davenport-Spencer <princesschristian@email.com>

At the sight of his name alone, my breath hitched in my throat and I had to stop and lean against a wall so I didn't fall over into the middle of the street. Upon closer review, the breath turned into a laugh rushing out of me so loud it drew the attention of passersby, which was saying something considering no one in the city cared about other people or loud noises.

It was true, I hadn't been able to stop thinking about him since he disappeared before sunrise after our night together, and also true that was extremely out of character for me. Another truth was that I'd jerked off once a day thinking about the outline of my hand against his gorgeous white ass and at least once more per day thinking about how good it felt to fuck him until we were both positively wrecked. All in all, it had been a lot of lonely hours spent with my hand because the memory of his mouth and his ass was unfortunately not enough to sustain me on its own. I'd even let my own primal urges get the better of me one night, and I'd wrapped that little blue ribbon of his around my cock, strangling my erection until I came so hard I almost lost consciousness. I'd soiled the already spit-stained piece of material, and then I'd spread it across the top of my dresser like a trophy.

Even with all of that in mind, I hadn't expected to hear from Christian ever again. I was, of course, sad at the thought of it, but I understood we were from different parts of the world and no matter how privileged I was, we led very different lives. I'd had no idea Christian was royalty when he ran into me on the street, and I'd like to say if I had known I would have done things differently, but I'm not sure I would have. His reappearance in my life cracked open a door that I was certain had previously been dead-bolted shut and bricked over.

Mr. Sheffield, the email started, and I rolled along the wall so I could change the angle of my body away from the street. The very careless yet contrived use of the honorific did something extremely troubling to my normal blood flow, and while pedestrians might ignore my ill-timed laughter, public indecency was another thing entirely.

Mr. Sheffield,

Apologies for emailing at such a late hour, but it's recently been brought to my attention I may have accidentally left my royal order, bestowed upon me by my father, in your possession, and I'm going to need it returned. I assure you I most definitely did not leave this esteemed decoration behind on purpose, at least not entirely, but I'll be happy to collect it at your leisure.

Best,
Christian

P.S. – Also, consider this an apology for the delay in contact even though I don't imagine you ever expected to hear from me again. My closest friend, Parrish, had to procure a phone for me as I don't have one of my own.

I read the email at least five times, hearing the inflection of Christian's voice in my head a little differently on each pass. The tone was exceedingly formal, but it felt flirty, and because I was an intelligent man, not a smart one, I latched on to that like it was a lifeboat in the middle of a storm.

I typed out a quick reply before I could overthink what I wanted to say to him. Christian and I hadn't fallen into bed together because either of us was discerning or thoughtful about choosing our partners. In fact, it had been quite the opposite that brought us together in that suite at The Plaza.

Princess,

I have your fancy little ribbon at home on my dresser, but it's a little worse for wear than when you left it under the couch in the hotel room. Admittedly, the damage is my own doing, but if you need it back, it's yours. Come and collect it.

Kale

I hit send and then switched off the screen and pushed away from the wall. The bar Ford had told me to meet him at was only four buildings down, and the soft amber glow of the sconces mounted on the brick facade washed over the sidewalk and into the street. Ford was in front of the door, talking on his phone and pacing back and forth the length of the bar windows. When he saw me, his lips pursed and he came to a stop. Once I reached him, he sighed, shaking his head.

"I told you before," he said into the phone, catching my stare with what I read to be an apology in his expression, "it was just casual. A one-time thing."

He opened his mouth and snapped it closed again, whoever was on the other end of the call replying in a raised voice. I could hear the abrupt cadence of their speech, and even unable to make out the words themselves, I knew the conversation wasn't something new to Ford. He'd always been a love 'em and leave 'em kind of man, much to the chagrin of all the men he left behind.

"You can tell him if you want, but it's not going to change anything," Ford said, and it was then I recognized the frenzied voice on the other end of the line. "Stefan...you're not making this any easier."

"You're a prick," I told him, pivoting on the ball of my foot and heading into the bar. He could clean up his mess on the sidewalk by himself and join me when he was finished. I'd told Ford on more than one occasion to keep his flirty little hands off my assistants, and even though he'd teased about sleeping with Stefan, I thought he was joking. Clearly not, and all that meant for me was that the time had come for me to find a new assistant.

Again.

Shrugging out of my coat, I took a seat at one of the small two-top tables against the far wall of the bar. I had a great view of the window and I could see Ford on the street, his features turning more tense by the second. I had to give it to him, at least he was doing his best to smooth things over with Stefan. Ford wasn't the softest with his demeanor sometimes, and once he made up his mind, there was hardly ever any turning back. He was a hell of a businessman because of it, a relentless lover, but also a bit of a bull when it came to handling other people's emotions.

I ordered myself a glass of wine, because the email from Christian had already done enough for my anxiety and whiskey wasn't going to make anything better. Ford was still outside when my screen lit up with another email from Christian. The waitress brought my wine, and I opened the message.

Damaged how?

Ford was off the phone and inside, slipping out of his coat and stalking toward the table. His face was flushed and he dropped his phone next to my wine, holding up his hands like he was ready to surrender.

"Please, don't even say it," he pleaded, collapsing into the chair opposite me.

"Say what?"

"Don't fuck my assistant, Ford." He bobbled his head back and forth, but there wasn't any fight in it. He knew he'd made a bad decision.

"You said he was good with his hands," I reminded him. "I hope it was worth it."

"I mean…" Ford cracked a smile, and I couldn't help but roll my eyes at him.

"The agency is going to stop sending me candidates if they all leave with the same complaint."

"You don't think they're really telling people their boss' best friend is taking them to bed, do you?" He arched a brow. "I make sure they don't."

"And what do you have them say instead?" I asked, not certain I wanted the answer.

"That you're too nice, of course." Ford flagged down the waitress and ordered himself a martini. "That the work is too easy and they're bored. They need something faster-paced."

"I'm not sure that's a better lie. No wonder I'm getting horrible candidates."

"They're not horrible at everything."

"My front office is not a goddamn dating pool for you, Ford." I scrubbed a hand down my face and my phone rattled against the tabletop.

"I don't date them," he promised, leaning back with a hearty laugh.

I knew there was no reasoning with him, but it would be

back to the drawing board when it came to my assistant once I was back in the office. Unfortunately, Ford had never met a man—or woman, for that matter—he didn't like. Maybe I could hire an old, retired grandmother or some no-nonsense paralegal from the eighties who would eat a man like Ford Carlisle for breakfast.

The waitress brought his drink and he eyed her appreciatively. I swiped open my phone, finding three emails when I had expected none. The first from Stefan, resigning due to a misrepresentation in the kinds of duties the job entailed, the second from the temp agency confirming I was aware of the resignation, and the third from Christian. I had half a mind to respond to Stefan and tell him fucking every handsome businessman who came into my office was not, in fact, a stipulation for continued employment, but I'd heard enough of him on the phone with Ford to know he was too riled up to see reason.

"How do you convince them to lie for you?" I asked, deleting the two emails about work and opening the only one I wanted to read.

"Do you really want to know?"

I sighed. "Yes."

"I bribe them."

I pinched the bridge of my nose between my thumb and forefinger. "With what?"

"Depends."

"What did you offer Stefan?" I asked.

"Another go."

"I appreciate that you have limited to non-existent morals," I told him. "Thank you."

"You're welcome." Ford grinned and took a drink of his

martini before popping one of the stuffed olives off with his teeth. "So, what's going on with you? Any word from that Christian man?"

I tapped my fingers against the black screen of my phone. "I was just chatting with him."

"Are you going to see him again?"

I swiped open the email.

Damaged how, Kale?
Hopefully you can spring for some dry cleaning before you post it back to me.

- C

No.

Nothing in that message would do for me, and I wrote out a reply telling him as much.

Back to a first name basis, are we? I have to admit, I liked you better when you knew your place. I'm happy to dry clean your spit and my cum out of the strip of ribbon if that's what you demand, but there's no way I'm mailing it back to you. If you want it, you can come and get it.

I hit send and glanced up at Ford, who eyed me with an indescribable kind of glint in his eyes.

"What?" I barked, swirling my wine before taking a sip.

"Just never seen that look on your face before."

"How would you read it?" I asked.

"If I didn't know better, I'd think there were feelings involved with whoever you just sent that message to."

"I do have feelings, Ford." I scoffed, the insinuation beyond ridiculous. "I'm not like you."

"I'll have you know I have feelings," he protested. "I feel lots of things."

"Like my assistants' hands?"

"And their mouths, if I'm lucky."

He laughed, and I took another drink of my wine. My phone flashed with another email, and I was going to have to switch to text because the formality was too much for me. I appreciated the honorifics, though. I was actually close to demanding them, but the prehistoric use of email felt beyond dated.

Apologies for the brevity, Mr. Sheffield.

That's curious. I don't remember leaving cum on one of the highest orders of my very own kingdom, but that's neither here nor there. Getting out of the county is a little harder than usual, on account of the fact last time I was abroad, I slipped my security detail, met a handsome stranger on the street, and eventually let him gag me with said royal order. As it is, I'm already risking life and limb by emailing you from a throw-away phone my best friend procured for me. To say I'm in a state of lockdown might be an understatement. As always, though, open to suggestions.

Your humble servant,
HRH Christian Davenport-Spencer

"Yeah." Ford smacked his lips together, eyeing me over the brim of his martini. "Definitely feelings."

"I don't know what you're talking about," I said, scratching my chin.

In light of Christian's most recent email, I found myself facing a series of problems, each one feeling a little more insurmountable than the last. Replacing Stefan, I could manage. Trying to find a way to see Christian again? That felt a little more out of the question, but I wasn't the kind of man to back away from a good challenge, as I'd already proven from the first night we met.

"Tell me what's going on in that pretty little farmer's brain of yours, Kale. I can tell you're going a mile a minute, but it doesn't look like you're going anywhere good."

"I just...I don't think you'll believe me if I tell you."

"Try me."

I gave Ford a helpless shrug and a cockeyed smile. "I'm just trying to figure out how to kidnap a prince."

CHAPTER 12
CHRISTIAN

"It's giving Rapunzel," Parrish said to me, reclining against a chaise lounge near the window. He mindlessly plucked at some fringe on a decorative pillow, mouth twisted into a disappointed frown.

I tugged at the end of my hair, barely long enough to graze the back of my neck.

"I think they're almost tired of the whole thing," I assured him.

"You're less fun here."

"I'm more of a prince here," I reminded him.

Parrish exhaled a heavy breath and spun toward me, dropping both of his loafer-clad feet onto the wood floor. Propping his elbows on his knees, he leveled a bored look at me, mouth still in that tight pucker of a frown.

"You're almost thirty," he said. "And you're not an heir. This is..."

"Too much," I supplied.

"It's overdone." Parrish stood and brushed his hands down the front of his gray tweed pants as if there were invisible wrinkles he was trying to press out with his fingertips. "Come on."

"Where are we going?"

I stood, even though I didn't think I would make it anywhere. The cell phone he'd gotten for me was tucked safely under my pillow, a slew of messages between Kale and me the only real contents of the device. It had been three days since I emailed him the first time, and three days of near constant communication, save for when we were sleeping. Kale, it turned out, was quite an insomniac, which I appreciated on account of the time difference. He was also a workaholic when he didn't have anything better to do, like me. And since I was a globe away, he was available.

"This isn't like you," Parrish said with a weak gesture toward the window. "You're a climber, a little escape artist. You always have been, but you're locked up here and you're *content* about it."

"I'm hardly content," I protested.

"You're not fighting."

I swallowed, reaching under the pillow to make sure the phone was where I'd left it. "I think I went too far this last time. I've never been basically kidnapped off the street and sent back home before."

"What did your father say when you got back?"

"He hasn't seen me," I said, biting the tip of my tongue between my sharpest teeth.

Parrish let out a low whistle and sat back down. "That's bad."

I waved my hand flippantly around the room. "Hence the imprisonment. I'm not trying to make this worse on myself."

"What has Phillip said?"

"So much I've lost track."

My oldest brother had been the first person to come visit me besides Niko, who'd been standing like a sentry outside the door of my apartments since I stepped foot back over the threshold. He started with a lot of big and intelligent-sounding words, but it wasn't long before the curse words began to slip out and then he was red-faced with spit flying from the corners of his mouth. I was an embarrassment, a mockery of the crown. The list of my wrongdoings went on and on. I tried to tell myself he was being overdramatic. All I'd done was sneak out of a boring ballet and kiss a handsome stranger. In the list of offenses I'd committed over the course of my life, it was relatively minor.

"Summarize," Parrish said.

"I'm a letdown."

Even though I'd spent my entire life taking everything Phillip ever said to me with a handful of grains of salt, something about the tone of his latest accusations had settled very heavily in the pit of my stomach and not bothered to leave. The problem was, at least as I saw it, he'd never understand what it was like to not be the heir. He was so much like our father because that was how he'd been raised to be. And then my other older brother, Edward, a carbon copy of Phillip, and me, a copy of Edward. But the edges had worn down after every imprint, the younger showing a few more flaws than the rest.

I hadn't realized how much the years of comparison had gotten to me until I'd been in that hotel room with Kale. Until I'd met the first person in my whole life who didn't see me as a copy of Edward, who was a copy of Phillip, who was a copy of our father and his father and his father and so on up the line.

There was no comparison in Kale's eyes when he looked at me, just desire. The singular focus made it easy to give him what he asked for. I'd have probably given him anything, all things considered. But he didn't ask for it. All he'd wanted was a night of orgasms for the both of us, which I'd give him a thousand times over if the situation allowed.

"I've had enough of this." Parrish pulled his phone out of his pocket and turned that lingering frown toward the screen. Had he always been as serious as all that? He hadn't cracked a smile since he showed up, which was unlike him. Though, he had encouraged me to climb out the window which was very much like him.

"Niko let me in, you know," he said, nodding at his phone before returning it to his pocket and marching over to my closet.

"I am still a prince. Not a prisoner."

Parrish pulled a small suitcase out of my closet and flung it open. He yanked shirts off of hangers, barely bothering to fold them before shoving them into the case. After he'd torn through my shirts and ties, he moved onto pants and underwear, and lastly socks. For good measure, I supposed, he shoved a pair of white sneakers on top of it all, and I found myself wondering if he'd ever packed a suitcase by himself in his entire life or if mine was the first.

"Then start acting like it."

He zipped the case closed and dragged it to the window he'd been sitting under.

"What are you doing?"

"Staging a jail break." Parris shoved the window open and pushed the suitcase out. It landed with a dull thump against the grass two floors down. I knew it would be behind a bush because, whenever I'd bothered to escape out the window, that was where I'd always ended up.

"Where exactly are we going to go?" I asked with a sigh. "Niko is right outside the door and my hips don't feel like crawling down a trellis."

Parrish went back into my closet and came back with another pair of sneakers, which he threw against my chest.

"Put these on," he demanded.

"I don't like when you're bossy."

I only liked when Kale was bossy, apparently.

"Then I need you to start thinking like my best friend again." He braced his hands against his hips, staring at me while I slid my feet into the shoes and tied up the laces.

"And how does your best friend act?" I pulled the phone out from under the pillow and slipped it into my pocket. There wasn't a message from Kale, I'd checked. The silence was a little out of character, but I wasn't ready to read into it yet.

"Like he has control over his life."

"It's a fallacy," I huffed.

"I don't know if that American fucked the sense out of you or what, but I'm hoping that's not the case."

Parrish yanked open the door to my apartments and glared across the hall at Niko, leaning against the wall with a weary look on his face.

"We're leaving," Parrish told him, glancing over his shoulder at me. "Aren't we, Christian?"

I cleared my throat and did my best to straighten my posture. I was wearing old jeans and a t-shirt that had seen better days long before it fell into my possession. I wasn't dressed to stage an escape, let alone step foot in public, but Parrish had called my bluff and I didn't have much of a choice.

I could have stayed, but it was the twenty-first century and I could take that small connection to Kale if I left, so it wasn't like there was so much a need for me to stay.

Not if I didn't really want to.

"I have orders," Niko said, tired like he'd already had this conversation a hundred times before.

"And he's a prince," Parrish snapped. "Aren't you?"

"I am."

Niko swallowed, lips pursed.

"Are you following?" I asked him. "What are your orders?"

"I'm supposed to let them know if you try to leave. Let them know who comes to see you."

"They know Parrish is here?"

Niko scratched the side of his nose, cheeks turning pink.

"Come on, Christian," Parrish said, throwing a look at Niko that was so fleeting, I couldn't make sense of the meaning behind it. "Niko will give you a head start, won't he?"

The flush on Niko's cheeks darkened, and I took that to be a yes.

I followed Parrish through the long halls of the palace and around the side to collect my bag. He carried it for me, almost like he knew I would hesitate and ruin his whole harebrained plan if he gave over the case.

"How long do you think he'll give me?" I asked, climbing into the passenger seat of Parrish's sports car.

He threw the bag into the trunk and came around the driver's side, checking his phone again before dropping it into the cup holder between us.

"He isn't going to come after you," he said.

"How do you know?"

I didn't bother trying to slump down or cover my face as Parrish zipped around the fountain and down the long gravel drive toward the road.

"Who is *my* father?" Parrish asked instead of answering.

"My father's most trusted advisor," I said. "Head of state, head of—"

He cut me off, "What do you think the most important skill is for that job?"

"Persuasion," I mumbled.

"I learned from the best."

Off the grounds, I unrolled the window and turned my face toward the breeze and the sunshine. I hadn't realized how cooped up I'd felt until the wind worked its way through my hair and the sun began to warm my cheeks. The air itself was chilly, but the combination was as invigorating as sex.

"Thank you," I said to him without opening my eyes. "Truly. I didn't realize…"

"It's easy to lose sight of life," he said. "But this has gone on long enough in every regard, Christian. You need to have a heart to heart with your father and redefine the expectations around your role and your life."

"I know," I grumbled, blinking my eyes open.

Parrish sped down side roads, navigating around the traffic in the city as best as the old and narrow streets would allow.

"You're too old for his," he chastised.

"I know."

"Too old to climb out windows and use employee exits to get out of functions."

"Phillip said the same thing," I muttered.

"I don't mean it the way he did and you know it." Parrish

pulled into a parking spot and cut the engine, casting the car into a near-deafening silence. "You're twenty-eight and they treat you like a child."

"Phillip would tell you they treat me like one because I act like one."

"Cause and effect works both ways. Maybe if they treated you like an adult for once, you would act like one." He checked his phone again and nodded, throwing open the driver's side door and shoving the device into his pocket.

"Why are you so impassioned about my role within the family?" I followed him out of the car, checking my own stolen phone to find no new messages.

"Because I'm too old for this." He popped the trunk and pulled out my suitcase, which he finally pushed into my hands.

"Last I checked, you got as much of a thrill slipping my detail as I do."

"That's spontaneous." He fished his keys out of his pocket and twisted one of them off, then shook it at me like it was a cat toy. I wasn't certain what he was on about, but I held out my hand, palm up, and he dropped it into my waiting hand. "This is too logistical."

"What are you talking about?" I asked, closing my fist around the sharp teeth of the key. They cut into my palm, and I dropped the key into my pocket because I was still at a loss for what he was trying to tell me. I had a key and a suitcase, and an undetermined head start before Niko came after me. He knew Parrish had come to visit, even if no one else did, so it wouldn't take long for him to know where to find me.

"It's a good thing you're the spare for the spare," Parrish said, mumbling something less flattering than that under his breath before continuing on. "Logistically, being tracked down by an American with more money than common sense who wants to see you again, as a *surprise*—" He paused for effect and shook his hands in the air, "to return some dry cleaning? I don't know, Christian, but this man…"

"Dry cleaning?" I croaked, stare flickering up toward the series of windows on the top floor of the building that I knew contained Parrish's apartment.

"Dry cleaning," he repeated, "which I'm assured is somehow a matter of state security."

"Kale?"

"My second least favorite kind of lettuce," Parrish went on, his longstanding frown finally cracking toward a smile.

"He…"

"You're daft."

"How did he find *you*?" I managed to ask.

"The internet is a vast and terrifying place." He shrugged. "Either that, or I'm not treated like an infant and I'm allowed to have social media, so it was easier to find me than it was to find you."

"We've been emailing for days," I cut in.

"You can sort out the details with him if it matters." Parrish pointed at my pocket, pointed at the key. "You can also pay me back for the vacation I'm taking so you can have free use of my apartment. You're welcome. Now, please, fuck off upstairs, Christian. Your American is waiting."

CHAPTER 13
KALE

Finding Parrish Bernadotte was easy. *Deciding* to find him had been the hard part, but frankly I was tired of jerking off and I had some vacation days left to burn before the end of the year. I could have asked Christian directly, but circumventing him was something Ford had come up with at the bar when I suggested he help me plan a royal kidnapping. When all was said and done, I'd hardly have called it kidnapping, more a facilitated rendezvous with a yet-to-be determined list of repercussions.

After landing at the airport, I'd caught a car directly to the address Parrish had given me. Jetlagged and in dire need of two minutes to brush my teeth, Christian's lifelong best friend sized me up, gave me a spare key, and set off to the palace. I'd offered to get a hotel, but he volunteered his apartment instead, and I'd found it hard to decline. The time was limited, with less than a week before I was due back in New York. Parrish wasn't sure how long Christian would be able to stay away from the palace without drawing security...or worse. The whole thing was a gamble, but when I had lay awake at night reading Christian's emails until I fell asleep, I knew it was worth it.

That didn't mean it was a good idea, though. It was probably anything but. Christian and I had exchanged messages about a lot of things, but none of them ever even touched on the future. We were both stuck in a cycle, a world apart but reliving the same handful of hours over and over. And since I clearly wasn't above hopping on a plane for a booty call, I found myself hunched over the sink in Parrish's bathroom, spitting toothpaste into the basin while I waited for Christian to arrive.

As the minutes creeped on, I worried I had overestimated the brilliance of my plan. Ford and I had come up with more than our fair share of bad ideas after drinking too much wine, and I didn't want this trip to see Christian to become one of them. I was neck deep in what that kind of catastrophe would look like when I heard the sound of a key in the front door and the lock disengaging.

My bag was in the bedroom, phone on the charger, and when Christian sheepishly stepped into the apartment, I didn't know what to do with my hands. He had a suitcase at his feet and a nervous look on his face. His shoulders were tense, but uneven, like he was ready to shrug me off at a moment's notice.

"My American," he murmured under his breath, stepping inside and closing the door behind him. He twisted all of the locks into place and sucked in a deep breath, finally meeting my stare.

"Is that what I am?"

"That's what Parrish calls you." He licked his lips, worrying the corner of his mouth with the tip of his tongue.

"What do you call me?" I asked.

He exhaled with a huff. "I call you Mr. Sheffield."

Heat flickered up my spine, and I flexed my fists, straightening my fingers at my sides and taking a step toward the door. Christian's nostrils flared, but he stood his ground, mouth pulling up into a bratty smile that I'd forgotten I missed until I saw it again.

"Come all the way 'round the world for that, then?" he asked.

"Get on your knees, princess."

"No kiss?" He teased the question, even as he sank down the ground. One knee, then the other, and all the earlier nervousness was gone from his face. He blinked up at me with heavy, hooded eyelids, waiting for his next instruction.

"I'll give you something to kiss."

I closed the space between us, my belt undone and my fly down before I reached him. Christian's mouth fell open, tongue out and ready. His lashes fluttered closed and I traced my dick across the perfect pout of his lips. It took every ounce of willpower that had ever or would ever exist in my body to not immediately bury myself into the back of his throat. My body was needy and loud, but we had enough time that I didn't need to rush through it like the last time.

"Tell me to stop if you want me to stop," I said.

"Go."

I slapped my dick against the flat of his tongue and slid one hand around the back of his head. He made an unimpressed sound and I snapped my hips, holding him in place as I pushed the head of my cock into the back of his throat. Christian glared up at me through watering eyes, gagging around my girth, but I didn't offer him any reprieve.

"Breathe through your nose," I said.

He huffed a hot breath against the base of my shaft, tickling my pubes.

I held myself in his mouth until the convulsions in his throat calmed down, then I slid all the way out and fucked back in. He gagged again, spit slicking around his lips and down his chin while I fucked his mouth like it was a sex toy. When I was close to coming, I pulled all the way out and stepped back. Christian leaned forward, chasing after my cock. His stare was hazy and his lips were already swollen. I took another step back toward the far end of the room.

"Crawl," I told him.

"Excuse me?" His eyes rolled a little bit before he blinked himself out of a stupor and back into the present.

I took a step backward, then another and another until my back was pressed against one of the open windows on the far wall of Parrish's apartment.

"Crawl," I repeated.

Christian spent less than ten seconds debating the demand before he went onto all fours and began the slow trek across the room. He started toward me, eyes narrowed, but the animosity only made my cock even harder than his mouth had.

"Put your ass in the air," I demanded. "Show me what I came all this way for."

Christian exhaled loudly, accentuating the arch in his back as he weaved his way around Parrish's furniture.

"Does crawling make you feel small?" I asked him.

"It should, shouldn't it?" Christian stopped in front of me, looking up at me like it was obedience that coursed through his veins, not rebellion.

"Does it?"

"No."

"How does it make you feel?"

"I don't know," he admitted, although the flush on his cheeks said otherwise.

"I haven't been able to stop thinking about you all week," I told him. As if to confirm it, precum leaked out the slit of my cock and mixed with Christian's spit. I tore open the buttons on my shirt and shrugged out of it, then rucked up my undershirt and held it against my chest with my chin.

"Me, or this ass you flew around the world for?" he asked.

"Aren't they the same thing?"

Christian made a noise in the back of his throat and shifted back onto his heels, palms resting on the tops of his thighs. "You came here to fuck me, Kale. What are you waiting for?"

"When you call me by my name, it makes my cock soft," I said, even though it was clearly a lie.

Christian angled his head to the side, the bulge between his legs impossible for either of us to ignore. He reached down and palmed himself over the fly of his jeans, groaning as he caused the friction we were both after.

"Sorry, Mr. Sheffield," he apologized with fake sincerity, using two of his fingers to wipe spit off his lower lip. "We can't have that now, can we?"

I fisted my cock around the base and aimed it back at his mouth. My pulse hammered against my fingers, beating in my ears, the last threads of my self-control ready to snap. How had it only been a week since I'd met this man? Since I'd last had him?

"Do you want me to stop?"

"I'll have you arrested for kidnapping if you do."

I fisted his hair and yanked him onto my cock.

The blow job was short and messy, and I came with my head against the cracked window and my dick on the tip of Christian's tongue. He moaned and sucked as I spilled into his mouth, taking all of my shaft into his mouth like the greedy little boy I already knew him to be. Even after my balls had emptied, Christian kissed and suckled my cock, and my grip on his head turned softer as he worked at me. He dragged his hands up my legs, shoving my pants down as he went, and then he found the bruise he'd left, pressing his finger into the pale yellow remnants of the mark on my thigh.

I winced, smacking his hand away, but I immediately missed the feel of him there. The reminder.

I eased my half-flaccid cock out of his hot mouth and slid down the wall until I was on the floor, eye level with him. Christian was already halfway to subspace, his stare glazed and happy, with a smear of cum and saliva across his chin.

"I think I missed *you*," I told him.

"More than my mouth?"

I chuckled, crooking my finger and beckoning him closer. He came without protest, which was novel for him, and then Christian was in my lap, half curled against my chest. He was still fully dressed, his skin hot and clammy where I could feel him against me. I wrapped my arms around him, stroking my hand over his head and smoothing out the hairs I'd pulled at minutes before.

"What are you doing here?" Christian finally asked, barely louder than a whisper.

"I don't know. I didn't think this all the way through."

"How far did you get?"

"I knew I wanted to see you again—"

He cut me off. "Aren't there men you can see in New York?"

"I needed to see you," I corrected.

His hand slid around the exposed skin of my waist, and he traced a soft swirl around the swell of my hipbone. "Why?" he asked.

"Why doesn't crawling make you feel small?"

He groaned, shifting in my lap so his back was against my chest. With his legs splayed out in front of him, he freed his cock from his pants. The tip of his dick was nearly purple, and the rest of his shaft strained for how swollen and hard it was. He licked his palm and curled his hand around himself, giving a slow stroke from root to tip.

"Crawling to *you* doesn't make me feel small," he said.

"I don't know why I needed to see you."

"Don't lie." Christian's shoulder blades dug into my chest as he arched up, hand moving quicker over his erection.

"I couldn't stop thinking about you," I repeated.

"I am unforgettable."

"I wanted you."

He hummed, head falling against my shoulder. I hooked my ankles around his calves, pulling his legs wide.

"You don't take no for an answer," he murmured, cupping his balls and tugging them away from his body. His other hand was slick with precum and spit, the sound of it louder than my heartbeat.

"Not from you, princess. And not from Parrish either."

"And that's why you're here?"

I covered his hand with mine, loose enough that I didn't interfere with the pace of his wrist. He was twitchy and sweaty, and he came on both of our hands with a strangled shout. Cum shot out of his cock like a geyser, and I caught as much of it as I could, waiting until his hand fell away to let mine move.

I spread his legs wider, far enough that I could feel the way his thighs trembled against mine. Reaching up behind us, I cradled the back of his head with my clean hand, then pressed my cum-stained fingers against his mouth. He let his lips part and I pushed right into his mouth, just like I'd done with my cock. And just like with my cock, Christian shuddered and gagged. I stretched my fingers deep, pushing his own cum back with mine, right into his throat, straight into his stomach.

I laid a kiss against the top of his ear.

"If my cum isn't inside of you, it goes here. Do you understand?"

He nodded, choking around my hand. I pulled it free and he coughed, chest heaving as he tried to catch his breath.

"Yes," he rasped, the single syllable rough as sandpaper.

"Yes, what?"

"Yes, Mr. Sheffield." Christian dropped his head against my shoulder again, and I loosened the tension of my legs around his. He immediately rolled and curled back into my lap, body vibrating like a happy little cat. With a long and slow exhale, I found myself with the distinct impression it was the first time Christian had been relaxed since his little jaunt to New York. I also realized, it was the first time *I* felt the same. With the weight of him in my lap, the heat of his mouth around my cock still a fresh memory, I closed my eyes and held him close.

"That's why I'm here, Christian."

It wasn't so much a coherent answer, but it made sense in

my heart and it was the absolute best I could offer him considering there were feelings and things floating around in my head that I hadn't had time to make sense of yet. Though, I hadn't much tried either. Up until that orgasm, I'd been running on bad ideas and adrenaline...and a decent amount of top shelf liquor.

He seemed to understand, at least, nodding against my chest, his warm exhale ghosting over the hair in the center of my chest.

"That's why," I said again.

He slid one hand up around the back of my neck, the other around my waist.

"Thank you, Mr. Sheffield."

CHAPTER 14
CHRISTIAN

LESS THAN FIVE MINUTES AND ALL WAS RIGHT IN THE WORLD. KALE'S arms were around me, his cum was in my stomach, and I could have died happy. Even if Niko had chosen that exact moment to burst through the doors and re-kidnap me, I could have endured it. Kale's fingers in my hair quieted any residual noise that tried to take up space in my mind, and I adjusted myself on his lap, but it was too late. The initial post-orgasm haze had worn off and the clothes were uncomfortable, the sweat was cold and sticky. I groaned, rolling off of him and flopping onto the floor like a dead fish.

"I hope you're here to return my royal order." A hint of a smile flashed across my mouth, and Kale rolled his eyes, resting his head against the windowsill.

"If you're a very good boy while I'm here, I imagine you can earn it back."

"Are you on about the whole listening and doing what I'm told bit again?" I turned onto my stomach, pushed onto all fours, then rocked back into a seated position.

"I'm never not on that," he said, crooking a finger and beckoning me closer.

I'd already crawled for him, and I crawled again, going soft when he took my face into his hands and slanted our mouths together. The kiss tasted like hello, and I had to flatten my palms against his chest to hold myself up. I would have been content to spend the rest of his stay just like that, on my knees with his tongue in my mouth, but I also knew that would have been a waste when he had other body parts I had already become so fond of.

Kale ended the kiss, and I leaned back to study his face. He was handsome as I remembered, slim and angular in the face with a barely contained mop of dark hair on top of his head. He styled it well, but I liked how it looked after he was well-fucked the best. I threaded my fingers through the silky, chestnut strands, and felt myself slipping again. Forcing myself to untangle from him, I stood up and propped my hands on my waist. He gazed up at me, eyes still heavy with desire.

"I still don't understand what are you doing here." I said.

"Hopefully more of that," he answered.

"Obviously, but I think you know what I meant."

I wanted to know why he wasn't in America. Why he was half-dressed on my best friend's living room floor. I wanted to know why he had come back for me...

"Your emails were getting a little bratty and I figured you needed to get put back into line."

"You did not fly here just to spank me again."

"Didn't I?"

"It cannot be the only reason," I conceded, cheeks inexplicably burning with embarrassment.

"Why not?" Kale shifted and climbed onto his feet, facing me head on.

"That's ridiculous," I whispered.

"What's so ridiculous about it?"

"I'm sure there are a thousand men in New York for you to spank and fuck."

"But none of them are you," he said.

Spit lodged in my throat, making it impossible to swallow, and the cold sweat that had started to dry across my collarbone suddenly felt slick and wet all over again. I rubbed my clammy palms down the sides of my thighs and took a step away from him.

"No," I said weakly, "I imagine they're not."

"Is it so hard to believe that I wanted *you?*" Kale reached behind him and rucked up his undershirt, pulling it over his head and tossing it on the floor next to his dress shirt. He yanked off his belt next, then his pants and socks. I stood rigid and unsure in front of him, for once in my life feeling too far out of my element.

I cleared my throat and gestured vaguely toward the hallway across the room.

"Did you want to take a shower?"

"I want you to answer me," he said.

"Yes." I shrugged. "It's impossible to believe. Did you want to take a shower now?"

He shook his head. "No."

"Alright."

"You had your friend steal a phone for you," Kale said, holding up a finger, then another, counting off his points as he talked. "You created a fake email to talk to me so you wouldn't get caught, and before you argue that one, I know for a fact that *Princess* Christian is not a state email."

"Could be."

"His Royal Highness, Prince Christian Davenport-Spencer." Kale pressed his hand against the center of his chest and then bowed.

"Don't you fucking dare." I surged toward him, fisting his hair and yanking him upright again. His eyes flashed with a resistance which quickly turned to stubborn arrogance. It was the look he'd had on his face the first night I met him when he decided to take me to a hotel instead of leaving me to hide from Niko on my own.

"Why not?" He pulled against my hand, but I didn't let go. "Don't you deserve respect too?"

"Not like that," I rasped.

He chuckled, giving his head another tug, and I released his hair. "You find your respect at my feet, don't you?"

I managed a nod.

"You don't understand that," he said, not asking.

I shook my head.

"The first night I had you, I didn't think it was worth explaining," he said, smoothing back the strands I'd ruffled. "I figured you could put the pieces together on your own. It was just a one-time thing for us."

"And yet."

"Have you thought about it at all? Since then?" Kale's dick was hard again, tenting his briefs and smearing a dark wet spot across the front.

"Not the details of it," I said.

"Just the acts."

"Yes."

"Do you want to think about the rest of it? Do you want to understand it?"

I took a step back from him as if another foot between us would somehow make it easier to breathe.

"It was one night then and it's two nights now. What difference does it make?" I asked.

"A world of it."

"Did you want to shower?" I asked again.

I had no idea why a shower felt so imperative, but the idea had taken root in my head and I couldn't get away from it. I needed to get Kale out of his underwear and into the shower, and I needed to get soap on my hands and his skin. I needed to wash him, and...

I let out a harsh breath, puffing out my cheeks. Recognition flashed across his face, and his expression softened, just enough for me to notice it.

"We can shower," he agreed.

"Thank you."

I spun on my heel and went into Parrish's bathroom. I could feel Kale behind me, a looming presence despite his slender form, and I imagined that spoke volumes about why it felt so good in my chest when I got on my knees for him or when I bent over his lap and let him spank me. He demanded it without even using words.

Kale had been here awhile, I realized, seeing his toiletry bag on the edge of the sink. His toothbrush was still wet, and I leaned over and used two of my fingers to spread the zipper apart to peer inside. I found all the usual suspects—toothbrush, toothpaste, deodorant, moisturizer and eye cream, a decent size bottle of lubricant and a fresh box of condoms. I pulled my hand away from the bag and turned my attention to the shower.

"It's called submission," he said after I turned on the water.

I cracked my neck, not daring to look at him. "I know what it's called."

"Alright," he said.

I tested the water to make sure it was warm enough to turn our skin pink, but not hot enough to peel it off. Stepping back, I gestured weakly toward the spray, turning my attention to the ceiling when he shoved his briefs down and stepped out of them. Once he was under the water, I put two towels on Parrish's towel warmer, turned it on, then followed Kale into the shower.

He'd already put his soap on the sill, a white bottle that looked far too modern even for Parrish's tastes. I leaned around him and picked it up, flipping the cap open to take a sniff. The soap was surprisingly spicy and clean at the same time, like ginger and linen. I squirted some onto a cloth and lathered it up, not asking permission before I started to drag the lather across his shoulder blades.

"Tell me more," I said, half hoping the sound of the shower would wash the words right down the drain.

"In simplest terms, it's about making a choice."

"A choice to kneel?" I asked, working down his spine and over his ribs with the soapy washcloth.

"A choice to let someone else make the choices," he said.

Why was it so impossible to breathe around him? Why were the words always tangling in my throat and turning into things I didn't understand? That wasn't me; it wasn't who I was. If anything, it put me at a disadvantage to not be the smartest person in the room, something I loathed beyond comprehension. But with Kale, it didn't feel like a weakness. It wasn't that he was smarter than me, not even that he had more practical knowledge, just that...he was my elder in some way. In a very sexy and non-threatening way, thank God.

"Just like that?"

"You did it in New York."

I reached the round globes of his ass, using my finger to clean between them. I traced the tip of my first finger around his pucker, then moved to his balls and the insides of his thighs. It was hard to reach him standing, so again I went to my knees.

"What was the choice, then?" I asked. "I asked you for help, I hardly knew what I was getting myself into if that was it."

"You're overthinking it," he said, turning and bringing his erection flush with my face.

I blinked slowly, focusing on washing his thighs and his knees instead of the way his cock bobbed in front of my mouth, the way I could smell his cum and the musky sweat of our earlier exertion over the crisp scent of his soap.

"One choice to submit, then a series of choices to keep going."

"That sounds contradictory to your first point, Mr. Sheffield." I was at his feet, and I used my trembling fingers to wash his toes before working my way back to my feet so I could tend his chest and shoulders from the front.

"It's a living thing," he went on, raising his arms so I could get into his pits. The sight of the wet and curly hair beneath his arms made my own cock spring back to life, but I ignored the dizziness from when the blood left my brain and flooded my cock. "After the first one, it's more the illusion of control."

"How do you figure?"

"When we were at the hotel and I had you over my lap, for example."

We were very nearly eye level, and I couldn't look at him, even as I felt his stare roaming over my face. He put his arms back down at his sides, and I busied myself with the sharp slope of his collarbone.

"Go on," I coaxed.

He was clean, standing in front of me covered in soap and he made no move to rinse. I reached around him and pulled the detachable head off the wall, doing it for him. He huffed a low noise in the back of his throat and smiled, tracing his finger across my cheek as I tended him.

"If your choice would have been to stop, we would have."

"That's called consent," I reminded him.

"You're a quick study."

I put the shower head back onto the wall, waiting for him to finish his explanation.

"At home, I don't imagine you get to say no often," he said.

"I say it all the time."

"But no one listens."

I licked my lips.

"I would have listened. With me, that night, you were the one in control," he said.

"I was ass up over your lap with handprint-shaped bruises on my ass," I said. "I'd hardly consider that control."

"But that was what you wanted."

His hand was on my face again, his thumb this time

stroking across my cheek while his fingers stretched past my ear and threaded into my hair.

"Yes," I agreed.

"Submission is getting what you want by asking for what you need," he said.

"What about punishments?" My voice cracked. "You talked about punishing me."

"You act out because you *need* to be punished." Kale tilted my head back and looked so deep into my eyes, I knew whatever he said next would be the truest observation anyone had ever made about me. "Because you're spinning out of control and you need that anchor again. You need to know that I'm a man of my word and I'll reel you back in, no matter how far away you drift."

CHAPTER 15
KALE

CHRISTIAN'S NOSTRILS FLARED AND HE LICKED HIS LIPS, MOUTH falling partway open like he had something to say that he couldn't find the words for. The blank confusion on his face gave me the impression that I'd dropped a pretty substantial bomb on him, and I imagined he would need time to process. Hell, *I* needed time the process.

The trip itself had been such a half-cocked whirlwind of an adventure. The jetlag and the insanity of the whole thing was finally starting to catch up with me, and I had genuine concerns my legs were going to give out. Even with Christian's careful and thorough hands working their way over every inch of my skin, I didn't trust my knees to keep me standing.

Taking the cloth from Christian's hand and giving him the same service he'd given me, I cleaned him a little quicker, then made sure we were both rinsed before grabbing a towel for him off the warming rack just outside the shower.

"I wish your friend had a jacuzzi," I said, wrapping him up before knotting one of the large bath towels around my own waist.

"I told him the same thing." Christian toweled off, padding barefoot back into the living room where most of his clothes lay discarded on the floor. He stepped into his underwear and then flopped down on Parrish's couch with a groan.

I dried off and put on a clean pair of underwear, then sat down beside him and closed my eyes. Christian curled his fingers around my bicep and tugged me closer, my head falling into his lap. I blinked up, studying the guarded look on his face.

"What are you really doing here?" he asked.

"Lying on the couch at your best friend's apartment while you play with my hair," I said. Christian rolled his eyes at me and I kissed his bare stomach. "Hoping that we can sneak out and grab a bite to eat before my stomach eats itself."

"We can't," he said quickly.

"Why not?"

"This isn't New York. I can't just..."

"Is it that bad?" I asked. "Honestly?"

"The rules are rigid."

I shoved up off of his lap so I could face him head on. His features were still marred with the tight lines of worry around the corners of his eyes, and I found I much preferred the relaxed state of his face post-orgasm to this constant tension and concern.

"Why, though? Aren't you the spare of the spare and then some?"

"Eleventh back," he muttered with a shrug. "I don't know why it's this way. Tradition... expectation. Take your pick."

"Is the expectation that you just do as you're told for the rest of your life? Like a servant?"

"Come on, Kale." Christian stood up and paced across the

room, stopping in front of the window and folding his arms in front of his chest. His shoulders were up high around his ears, tense and locked. "You're from money—you get it."

"I'm not *from* money," I corrected.

"You just flew around the world to fuck me. That couldn't have been cheap."

In all honestly, I'd flown around the world to *see* him, but mincing words at this point wouldn't add anything to the conversation.

"My parents own a farm in California," I said, stretching out my legs and crossing them at the ankle. He was still at the window, shoulders maybe an inch lower than before. "They raise goats and grow produce."

"Do the goats shit gold?"

I chuckled. "I see where you're going, and the answer is no, but they shed it. Technically. Not enough to fund my lifestyle, though. That's my grandparents. It's their money."

"Are you a kept man, Mr. Sheffield?" He finally turned, resting his ass on the windowsill and staring my way. The light beat against his back, casting him into shadow and making him look as much like an angel as he had the first night I met him.

"I had a leg up," I admitted. "My grandparents were fundamental in helping me get to where I am and a decent amount of money in my bank account has come from theirs, but I've done well on my own."

"Well enough to globetrot for a fuck?"

"Would you stop talking about yourself like that? Like you're just a piece of ass? I liked you better in the shower," I told him. "When you were leaning into your submission a little better."

Christian's mouth quirked up in the corner and realization dropped over me like a wet and heavy blanket. He was being a brat again. He was quite literally sitting across from me doing exactly what we'd talked about in the shower. He was asking me for what he needed, and I had almost missed it. After telling him how reliable and sure I wanted to be for him.

"Come over here, princess."

At the endearment, he pushed off the windowsill and stalked toward me. The light diffused around him and I was able to make out the deep flush on his cheeks and the erection thickening between his legs.

"What do you want?" he rasped.

The question felt weighty, loaded, in a way I hadn't been expecting. He wasn't asking about what I wanted in that moment, of that I was sure. The question was a throwback to the rest of the conversation, with him trying to get to the bottom of my motives, which...good luck there. I wasn't even sure what I'd been thinking when Ford and I came up with the plan in the first place. The only thing I knew was I needed to see Christian again.

"I want you to bend yourself over my lap so I can give you what you need," I said to him.

Christian bent himself in half with ease, the burning rod of his cock pressing hard against my thigh, even through the shield of his underwear. I didn't have much time to decide if I wanted to keep them on him or take them off, and at the last minute, I decided to keep them on. The first time I'd taken Christian over my knee, I'd tucked his cock between my legs and let him rut against me while I spanked him. I'd allowed that because it was what he'd needed, but it was different now. He was untrusting and uncertain of me and my motivation, and it was my responsibility to remind him of who I was and who I wanted to be...to him.

I yanked the waistband down below his ass cheeks, exposing his skin but keeping his cock and balls covered. He groaned, writhing against me and I delivered one sharp smack to the center of his right ass cheek. Christian yelped, and I pressed my left hand against the center of his back to keep him still and steady.

"It's been ten days since we met," I said, kneading my hand over the first place I'd spanked him. "Count them."

I spanked him a second time, and he called it one, which was fine with me. One after another after another until we reached ten, and his cock had leaked a river through his underwear, the precum smearing against my leg every time I hit him. Christian was close to babbling nonsense, but I was nowhere near done with him.

"It was an eight hour flight to get here," I said next, delivering another strike, this time lower against the tender fold where his ass met his thigh.

He counted it was one, and I hit him harder each time until the word eight sounded like a prayer in the back of his throat. My hand throbbed from how hard I'd been hitting him, and what I wouldn't have given to be back in the privacy of my house with a rack of paddles and toys at my disposal. The way he would cry for me if I struck him with a tawse was enough to send shocks up the back of my spine at the thought of it.

I'd played with a lot of partners in my life, men and women, but it was a rare thing to find a partner who truly enjoyed the masochism part of BDSM. Not that there was anything wrong with people who did it for fun. I did it for fun, but there was a stark difference between people who liked pain as part of their orgasm and those who needed it separately. Christian was very much the latter, even if he couldn't comprehend what that meant for him.

"Are you good?" I asked him after the eighth spank.

Christian's face was buried in the cushions of the couch and he shook his head furiously, muttering something into the fabric that I couldn't make sense of. Dragging my hand up the length of his spine, I fisted his hair and yanked his head back.

"What did you say?"

"More. More. More," he whined.

"Ask me nicely."

"More, please, Mr. Sheffield."

I dropped his head and raised my hand, delivering the hardest spank of the day. His back didn't bow—it arched—and he pressed up against my hand as I rained another flurry of strikes down against his already bruising skin. New marks popped up around the lingering yellow remnants from our first night together, and my arm was close to falling off from exertion when Christian's entire body went straight as a board on my lap. Wet heat pooled on the top of my thigh, and he seized, cock pressing insistently against my leg as he came.

"Did you just..."

"Oh, fuck," he moaned against the couch, humping my leg as the last jets of cum leaked out of his cock.

I shoved my hand past the pulled-down waistband of his underwear and took his balls into my fist. They shifted and churned against my palm as he finished spilling his release into his underwear, moaning when I touched him, whispering and begging and saying my name over and over again.

It was better than any drink I'd ever had. Better than any high.

It was like Christian had been made for me, in ways neither of us understood. Because until I met him, I thought for sure I knew who I was and what I wanted. I was always after a good time, a naked time, a short time. Not that I had been relationship averse, I just never saw the point in it. I'd never met anyone who *inspired* me to want to lock them down. But with Christian on my lap, covered in his own cum after nothing more than a spanking? The idea of sharing him with anyone ever again made me want to tear all of Parrish's pretty art off the walls and set it on fire.

"Am I in trouble?" he asked, turning his head so his cheek lay against the couch.

His pupils were blown wide and his lashes were clumped together like he'd been crying.

"I didn't tell you not to come," I said. "But…"

"It feels like I should have asked."

The perfectness of this man was unparalleled and unfair.

"Then ask next time," I told him.

He nodded and turned his face away from me.

I petted the back of his head, smoothing down the strands of hair that he'd twisted out of place, then I worked my way down his back until both of my hands were on his ass, tracing the shape of my palms against his skin. Christian sucked in a sharp breath, held it, then let it out with a long shudder.

"I want to take you to dinner," I finally said.

"Can't go out," he muttered, still keeping his face buried and out of sight.

The despondency in his voice almost broke my heart, and hearing him sound so miserable so soon after a hands-free orgasm that had sent him into another stratosphere felt patently unfair. I needed to fix it. Needed to make it right for us both.

"What will happen?" I asked.

"Someone will recognize me."

"And then?"

"Niko will show up."

I sighed, remembering the unwelcome appearance of his security detail at my room at The Plaza.

"Do they know you're gone yet?"

When I reached out to Parrish, he had promised me that he would buy us as much time from Niko as he could manage, though he hadn't said just how he would do that. Since Niko hadn't shown up yet, I imagined we still had a little more time left. I would have been shocked if we made it through the next two nights unbothered, though. And I hated that, like a snake coiled in my stomach. The idea of my time with Christian being interrupted again had me ready to unfurl and strike. I tried my hardest to remind myself that he had a life that didn't make sense to me, obligations I would never under-stand, but all I wanted was two nights and three days. A small fraction of time for us to explore ourselves together, uninter-rupted and undeterred.

And after that?

I wouldn't be content to let him go, but that was a problem for future Kale.

"Niko knows I'm gone, but he was giving me a head start."

"Do you have your passport?" I asked.

Christian shifted onto his elbow, pushing himself up into a half-seated position across my lap. The wet spot on his underwear was massive, and it was a shame to waste a load like that when my mouth—and his—were right there.

"Parrish put it in my bag."

"Alright." I grabbed him by the shoulders and stood, depositing him on his feet with as much grace as I could manage. His knees wobbled, and he caught himself on my shoulder, post-sex confusion washing across his face.

"Alright, what?" he asked, tugging down his underwear to free his cock from the sticky wet spot he'd just made.

"Get dressed," I told him, yanking his briefs back up. "We're going to America."

CHAPTER 16
CHRISTIAN

IF THERE WAS A WORD TO DESCRIBE MY LIFE, IT WOULD BE *WAIT*. Wait for my dad to die so Phillip takes the throne. Wait for everyone older and more senior than me to go into a room so I can follow behind. Wait to be told what to wear, where to dance, what fork to use. Wait until things are different and maybe then...

Wait.

Wait.

Wait.

I was tired of waiting.

As the wheels of Kale's private plane touched down back in New York, I untangled our hands, which had been tangled together for hours, and stared at my fingers. I'd expected my hand to tremble in the air, for what I'd just done was the greatest act of rebellion I'd ever dared to imagine. The whole flight, between Kale's gentle kisses and soft touches, I thought about the words that made up my life *before* him.

Wait, of course, being a prevalent one.

Leave, being another that came up often.

Patience.

Expectations.

Tradition.

Roles.

Rules.

And it felt like a silly thing to measure my life as before Kale and after Kale, but since I'd met him on a New York sidewalk weeks before, I'd also known pleasure, adventure, and more commonly—and surprisingly—submission.

The conversation we'd had at Parrish's apartment before he decided it was a good plan to kidnap a prince felt like it had barely grazed the surface of some of the things we did together, some of the things he *wanted* to do. Because my whole life had been people demanding that I submit to them, that I concede and give over bits and pieces of myself so I could fit in the mold they'd built for me generations before my parents had even been born.

Then—Kale. And he had demanded a different kind of submission from me. One that was taking much more time and work to understand. The one thing I knew, though, was that I wanted it.

I craved it.

"Are we just here for a meal?" I asked, trying to act casual as the door to the plane opened and a gust of sharp city air blew into the cabin.

"I think that's entirely up to you," he said.

"Is this more of that 'I have the control' thing?"

"Yes and no." His eyes sparkled and he held his hand out for me. "I don't know what it's going to be like for you to go home after this. Whether it would be better for you to stay a day and go back, or wait it out until they come to collect you."

I swallowed back bile because I didn't necessarily think one would be worse than the other. Both would draw equal amounts of scorn, but surely the punishment would be worse if I warranted an international search and recovery team.

"I don't think I have an answer for that, so let's start with a meal and we can go from there, I think."

"Do you want to rest awhile first? Get used to the time?" Kale led me down the stairs and straight into the back seat of a waiting black town car. As soon as the door closed behind us, it was like being sealed into a vacuum. The only sounds I could hear were our soft breaths and the incessant thrum of my pulse just beneath my skin.

"Are you taking me back to The Plaza?" I asked, leather seats creaking beneath my weight.

"I'd take you home."

Something about the word choice exploded in my chest like a barb, and I rubbed over my sternum, trying to soothe the unexpected ache that came with his broad usage of the word home instead of the personal. It was just...home. Not *his* home. A fantastical idea took root in the back of my head that one day I could have a home with him, but that was...

No.

That was a daydream too far because I didn't even know the man beside me beyond he made me come harder than I ever had in my life and he was sure nice to look at. I also knew he'd flown around the world to see me, then properly kidnapped me because he wanted to take me on a date without being interrupted by my security detail. Kale had shown me big things with small actions, and all of it added up to more than just sex.

"Home sounds nice," I said softly, even though I knew better than to allow myself the fantasy.

Even though I'd only used the stolen phone to communicate with Kale, and I was with him, the phone was still in my pocket. I pulled it out, swiping open the screen and pressing Parrish's phone number onto the keys so I could send him a text message.

Me: Can you do me a favor?
Parrish: Another one?
Me: Unfortunately.
Parrish: What do you need?
Me: I want them to know I'm gone.
Parrish: Have you lost your mind?
Me: Maybe, but once they know I'm gone, tell them I'm coming back.
Parrish: And when are you coming back?

I glanced at Kale, who was not even trying to hide the fact he was looking at my messages.

"How long had you planned on staying?" I asked. "Before we decided to leave?"

"Two nights."

I nodded, telling Parrish.

Me: I'll be home in three days.
Parrish: You...you're not at my apartment, are you?
Me: No
Parrish: You've lost it.
Me: Tell Niko I'll be home in three days. Tell him to tell my dad

or Phillip or whoever. Tell Niko not to come for me. Tell him I'm safe here.

Parrish: It's his JOB, Christian.

Me: Just a few days.

Parrish: No promises.

Me: Thank you.

Parrish didn't say anything to that, and I knew I'd really have to make it up to him once I got home. He'd gone above and beyond for me the past week, the past lifetime. He never shied away from using his freedoms to get me the relief I was so desperate for. Hell, he'd gotten me Kale. It was just one more ask, and then...I'd deal with the rest of it once I was home.

"Your friend cares about you a lot," Kale murmured as I slid the phone back into my pocket.

The windows of the town car were tinted, but I could still make out the connected concrete and brick structures that reached straight up toward the sky. There were dozens, hundreds of people on the street, bustling past each other, paying no mind to anyone else. Maybe that was what I loved about New York, the anonymity of it.

"His father is my father's most trusted advisor," I said.

He snorted an amused sound in the back of his throat. "Is that a real thing? Not just in the movies?"

"It's a very real thing."

"Can I ask you a question I have no right asking?" Kale propped his head against the window, angling his knees and body toward mine.

"I think we're past the point of formalities."

He gave a weak shrug. "If you hate it so much, why don't you abdicate?"

"Abdication would be for my older brother or my father," I said.

"Or just...I don't know what the term is, but you know what I mean."

"I've thought about it a lot more since I met you than I had before," I admitted.

My cheeks burned, but covering them would have been too obvious. Officially stepping back from my responsibilities and duties as a senior member of the royal family wouldn't have been as earth-shattering as if Phillip decided to denounce his role, and in a way, I wondered if my own rebellion had already paved the way for me to make that decision for myself. Sure, I had charities and all of that work that came with my title, but was any of it really important? It wouldn't hurt anyone if I was to turn my back on it, but what would my life look like if I were to actually leave the palace? I'd never had the opportunity to live on my own before, to have a job, and even though I could still live off the family money without being active, I wouldn't want to do that. I'd hate feeling like I was taking advantage, but...

"Don't do it for me," he said softly.

I barked out a low laugh, the idea not as preposterous as either of us wanted it to be. "I'd never."

Kale nodded, like it had been an instruction given during one of our little games and I'd done my part in the whole thing.

"Good," he said, avoiding my stare.

"Good."

The silence turned awkward and heavy, like we both knew

if he asked me to walk away for him, I'd do it without a second thought.

The drive from the airport to Kale's house took almost an hour, and he seemed content to let me wordlessly stew across from him for the rest of the drive. He fiddled on his phone with his right hand, left hand wound tight around mine as I stared out the opposite window. It was as if the last words spoken had carried far more weight than either of us expected, but they were in the open now and there wasn't anything either of us could do to take them back.

The car came to a stop alongside a curb, and Kale slid his phone back into his pocket with a sigh. Squeezing my hand, he waited until the driver came around to open the door.

"A short nap," he said, voice scratchy. "A little acclimation, then we'll eat."

"Then we'll eat," I agreed, stepping out after him onto the sidewalk.

Kale's house looked like every other building in New York. Too tall and too narrow, sandwiched tightly between two other buildings with a similar profile. But his was built from bricks with white framed windows and wrought iron flower boxes, a black front door, and a tiny little porch light. I didn't know what I'd expected for the interior, but it definitely wasn't the wide-planked wood floors and quaint homey feel the place gave off.

"Do you want a tour first or do you want to go to bed?" he asked, tossing his keys onto a small table in the entryway.

"Bed," I rasped, not because I was tired but because seeing Kale's *home* was more than I could bear. If I were to walk through the rooms and see his things, it would make him more real and that dangerous daydream would turn into something far too big for me to safely contain.

"Bed it is," he said.

I followed him up the stairs to a small bedroom with three tall windows and a painted brick fireplace. The floor was the same wood as the lower level, but he'd layered rugs on top of each other, overlapping shapes and colors and patterns beneath the simple king size bed that faced the fireplace. Anyone else would have looked at the room and said it lacked character, but I'd never seen a room that felt more like Kale to me. Even though *I* didn't know Kale at all.

"I have to catch up on some work," he said, pulling back the covers on the bed. "My office is one floor down if you need anything, but...you can make yourself at home."

"Don't threaten me with a good time, Mr. Sheffield," I teased, toeing off my sneakers and flopping dramatically onto his bed.

Kale breathed out on a smile, his entire body leaning forward like he wanted to crawl under the sheets with me, but at the last minute he went upright again. I smiled at him, eyelids closing in a slow blink. Maybe I was more tired than I'd realized, the whirlwind events of the past day finally catching up to me.

"Get some rest, princess," he said softly, taking a step back.

I reached for the button on my jeans, and Kale swallowed, shaking his head before turning away from me entirely and pulling the door closed behind him on his way out. It was easy to hear the echo of his footsteps down the hallway and then the stairs. The wood floors were gorgeous, but did little to muffle the sound. Then it was the low hum of his voice as he started a phone call, and I stripped out of my pants and my shirt before climbing under his blankets.

Kale's bed smelled like him in a near overwhelming way that made me sad and horny all at the same time. Rolling onto my side, I looked out the windows on the far wall, wondering if the trees blossomed in the spring and if so, what color were the flowers. I fell asleep quickly, the comforting sound of Kale's voice vibrating up through the floor, dancing with the legion of horrible ideas about a future with him that I knew I'd never be able to shake.

CHRISTIAN FELL ASLEEP IMMEDIATELY, BUT I MADE SURE TO STILL quietly close the door behind me as I stepped into my office. The room was one of the smaller ones in my house, but I loved it beyond measure. With an old roll top desk I'd inherited from my great-grandfather, the space felt rich and cozy at the same time. Like many other rooms in the house, it also had a fireplace, but one I rarely used on account of how small the room was.

Sitting down at my desk, I texted Parrish to let him know I'd absconded with his best friend, then immediately called Ford. He answered on the first ring.

"I've been waiting to hear from you," he said in lieu of hello. "What time is it there?"

"Same time as it is where you are. I'm in New York."

"What?" Ford scoffed. "After all that planning and chartering of private planes and you're still in the city?"

"I'm *back* in the city," I corrected, reclining slightly in my wood and leather office chair. It matched the desk, which felt a little over the top, but I loved it just the same. The way it rolled across the wood floor and how it creaked underneath my weight. The noises were familiar to me, and they all sounded like home.

"Did your prince send you away?" he asked.

"Quite the contrary." I lowered my voice even though there was no way Christian would hear me. "He welcomed me with open arms."

"And open other parts, I'm sure."

"Don't be lewd," I chided, cheeks heating at the memory of just how Christian had welcomed me.

"Since when can't I be lewd?" He placed a teasing emphasis on the last word like it was a pretend dirty word when it never had been before. "You're the king of kiss and tell."

"You have me confused with yourself."

"We're two peas in a pod, Kale," he said, not wrong.

Ford and I were sometimes more similar than my brother and I were. I often wondered if Boston would have been better suited for a life on the farm instead of in the city, but he'd made the same choice as me to come stay with our grandparents. Our mom and dad had always maintained an open door policy. In addition to our visits, if we wanted to come live with them long term, we were always given the chance to make the change. I couldn't conceive of being there for more than a week, more than a week*end*, but I could imagine my twin brother longing for the quiet that came with the farm.

Ford, though...Ford was built for a luxurious life with waterfalls of money at his disposal. Like my brother and me, he came from money that had served as a cushion to get him started with his own endeavors. He was arrogant, but not so much so that he believed any of his life to be possible without the handouts he'd been given as a child. After all, Ford was a Carlisle and that name came with as much, if not more, as Sheffield.

"Christian and I are in New York," I said, ignoring the comparison he'd made.

"That....that's probably literal kidnapping, Kale. I thought we were making a joke of the whole thing."

"He came willingly," I said.

"Will the king see it that way?"

I scrubbed a hand down my face, swiveling the chair so I could stare out the window into my back garden. It was mostly concrete and cobblestones with falling leaves across the stretch of it, but in the spring, it was a gorgeous space. With wrought iron tables and chairs beneath the trees and a brick pizza oven I'd never managed to use, the place gave me the same feelings of calm that I got at the farm...with 100% less animal shit.

"Considering Christian's security guard and the son of his main advisor are in on the plan, I think we'll have a little bit of leeway."

I hoped, at least.

"Do I get to meet him properly on this little jaunt of his, or is his visit purely for sex?"

I exhaled into the phone, scrunching my nose.

That was certainly the question of the hour, wasn't it?

"We only talked about coming for dinner," I admitted with a laugh. "He's taking a quick nap first, though."

"Bore him already?"

"More like wore him out," I countered.

Ford let out a hearty laugh. "There's the man I know and love. But you didn't answer my first question."

"He's here for two and a half days," I said, glancing at the clock and counting down the half day. "I'm sure I can find time for you to meet him if that's what you really want to do."

"Of course I want to meet the man who has my best friend ass up over him."

"I'm not ass up," I grumbled.

"Aren't you?" He laughed at me again. "You kidnapped a fucking prince, Kale. That's desperate and heroic all at the same time."

"He's plenty capable of kidnapping himself."

Ford brushed me off. "Dinner tonight, then?"

"As long as you promise to not be embarrassing."

"You don't need my help with that," he said.

"And if Christian hates the idea, I'm canceling on you," I said.

"I'm inviting Brooks."

"What about Alex?"

Our friend group had become a tight foursome—Ford, myself, Brooks, and Alex—but Alex hadn't quite been himself since our missing fifth fled the city for his husband in Los Angeles. Beamer was sorely missed, but it was hard to begrudge him for chasing after his happiness, even if I vehemently disliked his husband. Beamer's secret husband, Dalton, had been a point of contention between us before his move, and I'd definitely made an ass of myself over the whole thing. I'd set it right—enough—before Beamer left, but I probably owed him a little more than I'd offered. I wanted him to be happy, but I hoped he'd be happy with someone who loved New York as much as we did. I hadn't taken losing him well, and neither had Alex. Things between the two of them had been very new and very causal, not even more than one or two hookups as far as I knew. But the connection Alex found with Beamer had kicked something to life inside of him and he was still sort of floundering with how to handle it.

"Alex is sulking," Ford informed me. "You should check on him after your prince goes home."

"We'll all get together," I said. "A trip to The Black Door maybe."

"Probably the last thing he wants, but exactly what he needs." Ford cleared his throat. "Anyway. Dinner?"

"As long as it's okay with Christian."

"I'll text you an address," Ford said before hanging up the phone. Less than a minute later, I had a text message with a reservation confirmation for four at six. I dropped my phone down onto the desk and checked the clock. It was barely three, which meant Christian would have enough time to get a decent nap before I had to haul him up to go re-meet my friends.

It also gave me enough time to catch up on any work from the morning that I'd overlooked, but it was an email from my brother that caught my eye at the top of my inbox.

Kale,

Ran into Stefan and he said he didn't work for you anymore. Do you need another assistant?

- Boston

Hearing my most recently departed assistant's name was enough to sour the high I'd been riding since I tucked Christian into my bed upstairs. It was a firm reminder that while

Ford and I were very similar, there was a line, and my line was fucking my friends' employees. Ford, on the other hand, found that to be an aphrodisiac. He most preferred *my* assistants, which was earning both of us quite a reputation. One he didn't mind, but I didn't want.

Instead of answering his email, I decided to call him. Boston didn't answer, so like the annoying four-minutes older brother I was, I called him a second time.

"What, Kale?" he answered, breathy and exasperated.

"Why did you email me instead of just calling or texting?" I asked.

"I thought of it at my desk and it seemed easier."

"What did Stefan say?"

"That the job was not what he expected." Boston sounded amused, like he could see through the thinly-veiled lie.

"There are some unexpected tasks that come up on occasion. Why do you ask?"

"I wanted to offer my services," he said.

"No!" My answer came so quick and so loud, it startled us both. I fisted my free hand, then turned my cellphone to speaker mode and set it on the desk in front of me.

"You all right?" he asked, a hint of concern in the question.

"Yeah. Yes. I'm fine. I just...sorry. But no."

The last thing I wanted to do was bring one of my brother's friends onto the payroll, only for him to fall prey to Ford's ministrations.

"You need an assistant, don't you?"

One glance at my email confirmed I did need an assistant. Stefan's absence was already noticeable and once I was back in my actual office, it would only be more so.

"I don't want to hire one of your friends," I said.

"I wasn't suggesting you do that."

"What, then?"

"You could hire me."

I barked out a laugh, rolling my chair back from my desk. The wheels clattered over the uneven planks, and I pulled myself back in, the noise a steady hum that immediately began to calm my nerves over the conversation.

"You're too qualified," I said.

"What if I *want* to do it?"

"You have an MBA."

"And I'm bored," he said. "My job is boring, and it's monotonous, and it's not fun."

"Being an adult isn't fun," I reminded him.

"It would be fun on the farm," he muttered.

"Then go to the farm, Boston. Take a vacation for the winter. But being my assistant isn't any less predictable than your current position."

"But Stefan said—"

I cut him off, "No."

"Kale."

The doorknob to my office twisted and the giant wood door creaked as it was pushed open. Christian's sleep-drunk face appeared from around the corner, and my heart surged against my sternum.

"I'll think about it," I conceded, eyes immediately locked on Christian's. "We have to talk more. There's..."

"That's all I wanted," he said, giddy with excitement.

"Not now, though. Give me a few days."

"Sure. Yes. Of course."

"Bye, Boston. Love you," I said.

"Love you too."

The corner of Christian's eye twitched, and he waited until I disconnected the call to slink into my office. He pulled the door closed behind him and leaned against it.

"I didn't mean to interrupt," he said softly, his accent thicker when he was tired.

"Just my brother." I pushed the phone toward my computer and turned my chair toward him.

"His name is Boston?"

I nodded.

"Like the city?" Christian asked.

"Like the lettuce," I admitted.

Christian tilted his head back, mouth twitching up into a smirk. "Is there a reason you're both named after produce?"

"Our parents own a farm. Remember?" I crooked my finger, beckoning him closer.

Christian pushed away from the door and shuffled toward me, his bare feet pale against the wood-beamed floor.

"How was your rest?" I asked, tugging him onto my lap. He did his best to straddle me, the arms of the chair hindering his progress. "I thought you'd be out longer."

"It was enough."

"My friends invited us to dinner later," I said, resting my hands on the tops of his thighs. "We don't have to go if you don't want to."

"Isn't that the whole reason we fled the country?" he asked, shoulders wiggling a little with amusement. "For dinner?"

"A quiet dinner for two," I said.

"I don't mind sharing you with your friends while I'm here." Christian leaned closer, pressing a soft kiss against my temple. His lips tickled across the wisps of hair over my ear, and I wrapped my arms around his back and held him closer.

"Then a less quiet dinner for four it is," I murmured, using my head to nudge him around so I could get closer to his mouth. "But we have hours to ourselves before then, and I don't plan to waste a single one of them."

THE ROUNDED EDGE OF KALE'S DESK DUG INTO MY STOMACH, AND there was a paperclip stuck to my cheek. My pants were around my ankles, my shirt rucked up to the middle of my back, Kale's hand resting softly at the base of my spine. The calm tickle of his fingers against my sweaty skin was a sharp contrast to the painful *thwack* of the wooden ruler he was using on my ass. My cock was hard and leaking, smashed between the wood and my stomach, and we'd been at it for so long I was starting to worry Kale was going to send me to meet his friends—for the second time—with the heaviest balls I'd ever had.

"You're thinking too loud," he said, landing another strike against the backs of my thighs with the ruler.

I groaned, banging my head against his leather desk pad.

He had to know what I was after. The high from our first time together. That floaty kind of disconnect he'd taken me to with his hand against my ass, but for some reason it evaded me. The scenario was close enough to the same that it should have worked. Running free in a foreign city? Check. With a handsome man who was technically a stranger? Check. Hard enough to mine diamonds with nothing more than my dick? Triple check. Kale had done all the right things, said the correct words, and I'd played along with them, but the goal of it all continued to elude me.

Kale dropped the ruler in front of my face, then threw himself backward into his chair. The wheels rolled over the wood floor, loud as a train. I debated holding my position, but decided to straighten up and tug my pants back over my ass. Turning to face him, I leaned against his desk. There was no way my erection was going back into my pants, and the cradle of my underwear beneath my balls only made me look more endowed. Kale's face was flushed, the sleeves of his shirt rolled up to his forearms, and a steady trickle of sweat raced down his left temple.

Bless him, the man had tried.

"I'm sorry," I muttered with a shrug. My brain warred between frustrated and exhausted, unsure of where to settle. My knees trembled from the spanking, but my muscles were tired from hovering on the edge of perfection for so long. "I know this isn't what you expected."

Kale scoffed. "What are you talking about?"

"I can't..." I gestured weakly, blinking slowly. "Can't get there."

"Get where?"

"I don't know. What's it called?"

His mouth twitched in the corner. "You tell me, Christian. What are you after that you're not getting from me?"

The question was sharp as a spear in my side. I held up both hands, shaking my head so quick it made me dizzy.

"It's not you," I said quickly. "It's not you. It's me. I can't get there."

"Get where?" he asked again.

"That place where it feels so good." I pressed my chin against my chest, staring at my bare toes pointing toward his feet. He was still dressed from the flight, I realized, down to the shoes and the slacks.

"Did it not feel good?" he asked.

I dared a glance up at his face, finding his lower lip pushed out in the tease of a pout that wasn't quite ready to commit.

"It felt really good." I gave my ass a wiggle against the edge of his desk to remind me exactly how good it had felt.

"You're chasing after subspace," Kale said, tilting his head to the side.

"Is that what it's called?"

"Yes," he said simply. "It's a bonus, not a requirement."

"I liked it," I muttered.

"I imagine so." He leaned forward a little bit in his chair, resting his elbows on the tops of his knees. "I'm told it's unmatched."

"Does it not feel that way for you?"

"I get a different kind of high from it," Kale explained. "Sometimes I forget that you come by this naturally, but not on purpose."

My cock was still hard, but not as erect as when he'd been spanking me. I grasped the waistband of my underwear, ready to tuck myself away since we had moved onto the conversation piece of the day, but Kale stopped me with a frown and quick shake of his head.

"I didn't say you could put that away yet," he said softly, and I was immediately hard as steel again. I curled my fingers around the lip of his desk to hold myself up. "Good boy."

My eyes rolled back a little and a soft groan fell out of my mouth.

"You can't force yourself there," he went on, tipping his head back and looking up at me. "That defeats the whole point."

"How do I get there?" I asked.

"By surrendering," he said. "By not trying."

"But I want it."

"You can't fight your way into it, Christian. That's not how it works. Subspace comes from surrendering, from receiving."

"Why was it so easy before?"

"Because you surrendered." He smirked at me, arrogant asshole. "Because you received."

"Only because I didn't know it was a possibility."

"It's not a place for you to go. It's a place for me to take you."

I let out a long breath, looking up at the ceiling of Kale's office. "Why won't you, then?" I grumbled.

"Sometimes it can just be for fun, princess," he murmured, stretching one of his arms toward me. His fingertips danced across my painfully white knuckles, and I flexed my hand. The blood flow surged down my fingers and I managed another groan. "Haven't you enjoyed our time together so far?"

"Of course."

"Hmm?" Kale arched a brow and another rush of blood returned to my cock.

"Yes, of course, Mr. Sheffield."

"I think you've had enough spankings for today," he said,

standing slowly. His chair rolled across the floor until it bumped the wall. "I'm ready for you to suck my cock now."

Suddenly, the air was so dry and hot, it was impossible to breathe. I blinked at him a couple of times, because I'd heard the words, and yet...

"Get on your knees, Christian."

I hit the floor before my body even knew what I was doing. Tilting my head back, I stared up at him, a gorgeous gray halo radiating out from behind him. The sky outside was bright from clouds, not sunshine, and he stood out against the pale color like a painting that I could have found in one of the hallways at home. Kale had that aura about him. Regal enough to have been a painting, he was breathtaking. He made quick work of his fly, freeing his substantial erection and pointing his precum-slick tip toward my mouth.

"If it's too much and you can't speak, I want you to tap my thigh twice in a row." He tapped his fingers against the side of his thigh to demonstrate. "Do you understand?"

"Yes, Mr. Sheffield."

He did this little jerk with his head, mouth ticking up in the corner. It read like a subconscious reaction every time I called him Mr. Sheffield instead of Kale. A silent kind of approval that burned the center of my chest in the best kind of way. I would have been happy for him to always wear that expression, even though there was a quiet part in the back of my mind that wanted to know why I even cared about his reactions.

"This is for me," he said, using his cock to trace the outline of my lips. "Not for you."

I didn't have time to formulate a reply to that because his

cock was in my mouth and in my throat before I could blink. With no warning, Kale shoved his entire length past my lips, the short and trimmed hairs around the base of his shaft tickling my nose. I sputtered, my body immediately trying to fight against the intrusion, but he cradled the back of my head with his hand and shushed me.

"Through the nose, princess. You don't need your mouth to breathe, do you?"

I sucked in a desperate breath through my nostrils, and it was nowhere near enough.

"You only need your mouth to get me off. No arguing, no taunting." His exhale sounded like a growl and I huffed a breath against the base of his dick. "Just sucking. There you go. Just like that."

I wanted to suck him, but his erection was lodged so deep in my throat, the only thing I could do was flatten my tongue and focus on measured and steady breaths in and out of my nose.

"You're gorgeous like this," he whispered, still unmoving. The top of his dick pulsed against the roof of my mouth. "My beautiful little prince. My cock slut on his knees."

I groaned around his thickness, the words almost enough to make me come on their own. The lack of air, the ache in my jaw, and the pressure against my tongue all worked together like an aphrodisiac that I was quickly addicted to. There was another feeling then, creeping around the edges, and my eyes went wide at the recognition of it. That soft and hazy kind of float that I'd fallen into our first night together. It wasn't around me, but it was within reach. As soon as I recognized it, though, it was gone. I grumbled a protest around Kale's cock, and he added his other hand to my head.

He worked his fingers through my hair, stroking the strands back from my face and whispering gentle praises at me that I didn't deserve. I'd gotten so close to it again and then lost it. Just like everything else in my life, I made a mockery of it. I was hard and horny, but angry and annoyed, ready to tap out, when he eased his shaft an inch out of my mouth. His cock pressed against my tongue like one of those wooden sticks at the doctor's office.

"This is what you're good for," he said quietly, pushing back in another inch and sealing off my throat with the thick swell of his cock. Out an inch, back in, out, in. A slow and controlled pump of his hips. Blinking through tears, I watched Kale throw his head back, fingers digging into the sides of my head. He was on the brink of something too. I could see it in the tight stretch of his muscles, his entire body coiled like a snake ready to strike.

Between my legs, my own cock leaked copious amounts of precum, slick and warm, down the side of my shaft. I brought one hand to my balls, the other to my cock. I didn't stroke or pull. I simply held myself together. Balls in one hand and cock in the other like some kind of statue...or trophy.

"I'm going to fuck your throat, Christian." Kale petted his fingers through my hair before digging down into a hard grip on either side of my head. "I don't care if you spit or throw up or cry. Short of you tapping out, the only way I'm taking my dick out of your throat is if I come in it. Understand?"

I nodded quickly, tears racing down my cheeks. I'd gotten used to breathing with his cock lodged in my mouth, to the point where I almost found its presence a comfort. I was in his hands, in his care, making him feel good. There were a myriad of feelings to unpack, but Kale gave me time for none of them.

I was still mid-nod when he withdrew his cock from my mouth completely.

The air against my tongue and throat was cold, and my body worked on reflex, sucking in a desperate breath. It was too much, too fast, and I started to cough, but Kale was there still, his entire cock shoved back into my throat. The tip of his dick punched the rest of my breath inside, and then he was gone again. In and out with drawn-out snaps of his hips that withdrew him almost to the tip each time before he pushed back in.

My grip around my cock and balls was the first to go, quickly followed by the tension in my jaw. Kale properly skull-fucked me, the gurgling and gagging noises coming out of my mouth some of the most indecent things I'd ever heard in my life. The layer of tears in my eyes was so thick I couldn't even see his face above me. I could barely make out the haloed glow of his profile, but I didn't need to see him to know he was there. Kale was so deep inside of me, not just physically, that nothing else even mattered.

I came from the use, untouched and unallowed. Whimpering through my orgasm, the muscles in my throat gripped hungrily at the tip of Kale's cock, and he came right after me with a roar that should have rattled the windows. Buried into the back of my throat and bowed over me, his stomach against my forehead. For the first time in my life I didn't feel like a spare prince.

I felt like a fucking king.

The taste of cum flooded my mouth as he pulled his cock back past my lips, and then he lifted me onto his lap like I was a ragdoll. The wooden arm of his chair bit into my left, but my synapses were misfiring, because the hurt only forced another dribble of cum out of my cock. Kale's hands were still in my hair, not gripping, but stroking and petting. His lips against my ear, he whispered promises he had no right making, but I wanted them just the same.

I deserved his praise.

I'd *earned* it.

Kale's fingertips against my sweaty neck and the spit-slick skin of my chin and cheeks were soft as cashmere. My body felt like it was hovering in his lap, my brain a figurative organ that wasn't connected to the rest of me. I'd been reduced to feeling and need and *pleasure*.

The fucking pleasure.

"Come on back to me, princess." Kale kissed the top of my head, and I narrowed in on the feeling of his lips against my hair. The chair against my leg, his arms around my back. Slowly but surely, my brain came back online, my soul settled back into my body, and I burrowed against his chest, beyond grateful that he'd taken me back to the best place I'd ever been.

"I'm here." My voice didn't sound like my own. My throat burned from the rough fucking and my jaw ached from the stretch. Kale brought his hands around to my face, fingers gently massaging right in front of my ears. I inhaled deeply, leaning into him with a content groan.

"Yeah," he said, breath puffing out cold against the drying spit and tears on my cheeks. He traced his fingers across my cheekbones, and I shivered, eyes half open and mouth still slack.

"I'm here," I said again. Just as much for him as for me. I was in my body. My bones were mine. My muscles. My heart. I was in New York City, in America, in the lap of a man who'd turned my world upside down without even trying.

Something flashed in his eyes, but as soon as it was there, it was gone. He licked his lips and pressed our foreheads together, letting out a breath that trembled as much as my own.

"I see you, princess," he whispered. "I fucking see you."

I was falling in love with a prince.

Cursing myself the entire time I cleaned Christian up from the encounter over the top of my desk, I added some new personal insults for good measure while I watched him get dressed after a shower. He looked at home in my bedroom, and I found myself fighting back the unfairness of the whole thing. Christian wasn't the kind of man I should be developing feelings for. He was a goddamn prince of a foreign country and there was no life in that for us. I couldn't walk away from my friends and my family, and he couldn't escape the obligations of his title and his name.

"Do I look presentable?" he asked, undoing the top button of the short-sleeved button-up he'd just put on.

"More than," I assured him. "They've already met you anyway. You've made your first impression."

"I can't imagine it was a good one."

"I like you, so they'll like you."

I held out my hand to him and he walked easily into my waiting arms. Wrapping him up, I buried my nose in the dark tuft of his hair, breathing in the way my shampoo mixed with the residual of his styling product and committing it to memory. Christian rested his cheek against the front of my shoulder, and for a moment, everything was perfect. It was easy to pretend we were different people and there wasn't a deadline on our relationship.

He chuckled, giving his shoulders a little shrug until I let him free. "I don't know why it matters, to be honest."

"Why do you say that?"

"I'm leaving in a couple of days."

I rubbed at an itch on the side of my nostrils, knowing what he said was true, but hating it just the same.

"Are you ready?" I asked him instead of responding to the statement.

"As I'll ever be." Christian rolled his neck, giving it a crack before a soft mask of friendliness settled on his face. "My mind is going a mile a minute and my throat feels like...well...I don't know how to describe what's happening in my throat."

"The word you're looking for is well-fucked," I murmured, smoothing a hand down the front of my shirt to check for wrinkles.

"Right, well I don't think that's something I can say to your friends when they ask if I always sound this raspy." He cleared his throat and winked, inclining his head toward the door.

I knew we had to leave. We had this commitment with my friends, which was poor planning on my part. My time with Christian was beyond limited and I was far more inclined to tie him to my bed for the next two days and only let him up for food and water.

"It's the exact kind of thing you can say to my friends," I

promised. "For better or worse, we're very open with each other."

He gave me a deadpan look. "You don't say."

I shoved him out of the door and he made a quick turn down the stairs to the main level of the house. I watched his ass bounce as he moved through my house like he'd been there for years, not hours.

"Idiot," I muttered under my breath.

Christian threw a look over his shoulder at me, brows knit. "What?"

"Nothing."

I grabbed my wallet, phone, and keys from the table beside the door and then made sure everything was situated in my pockets.

"Do you have a scarf in your bag?" I asked, pulling my coat off the hook.

"I didn't quite pack for myself," he reminded me. "Or for America."

I pulled another of my coats off the hook and passed it to him, then one of the many cashmere scarfs sent by my parents. My coat was a little large around the shoulders on him, but something about seeing Christian in my clothes, even if it was only outerwear, sent a flare of ownership straight up my spine. If he hadn't been studying me with such an intense watchfulness, I would have smashed my face into the wall to clear my head of the intrusive thoughts.

"Is this more to your liking, Mr. Sheffield?" Christian smirked, tying a loose knot with the scarf at the base of his throat.

"Don't patronize me or you'll find out just how much my friends and I like to share," I warned.

The comment should have been out of line, so far out of bounds and beyond anything he and I had ever talked about before. But when I snapped my mouth closed, Christian's nostrils flared and his cheeks flushed. My hand was still against the fringe of the borrowed scarf and I wound it around my fist, pulling him against my chest.

"Did you like the idea of that?" I asked, dropping a kiss against the corner of his mouth.

"It's daunting."

"But?"

"You've shown me so many things already," Christian said quietly, almost shy. "I wouldn't be surprised to find out it's exactly the kind of thing I liked."

"I'm not going to share you with them." I kissed my way up the angle of his jaw until his ear was against my mouth. I nipped his earlobe and he moaned, arching into me like our bodies were made to be pressed together in that exact way. "But I'm not against telling them how pretty you look when you come."

"I'm about to come again," he whimpered, shoving me away from him and sucking in the largest breath I'd ever seen. "Please open the front door so I can get some air or I might combust on the spot."

"How are you so perfect?"

"Years of thoughtful breeding," he said, reaching past me and twisting the doorknob when I didn't do as he'd asked.

A cool gust of fall air blew into the entry, and Christian was out in the front garden before I could blink. The fresh air helped enough to clear my head, as well. To remind me that the only thing to come from keeping him sexed up and tied down in my bedroom for his whole stay would be broken hearts for both of us.

"Oh, lovely," a familiar voice said from my front gate.

I looked past Christian to find Ford and Brooks together on the sidewalk.

"What are you doing here?" I asked, locking the door and coming to stand beside Christian. He reached for my hand, and I happily threaded our fingers together. Ford's stare flickered down to our joined hands, but besides a twitch at the corner of his left eye, he didn't say a word.

"We figured—" Ford started, only to be interrupted.

"*He* figured."

"I figured," Ford corrected, "that it was going to take the jaws of life to pry your cock out of your new favorite foreign dignitary and I wasn't interested in missing our dinner reservations."

"Did you bring the fire department?" I asked, pretending to look around for a man in uniform who'd been prepared to separate Christian and me from each other.

"Just some Crisco." Ford patted the pocket of his coat. "Worst case, I would have lubed you up until you slid apart and fell onto the floor."

"Very thoughtful," Christian muttered, giving my hand a squeeze.

"Can we please get going?" Brooks gestured toward the corner. "I'm starving."

Christian and I joined them on the sidewalk, walking behind. Ford chattered on mindlessly about a whole array of things I didn't care enough to ask for clarification on, but as soon as we were divested of our outerwear and seated at the restaurant, he turned his sights onto Christian.

"So, we hear you're a prince."

"Which one of you helped stage the kidnapping?" Christian asked, amusement coloring the cadence of his voice.

"That was definitely me." Ford grinned. "Ford Carlisle, in case you forgot."

"I'm Christian Davenport-Spencer," he said, tilting his head to the side.

"Prince of...?"

"Princess," I corrected. Christian reached under the table and dug his fingernails into my thighs.

Brooks' mouth twitched in the corner. "Cute."

"I very much like that I'm not a prince here," Christian told Ford.

"I wasn't aware it was something you could take off like a coat."

"Don't start," I warned.

"I'm just getting to know your friend," Ford said, throwing a look at me before focusing back on Christian.

"You can't get mad," Brooks said. "This is how you treated Beamer's husband."

I scoffed, the protest already tasting like a lie in the back of my throat. "No it's not."

"It is," Ford agreed, flagging down a waitress and ordering a round of drinks for the four of us.

"I was nowhere near as insulting as you've managed to be."

"He's fine," Christian promised. "I've verbally sparred with men far more competent at the sport than him."

Brooks barked out a laugh, and I reached to my side, taking Christian's face into my hands and kissing him wet and hard against the mouth. He let out a surprised little sound, but quickly melted into me. His lips parted enough for my tongue to sneak past for a taste, and the moan he breathed into my mouth rattled me down to my bones.

"I like him," Brooks said. The waitress brought our drinks and he raised his glass for a toast. "To Kale's smart-mouth princess."

Christian did a royal-looking little swirl with his hand and dipped his head in a sort of bow, then raised his glass and clinked it against Brooks' drink. I joined my glass with theirs, and Ford, finally made the fourth.

"So," Brooks sipped his drink and leaned back in his seat. "Tell me how the two of you met."

"It was a very dramatic kidnapping," Christian started to explain, and I smacked the side of his arm. He laughed and leaned toward me, affection rolling off of him in waves. "I'd just snuck out of the ballet and I ran right into your friend here. He kissed me senseless, took me to a sex club, and then a rather posh hotel for the night."

"The rest is history," I finished.

Christian chuckled and I admired his profile while he fell into an easy conversation with Brooks that didn't involve me in the slightest. He was handsome and animated. He was engaging, and it came as easy as breathing. I didn't know Christian well, but I'd watched him talk to Niko and I'd seen him talk to me. With Brooks, he wasn't pretending. He was being honest and real, and that understanding only served to push me deeper into the realm of feelings that weren't going to do me any favors.

"You're fucked," Ford murmured under his breath.

I inhaled slowly through my teeth, groaning before I angled myself away from Christian so I could talk to Ford without breaking up the conversation at the other end of the table. Christian's hand was still on my thigh, his fingers less tense than before.

"I know."

"Are you going to pack up like Beamer did and leave us too?" Ford arched a brow, the words sounding much more like a taunt than a question.

"I'm not absconding to a foreign nation," I assured him.

"What next, then?"

I swallowed, looking at Christian. He laughed at something Brooks said, and I wished I had an answer.

"I don't know," I admitted. "Nothing good, though."

"Yeah." Ford exhaled heavily. "I hate to say this, but you should call Beamer. This is right up his alley."

"Dalton Fox isn't a prince," I said.

Our missing fifth friend had gotten married in college, then promptly forgot his husband existed. They'd reconnected fifteen years later and apparently there'd been something to the initial pairing worth remembering. Beamer—or Carter Royce IV, as his parents knew him, Ivey as his husband called him—and Dalton had ended up in Los Angeles when all was said and done.

"He's not," Ford agreed. "Still I can't help but think there are similarities here."

"Beamer isn't going to want to talk to me about Dalton."

"Not until you offer up a proper apology to his husband, no." Ford's eyes sparkled as he studied me over the rim of his drink.

"I've apologized."

"You reached a tentative agreement on the counsel of overbearing assholes," he said.

"That's rich, considering how you just talked to Christian."

"Your own medicine and all that," he said, waving me off. "I'm only saying that I think Beamer *and his husband* would have some advice you might find useful."

"This isn't anything serious," I grumbled. Much like earlier, the words tasted like poison on my tongue.

Ford's mouth twisted into a frown and he shook his head, attention drifting to Brooks and Christian at the other side of the table, engaged in conversation like they were the longtime friends and we were the newcomers.

"You've never lied to me before, Sheffield," Ford warned. "Don't start now."

ONE THING I'D LEARNED OVER DINNER WITH KALE AND HIS FRIENDS was that his stomach was a seemingly endless pit. He drank whiskey, he ate oysters, he had salad and soup, then pasta and bread. There didn't seem to be an end to the volume of food he was capable of consuming, and by the time the waitress came through with a dessert menu, I worried the button on my pants would burst.

I'd spent most of the meal talking with Kale's friend Brooks, whom I found to be a more tempered version of him and Ford. He was witty without being over the top and almost soft-spoken, though I imagined that was a side effect of having friends like the two of them.

"What was your other friend like?" I asked, shoving the dessert menu toward Kale, who eyed it with an unnatural level of interest.

The question caught Ford's attention and he leaned closer to Brooks, pushing into our conversation. "Are you talking about Beamer?"

"That's such a horrible nickname," I said, "but yes."

"He was more like you," Kale answered, and Brooks nodded his confirmation.

"In what ways?"

"Submissive and breedable," Ford answered.

Kale balled up the napkin on his lap and flung it directly into Ford's face. "Don't be crass."

Ford threw the napkin back, and I snatched it before Kale could return the volley.

"Take the stick out of your ass," Ford teased, mouth twisting into a baiting grin. "I'd bet my 401k on how your prince likes it in bed."

Heat flooded my cheeks, and I threw a glance at Kale from the corner of my eye. It looked like steam was ready to billow out of his ears. While the conversation bordered on embarrassing, it was only because I wasn't as familiar with Brooks and Ford as I was with Kale. The thought that I considered myself familiar with him should have been absurd, but it had only taken a handful of encounters with his nimble fingers and talented tongue to pull back the layers that I'd always imagined kept me so well hidden. The conversations weren't anything Parrish and I hadn't talked about before either, so I swallowed down any ill-placed sense of propriety and decided I was game to play along.

"Don't take the bet," I stage-whispered to Kale, shifting in my seat to alleviate some of the pressure on my bruised backside. Ford smirked and Kale's nostrils flared. I settled my hand again on the top of his thigh and whispered into his ear, "I'm not ashamed of the things we do together."

"Neither am I," he grumbled, stare still steady on Ford across the table.

"You're far more protective than I ever thought," Brooks

said. "First with Beamer and now with Christian. Do you just have a thing for submissive men?"

"I don't have *a thing* for submissive men," Kale snapped.

"Don't you, though?" I slid my hand a little higher up his thigh. Heat radiated from between his legs like there was an open-door furnace blazing inches away from my fingertips.

"I like him," Ford said, giving his head a playful little shake to the side. "Let's take him to The Black Door."

"No," Kale answered at the same time I said, "Yes."

"If you don't want me to play, I'm more than happy to call up Stefan again," Ford said.

"He doesn't work for me anymore, I'm surprised you're interested."

An unexplained feeling bubbled up in the pit of my stomach, and I tried to get an answer from either of their faces before I asked the question. I raised a brow, ready to ask when Ford answered for me.

"Kale's former assistant," he said, looking proud.

"Ford can't stop fucking the help."

Ford's grin split his mouth and he let out a giddy little laugh, leaning back in his chair and tossing his napkin onto his plate. "Can we please go to The Black Door tonight?" he asked again.

"Don't you have the staffing agency on speed dial?" Kale questioned.

"I might, and if you don't want me to fuck my way through your list of talented candidates, we should get going."

"I'd like to go," I said, low enough for only Kale to hear me.

"I'm sure you would."

"You took me there the night we met," I reminded him, the earlier feeling in my stomach turning into something hotter and more consuming. From jealousy to arousal, my nerves were a live wire, ready to combust at the slightest spark.

It was all Kale's fault, of course.

Whatever happened between us at the house after my nap had seemingly rewired the circuitry in my brain because trying to make someone happy by acting right had never felt so good. We'd danced around it at The Plaza, and I'd had the orgasms to prove it. Coming my brains out with his handprints emblazoned against my ass had given me enough to think about. But it was more than the pain that had gotten me off better than anything else ever had before. There was something in the acts of it. Of the listening, of the receiving, of the *choosing*. I'd consciously made the choice to let Kale control my body, my orgasms, my decisions. Not outside of the bedroom, or not outside of sex, rather, but...

I ached with the need to understand these new feelings, the motivation for all of them. After a lifetime of fighting against people who made decisions for me, why was Kale's control so goddamn appealing? I craved it, which wasn't good for either of us. I had two days at most left with him before I had to go back home, and what kind of life would that be for us? Even if I dared give myself the leeway to entertain a relationship with him...what would it be like? It would take this perfect kind of control and ruin it with the kind I'd spent years running from. I didn't want whatever this thing was with Kale to get tainted by home. It was better for us to only have it now and to only have it in America.

"I didn't think I'd ever see you again," he reminded me, but I knew after this current stay, that possibility might still ring true.

I swallowed down that truth and turned my gaze toward the place my hand rested on his thigh like it was home.

"I'm here now," I told him. "Let's just have some fun."

He clenched his jaw, and I rolled my eyes.

"We talked about this before we left your house," I reminded him. "You told me what your friends were like, what they would know about us. You can't seriously be mad now that you were right."

"Kale loves to be right," Brooks said, pushing his chair back and standing up from the table.

"He does," Ford agreed, standing and smoothing his hands down the front of his black slacks. "We should celebrate just how right he is. By going to The Black Door."

"Give us a second," I said to Brooks, because I knew between the three of them, he was the voice of reason.

Brooks pushed a giggling Ford toward the front of the restaurant, and I turned to face Kale, the look on his face beyond stressed.

"What's your problem?" I asked.

His brows knit together. "I don't have a problem."

"You're acting like you have a problem. Why don't you want to go to your little club? What are you scared of?"

"I'm not scared." He was quick to answer, but some unclear emotion flashed behind his eyes before his normal resting arrogant face was back.

"They're not here." I waved my hand toward the two recently vacated seats across from us. "You can drop the mask."

"Not a mask."

"You're not acting the same as you were when you bent me over your desk and spanked me black and blue," I said.

Kale let out a low growl, sucking in a breath that puffed his chest up like the demonstrative little predator he fancied himself to be.

"I can handle the sex jokes from your friends," I said. "I thought you could too."

"It's different." The tip of Kale's tongue darted out, worrying the corner of his mouth nervously.

"Why?"

He shook his head.

I grabbed his face. "Why?" I asked again.

He squeezed his eyes closed like a petulant child.

"Why, Kale?"

"Stop." He ground the word out as if it hurt him.

I was going to have to try another tactic if I wanted to get an answer out of him. It wasn't a surprise to me that Kale was stubborn and immovable, but I also knew there had to be a way to get through to him. I was fairly certain I had the key, so I batted my lashes together, tilting my chin toward my chest and looking up at him as demure as I could manage.

"Mr. Sheffield," I whispered.

"Don't manipulate me."

He was harder to crack than I'd expected. I dropped my hands from his face, making a mental note of the way his mouth twisted into a frown when I let him go.

"I'm not here for a long time," I said, running out of ideas. "I'm here for a good time, remember? Just like the first night. This is all we've ever had, so what's different?"

"This is all we have," he repeated. "That's the fucking problem, Christian."

I pursed my lips, rubbing them together while I waited for him to finish his thought. There were a hundred different things for him to follow that up with, and for as much as he'd had me on my back since I arrived, I'd never been more on my toes. I had no idea what was about to come out of his mouth, but if anyone had read through the laundry list of possibilities, the reality of his next confession wouldn't have been anywhere in the notebook, let alone on the page.

"I didn't love you then," he said with a sigh, like the act of loving me caused him physical harm.

"I'm sorry. You what?"

My heart was in my throat, and Kale looked like he wanted to throw up in both of our laps. He shook his head, eyes darting in every which way except toward my face.

"Forget I said that," he mumbled.

"Absolutely not."

"Please?"

"No," I said.

"I like it better when you do what you're told."

Finally, an embarrassed glance in my direction.

"You know I'm not a good listener," I said softly.

In a sharp contrast to what had naturally become our standard roles, I reached toward him and pressed the side of my finger against the bottom of his chin, tipping his face level with mine. His eyes were wide and a little frantic, the muscle in his jaw ticking as he worked it back and forth.

"You are when you want to be," he said.

"Then give me a reason to want to be."

He swallowed, another shake of his head and the misdirection of his stare, but I grabbed his chin and pulled him back to my level. Kale sucked in a breath and looked at me for what felt like the first time since we'd sat down for dinner. I didn't need him to repeat himself, because the words—the feeling—it was clear as day all over every curve and angle of his face.

"Give me something worth listening to," I whispered.

Another muscle twitch in his jaw, and then the concession rolled off his shoulders, sending all of the nerves down to his feet. He visibly relaxed, save for the panicked look in the depths of his eyes.

"I didn't love you then," he said quietly, almost under his breath.

"And now?"

He nodded.

I leveled him with an unimpressed look that had him huffing out a low laugh that almost sounded like the man I knew him to be. Though, that felt unfair to say. This man in front of me, he was also Kale Sheffield. Just a very hidden version of himself that I didn't think many people had the luxury of knowing. And here he was, bared and raw for *me*.

"I didn't mean to." It sounded like an apology, and I couldn't think of anything worse than someone feeling sorry for falling in love with me.

I swallowed back bile and cleared my throat, fighting down a surge of biting commentary that I wanted to deliver in response to his bullshit apology.

"But I'm not sorry for it," he continued. "I know it's...not ideal."

I scoffed, and he shrugged helplessly, eyes lightening back to their normal shade of brown.

"It's far from ideal," I agreed.

"I don't think I stood a chance, though." Kale reached for my face, cradling my cheek in his hand. I leaned into the softness of his palm, enjoying the way his fingers danced across my cheekbone and toward my hairline.

"No," I said. "I don't think you did."

Because the truth of the whole matter was...

Neither did I.

CHRISTIAN AND I TRAILED BEHIND FORD AND BROOKS ON THE WALK to The Black Door. It was a wonder my legs even worked for how much adrenaline coursed through my system after my unplanned confession of love to Christian after dinner. It was the absolute last thing I ever wanted to tell him, but at the same time, the confession had felt entirely unavoidable. The feeling had been swirling around my chest from the second he stepped into my house, probably the first second he stepped into my life, and it expanded and grew with every breath, every touch. Taking up space and air until the only way to live with it inside of me was to address its presence.

Christian didn't say it back to me, but that hadn't felt important at the time. With his hand in mine, my scarf wrapped around his throat, it still wasn't important. The man I loved was beside me and that was the only thing that mattered. Jesus, was this how Beamer had felt when he fell in love with Dalton? What a consuming, terrifying and honestly unwelcome feeling.

When we reached the entrance for The Black Door, Christian gave my hand a squeeze. I looked over at him, immediately noticing the worried knit of his brows.

"What's wrong?" I asked.

He fished his passport out of his pocket to show at the desk for his identification. "I'm just thinking about what you said at the restaurant."

"Did I ruin everything?"

"It just warrants a broader conversation," he said, flashing a bright smile to Avery at the desk.

"Mr. Sheffield, Your R—"

Christian held up his hand and shook his head.

"Not here," he murmured.

Avery gave him a jerky nod and handed him back his passport. "Have a good evening, gentlemen."

By the time we got inside, Ford and Brooks were already lost in the crowd, and I pulled Christian through to the bar. The place was quiet, but not quiet enough for the conversation that Christian and I were apparently about to have. Admittedly, not what I'd had in mind when I caved to pressure about coming in the first place, but discussing my unrequited love for a foreign royal felt like an appropriate level of masochism for the building.

From the far end of the bar, Brooks caught my eye and I pointed up, letting them both know I was taking Christian upstairs. It was more exposed up there, but more private at the same time. Even with the floor-to-ceiling glass windows in lieu of covered walls, something about the height and the exclusivity made the top floor feel like a secure little safe haven. It was one of my most favorite places that wasn't my house. Even if I wasn't with a partner, something about the way discretion and privacy seemed to float through the air had always been calming to me.

Brooks pointed up as well and I shook my head before tilting it to the side toward Christian. He answered that with a knowing nod, but tapped his watch, indicating he wasn't going to give me all night. With that out of the way, I procured drinks for me and Christian, then headed for the elevators and up to the next floor.

The view of the city from that high up had never gotten boring, and I gave Christian's hand a squeeze as we stepped off the elevator.

"They don't have views like this at home," he said to no one in particular.

It took some time, but I found us a secluded enough seat near the back of the room, and we settled in. Christian looked in his element, leaning back and taking a slow swallow of his drink. He surveyed the room with all the arrogance and authority of a king he'd never be before turning his attention to me.

"It just warrants a broader conversation," he repeated his line from earlier, and I gave him a nod in return.

"Normally I'd start, but..."

"You're not quite yourself," Christian supplied.

"You have that effect on me."

He smirked, shifting his weight with a quick grimace.

"Does it hurt?" I asked.

"You have that effect on me," he said, taking another sip of his drink.

I watched the way his lips wrapped around the rim of the

glass, and I swallowed back a groan at how horny the simple action made me. This warranted a whole different kind of conversation entirely. I wasn't just in love; I was in way over my head with him, and he knew it.

"I think your confession at dinner changes everything," he finally said.

"It shouldn't."

I wanted it to.

"No?" He arched a doubtful brow at me.

"My feelings are my own," I assured him. "It doesn't need to change what we have."

"And what do we have, Kale? A felony kidnapping charge and enough orgasms to last me through until the next one?"

I snorted, not enjoying the way he diminished our time together. But he also wasn't entirely wrong. At the end of the day, though, I didn't want to lose the connection between us just because I had done something stupid like fall in love with him. I'd figure out how to manage my own expectations, my own heart. I couldn't lose the parts of him I had. It was positively out of the question.

"This wasn't ever anything serious," I started to explain and his eyebrow raised higher into his hairline.

"Do you fly around the world for sex often?" he asked.

"No, but—"

"Do you make a habit of kissing strangers on the street and then taking them to fancy hotels to fuck?" He must have read the answer on my face, because he laughed and shook his head. "Don't answer that one."

"I'm just saying this wasn't what we agreed on."

"We didn't agree on anything besides dinner in America and we're already well past that," he said.

I hated how calm he was, how cool and collected about the whole thing like it wasn't my heart on the line. I knew that made me a hypocrite for somehow wanting him to take my feelings into consideration and ignore them at the same time. I'd never imagined myself to be a fair or balanced sort of man, though, and that was never more evident than right now.

"I just want to enjoy the limited time we have together," I said.

"But you don't want it to be limited, do you?"

I took a healthy swallow of my drink, looking for the answer beneath the ice. "No."

Christian moved, stretching out and crossing one leg over the other and casually resting his drink on his knee. Based on appearance alone, we could have been talking about the weather or the quality of the seafood at dinner. He looked absolutely unfazed by my confession, almost like he'd expected it.

"Then tell me that," he said.

"I just did." I scrubbed a hand down my face, wishing I could dig into the floor and bury myself in the dirt beneath the garage level of the building.

"No, you misunderstand me," Christian said, throwing me a smug look that dripped with desire. "Then *tell me* that."

"I just did," I repeated, finishing off my drink and setting it on the table in front of us. My frustration was mounting, and I tried to swallow it down to save myself from lashing out. I hated being misunderstood, and it was clear Christian and I were not having the same conversation. This was exactly what I'd been worried about after I spilled my heart to him. It would have been better to keep my feelings to myself so things could have carried on as we'd both intended.

"You're not listening to me, Mr. Sheffield." Christian leaned forward and set his drink beside mine, then he slid off the seat and onto his knees at my feet. "Tell me what you want."

It hurt to breathe.

Seeing him on his knees like that was perfection, better than having him over my lap with my handprints all over his ass, better than seeing his lips swollen and shiny from sucking my cock to completion, better than anything I'd ever seen in my life.

"I don't want you to leave," I finally whispered, the words jagged and sharp like razor wire in my throat. "I don't want this to be over."

"Then tell me to stay."

"You can't," I said.

"Can't I?" He sank down, dropping his ass onto his heels.

"I thought that was the whole kidnapping part, princess." At my use of the endearment, his entire face softened. I took his face into my hand, committing the way he leaned into me like it was second nature to memory. Just one more perfect moment with a man that could never truly be mine.

"Be honest with me," Christian said, his eyes closed. He reached up and covered my hand with both of his, keeping my fingers pressed against his face. He was so beautiful, so at peace. My heart twisted, fighting for space with the other feelings that were still far too big for my chest to contain.

"I can't ask you for the things I want."

"Why not?" He opened his eyes and locked his stare onto mine like he could see right through me. "You haven't had a problem asking for anything you wanted so far."

He slid my hand off his face and toward his throat, the

underside of his chin. My fingers curled up and over, pressing against his lips which were still puffy from the way I'd fucked his face earlier in the day. He was correct with his statement, and I owed him as much of my own truth as I could manage.

When Ford and I hatched the plan to pretend kidnap Christian, I didn't have any expectations beyond a fun weekend of sex that I imagined would be our last. Maybe I'd pretended it was going to be a sendoff before I ended up spending the rest of my life chasing the high I found when I was with him. Nothing more than that. But from the moment he walked through the door at Parrish's apartment, I knew it was different. Knew I wanted more.

Wanted everything.

And that was the thing about me. I was a man of money and a man of means. I very rarely took no for an answer, and Christian's gentle prodding reminded me of that.

"I want to be with you," I said.

He smiled, and I hooked my fingers over his lower lip, over his teeth. He let me pull his mouth open, shoulders jerking when I depressed his tongue and worked my way toward the back of his throat.

"I want to do dirty fucking things to you, princess. For a very long time."

Christian made a quiet choking sound, but he didn't even try to force my hand out of his mouth. His eyes had already started to take on that glassy sort of look that happened when he was falling deep into subspace, and I relished how easy it was to get him there. My chest swelled with pride, with need.

"It's more than that, though."

A tear slipped out from the corner of his eye, and I withdrew my fingers from his mouth, wiping them dry against his cheek. Christian's eyes rolled back in his head and he left his mouth open.

It was an invitation for me to continue.

Swiping the tear with the side of my knuckle, I took a deep breath. "I want to find a way to be with you for real," I admitted.

Christian's nostrils flared and his tongue darted out, licking the corner of his lower lip. Even as his expression had gone hazy, he held my gaze, attention rapt.

"I want you here. I want you in my home. In my bed. I want you marked. I want you to be mine."

I needed to stop before I said something embarrassing, but much like at dinner, the confession poured out of me with so much sincerity I could almost see Christian's pupils turn from black circles into hearts. This was what he'd really been after, I realized. The transparency, the honesty, the sincerity. I didn't know a single thing about Christian's life at home, but through his submission I'd picked up bits and pieces about him that others had seemingly spent his entire life either missing or ignoring.

There had to be a special kind of torment that came with being so far down the line of succession that your ascension was beyond improbable, but you were still held to all the same expectations and restrictions as everyone else. To spend your entire life as an afterthought? I couldn't imagine. And with me, Christian was the first thought, the only thought.

He was everything I'd ever wanted, and I wanted him to be all in.

What was the saying?

In for a penny, in for a pound.

I licked my lips and gave him one more answer, "More

than all of that, I want to take care of you and I want you to love me back. Holy shit, Christian, I know I have no right to ask it, but one day I want you to love me too."

A flash of clarity shot out of his eyes, and he swayed forward, mouth angling up at the corner. "Well. You're in luck, Mr. Sheffield. It does seem today is the day."

CHAPTER 22

CHRISTIAN

Maybe I'd been riding some kind of sexual high since Kale had choked me out with his cock earlier in the day, but I was certain I'd never been happier. Every nerve ending in my body hummed with approval, swaying like a tide until I found myself leaning toward Kale. He closed the space between us, pressing our mouths together in a kiss that quickly went from soft to ravenous. He wrapped his arms around my waist and hauled me onto his lap, hands roaming desperately over my back while his tongue explored the depths of mouth. I wondered if he could still taste himself there.

The energy of the kiss once again shifted, from furiously hard to something far more languid. The new kiss spoke of having nothing but time when I knew that couldn't have been further from the truth. I waited until he'd had his fill, which unfortunately went on forever. I didn't want to care, but my mind was loud as it ever was, and I was ready to take my clothes off right there in front of the crowded room and promise Kale Sheffield the whole goddamn world.

"What are we going to do?" I whispered against the corner of his mouth.

My lips tingled, and I let his body hold my weight. It was a surreal thing, to have someone to hold me up like that. Sure, I had Parrish, but our relationship was supportive in the way best friends were supportive. Much the way I'd watched Ford and Brooks offer Kale support, though their attitude was far more biting than Parrish's. Those dynamics mattered, but they weren't the same, and I'd never been as sure of anything as I was about that when Kale pressed the side of his head against mine.

"Are you talking about long term?" he asked.

I nodded.

"Let that be a problem for future us," he said, shifting and kissing my temple. "Right now, let's just enjoy the time. Enjoy each other."

"It's not going to be easy," I whispered.

I wasn't sure if it was even *possible*.

I had no idea what a future looked like for the two of us... for me. It wasn't something as simple as packing my things up and moving to America. There were rules and I was still a prince. It was a conversation I needed to have with Phillip, with my father, but I could already hear it playing out in my head.

You don't know him, Christian.

He's a commoner, Christian.

He's not from here, Christian.

You're embarrassing yourself, Christian.

No one would understand, because marriage in my family had always been a strategic game. Even though Phillip was of course fond of his wife and had affection for his family, the match had been orchestrated. Was it archaic? Of course. But it was generations of that kind of machinations that had made me a prince in the first place. The credit was owed where it was due. I wouldn't have met Kale if not for decades of everything going the way it had for my family.

"I'm not scared of a challenge," Kale said.

I leaned back, reaching up and curling my fingers around his neck. His skin was warm and his pulse thrummed under my palms, a steady beat that helped me to catch my breath.

"I need you to be sure about this, though," he went on, dark eyes scanning over my face. "This changes your life much more than mine and you're a little high on—"

I interrupted him, pressing my fingers against his bottom lip. I was not interested in hearing *his* ideas about the things that made me fall in love with him. "I have my wits about me."

He puckered his lips and kissed the pads of my fingers.

"We have time to make a plan," he said.

"There you are." Ford's voice rang out like an unwelcome alarm, and he threw himself down on a couch opposite where Kale and I sat. I closed my eyes, sucking in a deep breath and lifting my leg to untangle myself from Kale's lap. Insistent hands around my waist stilled me, and then his mouth was right beside my ear.

"You can stay as you are or you can get on your knees again," he whispered, smiling. "Or you can tell me no, and I'll let you sit however you want. I know we haven't discussed this yet, but—"

"If we had discussed it?"

"Here or the floor," he answered.

Heat rushed down my spine and between my legs. My cock was already hard enough to be indecent if we were to step out of this little club of theirs and the command didn't help the situation at all. It was another new thing, another interest I didn't know I had until Kale showed it to me. I quietly weighed the options he'd given me, testing how I imagined each of them would make me feel.

If I sat beside him on the couch, we'd be equals. I'd have a funny conversation with his arrogant friends and we'd have some drinks and then call it a night. There wasn't anything wrong with that, but we'd done it over dinner.

If I went back onto my knees, there's be no doubt in any of our minds about who I was and who I was *to* Kale. Not that I imagined there was any doubt at this point. We all knew what kind of man he was and what kind of man he attracted. We were, after all, in a club designed exactly for that. The third option had the most open ends.

If I stayed on his lap with my back to his friends, what would that play out like? Would they pretend I wasn't there? Would they still try to engage me in conversation even though they couldn't see my face? The position would reduce me to that of a sex toy, a distraction for Kale to play with while he talked with his friends. I was more than that to him—I knew it and I knew he knew it, but...

"I'll stay," I finally said.

The curiosity for the unknown caused gooseflesh to prickle up the back of my neck, and at my answer, Kale let out a satisfied groan that rattled through my thighs and down my legs.

"Here we are, indeed," Kale said to his friend, shifting me more to one thigh than both so he could look over me and talk to his friends. Heat radiated off of him, his face so close to mine, even though we faced opposite directions. I closed my eyes and rested my forehead against his shoulder.

"Where is Brooks?" Kale asked Ford.

"Chatting up a thick young thing with a pain kink," Ford answered.

"Just you and me, then?"

I groaned, body coming alive.

Ford chuckled. "Seems like it. Let me get you a fresh drink and we can people-watch awhile."

"Thanks." Kale moved, passing his empty glass to Ford, then he kissed the side of my head and spoke to me, "I want you to come tonight. While we're here."

"Right now?"

"After Ford is back. I want you to touch yourself while he and I are talking. Is that something you're comfortable with?"

My cheeks burned. "Please don't ask."

"I need to know."

"Just tell me," I begged, my brain already starting to misfire for how much I wanted exactly what he was asking me.

"What if I asked you to jerk off while you sucked my cock?" he asked, flicking his hand toward the couch Ford had just vacated. "While he sat right there and we talked about that twink across the room who's about to get railed against the window."

I didn't even bother looking toward the window because the twink in question didn't exist to me. The only thing that mattered was Kale and the insistent ache that had taken up residence in the middle of my chest and right between my legs. Like a tether ran between the two focus points, I was pulled taut at his whim.

There was appeal in the question, and sucking his dick in public, in front of his friends...it was something so far out of the realm of my comfort zone it gave me pause. I swallowed, sucking in a breath and drawing myself back into the moment with him, focusing on the warmth of his hands and his body against mine.

"Not yet," I answered.

The sound that left Kale's mouth sounded like the happy hum he made after he got off. I leaned up so I could see his face, finding a small and very content smile resting against his mouth.

"I'm proud of you, princess," he said, licking his lips. "You can always tell me no."

"I never want to."

"But I need you to know that you can."

How was everything with Kale so much? So different? How did he give me so much control over my life while actively also taking it away?

"Can I still stay on your lap?" I asked.

"Always."

"Can I still come?"

Kale laughed, and Ford was back, handing off a tumbler full of amber liquid and ice. He didn't acknowledge me in any way.

"You'll be in big trouble if you don't," Kale confirmed, raising his glass to my lips. I took a small sip, the scotch burning as it slid down my throat. "You'll also be in big trouble if anyone in this room sees your dick, princess. So show some discretion."

He leaned close and traced his tongue across the seam of my lips, licking off a drop of scotch I hadn't managed to get into my mouth.

And then I was dismissed.

It should have been demeaning, but my body reacted as if it was anything but. I closed my eyes, content to listen to Kale talk to Ford about mundane things that had no bearing on me in any way. At home, I attended many meetings and councils where my presence was demanded, but not needed. Sitting on Kale's lap with my back to his friend and a rock hard cock between my legs while they both ignored me should have resonated in my chest the same way that other kind of dismissal did, but...

I did have something to do. There was instruction I'd been given. Kale wanted me to sit on his lap, he wanted me to keep my cock hidden, and he wanted me to come. My presence *was* important, and I had things to do. I struggled to try and piece together the comparisons, the understanding of why I was so hard for this flavor of being demeaned and not the other ones that had made up my whole life. My dick started to deflate, and I grunted, squeezing my eyes closed while I tried to quiet the argument in the back of my brain.

"Excuse me one moment," Kale said, not to me. His hands bracketed my waist and he pressed his mouth against my ear so hard, the sound of his voice was muffled when he spoke next, that time *to* me. "I've made men with soft cocks come before, but it's not my job to get you off tonight."

"I'm overthinking this," I admitted.

"You don't need to think at all. You just need to grind against my leg like the horny little cock slut we both know you are." He moved me against his thigh, the friction of our bodies and the rough material of our pants almost immediately sparking my dick back to life.

I groaned, less frustrated, but still far from where I wanted to be.

"If it's too much—"

"It's not," I said quickly. "It's not. It's just new."

"I know," he whispered. "You're being so brave."

"Don't patronize me, please."

He pinched my side, and I grimaced, yanking my body out of his reach. His other hand was still firm around my waist, making it impossible to get far. His fingertips squeezed, a fatty piece of skin caught between them, and then he pulled and twisted, drawing a soft cry out of my mouth. My head fell forward and I gasped, hips doing a slow circle against his thigh as he tugged again at my skin. My brain caught up to my body, and my hips made another circle, pressing down hard against his thigh, pushing into the crook of his stomach.

"Oh," I breathed out.

"So brave," he murmured again, letting go of the spot where he'd pinched me.

Disappointment rushed through me, but before I could express it, he had his fingers digging into my skin again, another flash of pain radiating through my ribs. My lashes fluttered until my eyes fell all the way closed, and I swayed right into that comfortable and floaty place I'd been unable to find on my own.

"What do you say?" he asked, kissing the shell of my ear.

"Th..." Words were already hard, sensation and feeling washing over me like a rougher than usual sort of high tide. "Thank you, Mr. Sheffield."

"On with it, then," he said, releasing a piece of my skin

and digging his fingernails into the small sliver left between his fingers.

My hips bucked, then began to move on their own. Kale resumed his conversation with Ford, sipping slowly at his whiskey. Every now and then, his fingers grazed over what was undoubtedly a blossoming bruise on the bottom of my rib cage and my balls throbbed at the touch. Their voices behind me turned into a quiet hum, like background noise to the steady beat of my pulse in my ears.

Kale once again pressed his glass against my lips and I tried to drink, but the amber liquor dribbled down my chin instead. He flattened his tongue against the spot and licked, a hot stripe over my skin and across my mouth. My cock jerked and spasmed, shooting cum against the already wet cotton of my underwear, the expensive wool of my slacks. On his lap, my body undulated until my muscles ached from the uncontrolled force of my orgasm, the aftershocks finally dying down into a sporadic twitch.

Kale kissed me, more a sound than actual contact of his lips against mine. I was tangled and messy in his lap, but if it bothered him, he didn't give me any indication. Slowly the voices came back into focus. I recognized Brooks' voice, even though I had no recollection of when he'd sat down beside Ford. It was almost like a switch flipped when my awareness slipped back into my body.

I didn't know how Kale did it.

I didn't understand how he'd taken all of these things I hated about my life and made them powerful, put them in my control. Kale had somehow given me back my life when I hadn't even realized I'd lost it.

"I love you," I whispered the words against his shoulder,

turning my head to the side and collapsing against him. I hoped the confession hadn't been loud enough for Ford to hear, because the feelings felt so new and secret. I wanted it to be ours for a little while longer. Everything was going to change in a matter of days, and I wanted to stay in this bubble with him for as long as possible.

CHRISTIAN LOOKED AT HOME IN MY BED. WITH THE SUNLIGHT FANNED out across the foot of the bed, his hair tousled from sleep and sex, with the sheets pooled loose around his waist, he seemed like something out of a fairytale. Maybe I'd conjured him out of my dreams, I wasn't certain. I didn't think too hard on it, on the off chance he wasn't real and thinking too hard would send my subconscious into some sort of crisis that would have Christian evaporating from my life if I blinked too slowly.

I was content to leave him in my bed because I liked him there, and because I needed coffee. The wood floors in my house were cool against my bare feet, and I turned up the heat on my way to the kitchen. Fall was fully wrapping itself around New York, and the pumpkins from my parents were already starting to rot in the back garden.

Thinking about my parents had me thinking about my brother and the distress of our last phone call. I hoped he'd decided to go visit our parents instead of doing something spontaneous, but that hadn't ever been his style. Boston had always been better suited for an unpredictable life. He loved the city, though not as much as me. He needed the fresh air of the farm on occasion, but he'd always been horrible at asking for what he needed. I was proud of him for realizing he needed *something* new, but as always, he was ever the romantic optimist, believing the grass would be greener anywhere he *wasn't*.

I made a note to offer him a job, which would effectively kill two birds with one stone. It would keep him in the city, and it would keep an assistant at the desk long enough to get him trained and running. Ford was many things, but he knew better than to sleep with my very straight brother. Hopefully, the tedium of entry-level work would remind Boston of his capabilities, which were far beyond scheduling my meetings and fielding phone calls, and he'd get his head out of his ass and back on track. And Ford could go entertain himself with someone else's employment pool.

I finished adding things to the mental to-do list of shit I had to do once Christian's little trip to New York was over just as my coffee finished brewing. I debated making a mug for Christian and taking it into the bedroom, but the hours of travel and the excitement of our little adventure had undoubtedly taken a toll on him. I decided to let him sleep a little longer. That would give me an opportunity to play back through the events of the night before uninterrupted, with no one to judge any sort of panic that might flash across my face when I remembered the fact I'd confessed my love to a man I barely knew.

It wasn't so much that I was avoidant of the four-letter word, but I hadn't been looking for it and I surely hadn't expected to find it. Unlike my brother, I thrived with predictability. Christian had come around and turned everything about my life on its head. Ford had called me out on as much, and I made sure to move calling Beamer to the top of my list. I owed him a much bigger apology than I'd managed before his move, and it was embarrassing that it had taken kidnapping a prince for me to realize that love could do crazy things to a man.

A knock on the door startled me, and I narrowed my eyes in the direction of the noise. My friends absolutely made a habit of coming by unannounced, but it was too early for any of them to even be coherent, let alone dressed and on my stoop. I took a fortifying drink of my coffee and headed toward the door, if for no other reason than I didn't want them to knock again and wake Christian prematurely.

I don't know who I expected to be on the porch, but it definitely wasn't Christian's security lead, Niko. I recognized him immediately, breath rushing out of me in a long and audible exhale. He was in a sharp black suit, like the last time I saw him, a in stark contrast to my loose navy pajamas and plain white undershirt. I ran a hand through my hair and leaned against the doorjamb.

"I thought we had more time," I said.

He worked his jaw back and forth, tilting his head to look up the front facade of my home.

"I tried." He raised his hand and crooked two fingers in a familiar *come here* gesture. It was only then that I noticed the sleek black town car double-parked on the street. I lived on the Upper East Side, town cars were a common sight here, after all. A man in a suit that looked much like Niko's opened the back passenger door of the car at his beckoning, and another man, one who looked like a less happy version of Christian, stepped onto the sidewalk.

"I see," I murmured, taking a drink of my coffee and eyeing the new third party as he crossed the sidewalk and unlatched the gate that led into my front garden.

"Parrish asked that you please don't make it harder for him," Niko said softly, stepping aside to make way for the man I assumed to be one of Christian's brothers. I didn't have time to ask if Parrish had wanted me to make it easy on this man or on Christian, but I imagined it was somehow one and the same.

The man gave my home a much more judgmental onceover than Niko had, and I frowned at the distaste that colored his expression when he turned his attention to me.

"Do you have my brother?" he asked.

"I don't know," I said, crossing my legs at the ankle and matching his frown with one of my own. "I don't even know who you are."

Niko groaned, and the man affected a tight and unimpressed look that I imagined worked on a person who cared about royalty and rank and social status. Fortunately for me, and unfortunately for him, I was not one of those people. I came from old money. A man who had enough of those things, the social status notwithstanding, on account of my name and my lineage, but I'd never dictate someone's life the way Christian's family tried to do to him. I couldn't have been more different from the man standing on my doorstep.

"I am Phillip Davenport-Spencer, Prince of—"

I cut him off with a smirk, "Oh, you're Christian's brother. Yes, he's here."

My response clearly caught him off-guard, and I liked that. Phillip was likely not a man who'd ever been told no in his life, let alone been back-talked by a stranger. He was in America now, though. And respect wasn't freely given in the circles I moved in—it was earned.

He was no exception to the rule.

"It's time for him to come home," Phillip said.

"I have a flight on schedule for the day after tomorrow," I countered. "Happy to provide the details."

"He's needed now."

"Is he?" I arched a brow.

"Yes," Phillip grit out the single syllable.

"Well, there seems to be a conflict then, because he's needed *here* as well."

My statement couldn't have been closer to the truth. I did need Christian. Needed him naked in my bed, snoring softly until his body caught up on all the sleep he'd lost. He was exactly where he was supposed to be, and the only way his brother was going to get him out of my house was if Christian either went willingly or if Niko physically subdued me to get inside. Niko, thankfully, didn't strike me as the type for hand-to-hand combat, which was a relief because it was too early for that level of conflict. I took another drink of my coffee.

"My brother has obligations at home," Phillip said.

"Well, we did try to stay, but I wanted to take him out to dinner and we both decided that the restaurants in New York are more his speed."

"New York is nothing if not less respectful," Phillip said pointedly.

"I don't know." I gave him a lopsided shrug. "I've never had a problem."

"Go tell Christian I'm here. He's had his fun, and now it's time for him to come home."

I licked my lips, drawing them back between my teeth and

biting down hard to stop myself from saying the first words that came to mind, which were *he is home*. I wanted my home to be his, my bed to be his, my kitchen, my closet, my friends, all of it. I loved the man asleep in my bed and I wanted him to stay with me for more than another day.

"I'm trying to do you a favor," Phillip said next, which felt like a deflection.

"Is that so?"

"There's no future in whatever this little tryst is." Christian's brother waved dismissively at me, and I straightened to my full height, eager to hear the rest of his assumptions. "Christian knows who he is and where he comes from. He'll come home and fall in line, and you'll be left alone again in this horrible little city."

I scoffed, smirking as I took another drink of my coffee.

Phillip was right about one thing. Christian did know who he was, but it was something he'd learned at my feet, not in the throne room of the palace he'd grown up in. Before me, Christian had only known ideas of the kind of man his father had meant for him to be. With me, he knew the man he truly was in his heart.

"I'd love to make a bet on that one," I said.

"If you'll go collect my brother, we'll be out of your hair."

"He's asleep," I countered.

"Wake him up."

"He'll be home the day after tomorrow." I scratched the side of my cheek, close to my mouth. "Before dinner."

"I don't think you understand that my brother is a *prince*," Phillip said, lowering his voice.

"I'm well aware." I didn't think Christian would want me

to tell his brother about my favorite pet name for him, so I kept it tucked in the back of my mouth.

"He cannot just *abscond*."

"It was more like a kidnapping if that's easier for you to digest," I offered. "I planned it with my best friend before I chartered my flight."

"You're not doing yourself any favors, Mr. Sheffield."

I grimaced, hearing my full name roll off his tongue with so much disdain when his brother offered it up with so much admiration and affection. It was amazing how two men who shared the same DNA could be so grossly opposite each other. Phillip had flown halfway around the world to try and intimidate me, and he was about to fly the rest of the way back after learning the lesson I wasn't afraid of anyone, least of all him.

"I'm not letting you in and I'm not waking him up," I said, tired of the conversation and unsure of how much longer Christian would sleep through the commotion. "You know who I am, you know where he is, and you know when he'll be back. That needs to be enough."

I stepped back, hand around the door. I pushed it halfway closed, but not before I caught the frustrated flare of Phillip's nostrils.

"Is this the first time you've been told no?" I asked.

Niko snorted, then sputtered and coughed. Phillip's head swung around, giving him a sharp and disapproving look. Niko patted his chest, staring at the cobblestones beneath his feet until he was able to get himself back under control.

"Someone has to stay with him," Phillip said.

"I'm right here."

"Someone who can protect him."

I angled my head to the side, brow raised and ready for his

next comment. There wasn't anyone who could take better care of Christian than me. I knew it, Christian knew it, and Phillip was about to learn it for himself.

"The day after tomorrow, he'll be home," I said again.

"Niko stays."

"He's welcome to explore the city." I smiled, gesturing toward the city behind them. "I don't have room for him here."

"I find that hard to believe," Phillip challenged.

"You can think about it on your trip home." I gave Niko an apologetic look. He'd done plenty for Christian and me in the short time we'd known each other and I hoped my sparring with Phillip wasn't going to make things harder for him. "And, besides, if I can get Christian out from under Niko once, what makes you think I won't do it again?"

"You have no idea what you're dealing with," Phillip said, smoothing his hand down the front of his suit jacket, as if he'd ever had a button out of place in his entire life.

"I'm sure I can manage it. Now, as fond as I already am of Niko here, I have to ask you to please take your security detail with you and get off my property."

"The day after tomorrow," Phillip grit out.

"Before dinner."

"If he's late, I'll be back for you and no one with me will take no for an answer," he warned.

"Duly noted." I offered Phillip half of a bow and closed the door in their faces.

From behind me, I heard a noise, and my heart skipped and lodged itself in my throat. I turned quickly, biting the inside of my cheek in an attempt to bring down my pulse and school my features. I was many things, but unflappable was not one of them, and Phillip's impromptu call was far from how I wanted to spend my morning. The fact that Christian's father had undoubtedly sent him to New York with the sole intention of collecting his wayward brother should have been proof enough that I was in over my head.

But Christian looked perfect, with his hair sticking up every which way and a pair of my pajamas cinched tight and low around his waist, and I couldn't find it in myself to care. I would happily drown if it meant I got to wake up one more morning with this man beside me.

"Who were you talking to?" Christian asked, scrubbing a hand over his face.

I locked the deadbolt and closed the space between us, taking him into my arms and kissing the side of his head.

"No one important," I promised, hoping it was true. "Let's get you some coffee."

CHAPTER 24
CHRISTIAN

I'D RECOGNIZE THE SOUND OF MY BROTHER'S VOICE ANYWHERE, EVEN in my sleep. It was his chopped and constantly annoyed tone that had brought me around, immediately throwing me into a state of confusion because the softness of the sheets and the smell of the pillows confirmed I was still in America, in Kale's bed. But when I shuffled downstairs, Kale slammed the door closed and faced me with a cup of coffee in hand and the same unaffected look that sat on his face when he was in the middle of something serious.

He opened his arms to me, and if Phillip wasn't banging down the door in a fit of anger, Kale's arms were the only place I wanted to be. I nuzzled against his chest, breathing in the warm and spicy smell of his skin.

"What's on the agenda for today?" I asked, tracing my nose across the dip of his throat.

"First, coffee." He herded me into the kitchen, the terra-cotta tiles cool under my feet. I took a seat at the small dine-in table tucked under one of the windows while Kale busied himself with preparing a coffee for me.

"Shouldn't I get coffee for us both?" I asked when he joined me at the table. He brought a plate with two croissants with him, and I picked at the flaky corner of the one closest to me.

"You're my guest."

"But, like…" I cleared my throat, searching for the words and not wanting to come off sounding ignorant. "With the way things are between us."

Kale arched a brow. "How are things between us?"

"Are you really going to make me say it?" I asked.

"I really don't know where you're going, so…yes." He situated himself in his seat, a casual recline that screamed in sharp contrast compared to how uncomfortable *I* was feeling. Raising his coffee to his mouth, he took a drink and waited.

"I don't know a lot about domination." My cheeks immediately burned like I'd pressed them directly against the sun. "But isn't the serving meant to be my job?"

"Sex isn't a job, for one." Kale bobbled his head from side to side, a soft smile playing across his mouth. He wasn't teasing, but he was enjoying himself.

"This isn't sex," I blurted.

"But you're hard." He stretched one of his legs toward me, pressing his toes between my legs, against the tip of my slowly swelling cock.

"Because you're touching my dick."

"You were hard before," he said, withdrawing his leg and resting his ankle on the top of his other knee. "Was it thinking about serving me coffee that did it?"

"I'm always hard around you," I said, running my hands through my hair. I was inclined to pull it all out at the roots, but I wasn't quite there yet.

"What we do in the bedroom doesn't have to be what we do in every room," he said gently.

"We did it at a club last night," I reminded him, cock thickening even more as if to prove his earlier point. "Last time I checked, they didn't have any bedrooms."

"Oh, but they do."

I let out an audible sigh. "Point taken."

He smiled at me and dipped his chin toward his chest. "And I take yours. But to your point, no, Christian. You aren't supposed to serve me coffee unless you want to."

"What do *you* want?"

I was spoiled on account of my upbringing, but I strived to never be selfish. Even though that was the only thing I'd been when it came to him. The entirety of our relationship had been Kale doing things for me, whether it was hiding me from Niko, flying me around the world for dinner, or making me come so hard I saw stars. For weeks now, between the sex and the emails, everything Kale had done was *for* me. I hadn't even asked what he wanted, what he preferred.

"That's complicated."

"Then make it easy for me," I said.

He chewed his cheek, hollowing the skin while he worried himself over whatever answer he was preparing to give me.

"It's not as cut and dried as you're making it out to be. And none of the formalities of what this relationship *could* be matter. You're going back home the day after tomorrow and everything is going to be different then anyway."

Kale's expression turned sour, and he tore off a chunk of a croissant. Popping it into his mouth, he chewed and swallowed, then repeated the action eight times until the croissant was nothing but crumbs on the plate.

"What if I decide I don't want to go home?" I asked, peeling the buttery top layer off my croissant and folding it in on itself before shoving it into my mouth.

"You have to," he said quickly. "Do you want more coffee?"

He was up before I could read his expression and back with a full mug of steaming brown liquid.

"To your earlier question, the answer is no. I didn't get hard thinking about getting you coffee. At least, it wasn't just getting you coffee that did it. Now answer me."

"What do I want?" he repeated the question back at me and I nodded.

Kale studied my face in silence, eyes dragging from left to right and back, then up and down and around before his left eye twitched closed. It was almost a grimace, but not quite.

"I want to remember everything," he whispered, letting out a slow breath. "When you're gone."

Spit lodged in my throat, and I forced myself to swallow it down, the cursed echo of Phillip's voice still ringing in my ears.

"You're talking like when I leave, you're never going to see me again."

"It's different with the distance."

"Do you think if you tell me what to do over email that I'll ignore you?" I asked, snorting in amusement at the idea of Kale sending me a list of tasks that I would read and promptly ignore. He was delirious if that was his concern, because there wasn't a single word of his that I didn't hang off of. An ocean between us wasn't going to change that.

"There's just...different ways to do this." He gave me a weak shrug. "There's people who do it for fun during sex, people who take it a little bit further than that, and people who do it all the time. It's not one size fits all."

"And what do you want?" I asked again.

"Something in the middle, I think," he murmured, shoving the plate aside and reaching for my hand. I gave it without concern, and he threaded our fingers together, turning my palm up so my knuckles dusted across the rustic wood of the breakfast table.

"Tell me about it," I whispered. "I need your help here. I don't know how to ask for what I need because I don't have the words for it."

I hadn't been searching for *the right* thing to say, but I must have found it just the same. The stress that had wrinkled the corners of Kale's eyes turned soft and his mouth twisted up at the corner, a smile that almost looked like an apology. I wanted to move, to go to him. Wanted to crawl into his lap and curl against his chest, but I didn't know if that was appropriate or reasonable.

Normally, at home, when I was out of my depth with something, it made me angry. Nothing made me more upset than feeling—or looking—stupid, but even though I was the one at a clear disadvantage, nothing about Kale's demeanor brought up those feelings for me. The space felt safe and tender, giving me the feeling of being in his arms even if I was on the other side of the table.

"Most of my relationships have been inconsequential, Christian," he explained, turning our joined hands over. "Not all of them, but..."

"I've never had a relationship," I offered.

"Why not?"

"I've never been interested in anyone that my father or

Phillip would approve of," I admitted. "And it's honestly too fun to make them mad, so I've not cared to try and find anyone they'd consider respectable."

"What would they think of me?" he asked.

The fact that Kale had closed the door in Phillip's face and lived to tell about it was more of an answer to the question than I'd ever be able to give him.

"I think you'd be tolerable," I answered.

His mouth quirked into a brief smile.

"I enjoy the way things are between us." Kale picked his words carefully, gaze flickering toward the ceiling like the rest of the answer might be written above our heads. "I like when you let me choose for us, but I have no interest in being in a relationship with someone who doesn't have opinions of his own."

"I have plenty of opinions."

He chuckled, yanking our hands across the table and raising them to his mouth. He kissed each of my knuckles, then each of my fingertips.

"I know you do," he said, angling his arm so he could kiss the thin skin on the inside of my wrist. "It's one of the things I love about you."

I closed my eyes, humming softly to match the way his confession felt in my bones. "What else do you love about me?"

"I love how you look on your knees with my cock in your mouth."

I opened my eyes in time to see him smirk.

"I love how my sheets smell after you've slept in my bed."

My lashes fluttered, and I let my eyes fall closed again.

"I love that you asked me to tell you what I loved about you because you needed the reassurance," he said.

"That's no—" I snapped my mouth closed before the rest of the sentence could escape my mouth.

That was *exactly* the reason I'd asked the question, and somehow he'd realized it before I did. I didn't know if he was simply that observant, that good, or some combination of both. But it was really sexy to recognize how in tune with me he already was.

"And what I want, Christian, is for you to continue asking me for the things you need. Whether you ask with your mouth, or your body, or that ever-hard cock of yours. What I want is to give you what you need."

My eyes were still closed, so I heard, rather than saw, when Kale went to his knees in front of me. Without looking, I tangled my fingers through his hair, relishing the silky softness of the strands as they wove through my fingers. I knew where he was, and one part of me wanted to open my eyes and see him there, but the other part...

There was a lot I didn't understand about the dynamic of my relationship with Kale, but one thing I knew for certain was having him on his knees for me was a sacred offering that deserved to be treated with reverence. When he reached for the waistband of my pajama pants, which were his pajama pants, I squeezed my eyes closed tighter. Lifting off the seat so he could tug them down to my thighs, I dropped my head back to give me double protection from seeing him between my legs.

When his mouth sealed around the tip of my cock, I let go of his hair and covered my face with both of my hands. Digging the heels of my palms against my closed eyelids, my entire body burned like a bomb had centered itself in the middle of my chest before detonating outward to every nerve ending in my body.

"Kale," I whimpered his name, and he hummed happily, taking the rest of my length into his mouth.

His mouth was hot and wet, tongue wrapping around my shaft as he worked his way up and down. For every disheveled noise I made, Kale doubled his efforts, and by the time an orgasm shimmered around the edges of my vision, I was sitting in a pool of spit, my bruised thighs sliding around the chair. Kale's fingers dug into my legs, spreading them apart and while he bobbed up and down my shaft, groaning like I was the best meal he'd ever had.

The orgasm was a heavy and intense wave that slammed into me so hard, my back bowed and I curled over the top of Kale's head. Hips bucking madly as hot jets of cum streaked out of my dick, my fingers gripped the seat of the chair to keep myself rooted to the ground. My eyes flew open in time for me to realize Kale had been watching me the whole time. With his lips spread around the thick girth of my shaft, his stare was focused upward at my face. His brown eyes shone with unshed tears, and spit shined across his hollowed cheeks.

He sucked at my dick, swallowing the last pulses of my orgasm with a low growl of approval. He kept his mouth around me until the touch of his tongue against my shaft hurt, and only then did he carefully ease me out of his mouth. He didn't bother tucking me back into my pajamas, as they were wet and soiled like the rest of me. His lips were shiny and swollen, and while I'd wanted many things in my life, I'd never *needed* anything more than I needed to kiss him in that moment.

The chair made a loud and grating sound as it slid back across the tiles, and I was on my knees with Kale's face in my hands, crashing our mouths together. He opened for me readily, going pliant while I used my tongue to scoop the taste of my cum from his mouth. It mixed with my spit and his spit, swirling between our tongues and our mouths, not even stopping when my back hit the floor.

Kale's weight on top of me was a welcome presence, and I spread my legs to make room for him there. He didn't break the kiss, not even when he reached down between his legs to jerk off. With his other hand braced beside my head, hips rutting against me, Kale shot his load across my stomach with another rough grunt before he collapsed, dropping his forehead against mine.

The entire scene felt frantic, but those moments at the end were the most peaceful of my life. I sighed softly, letting my eyes fall closed again. The sharp pain of the tile against my shoulder blades faded into nothing, the sticky wetness between my legs was nothing more than another piece of me. A piece of us.

Kale kissed me again.

The corner of my mouth, my chin, my cheeks, my nose. Humming contentedly, I wrapped my arms around him, tracing my hands down to his exposed ass and digging in. Kale kissed each of my eyelids before pressing our foreheads together and going still.

"I don't know how to be with you, princess," he whispered, "but I promise you, I'm going to figure it out."

And I believed him.

Something like warmth bloomed in my chest, spreading through my whole body when Christian very studiously adjusted the ends of my scarf around my neck. I didn't need—or expect—him to serve me in some of the ways we'd talked about over coffee, but I was content to let him explore as much as he wanted for the rest of our limited time together. I wasn't sure if he'd heard his brother and me speaking, but he hadn't said anything and I wasn't going to bring it up. We had two days and two nights left, and I was going to make the most of them. So, when he asked to see the city, the answer was an immediate yes.

After breakfast and after our after-breakfast fuck, we took a hot and slow shower together, then dressed and kissed, and kissed some more. It was nearly two in the afternoon by the time we made it out of the house on our way to Central Park. While I'd always loved the city, I'd long ago grown familiar and bored with the tourist traps. There were always more people, and while money wasn't an issue for me, things were more expensive too. I preferred the higher-class establishments that were harder for people to gain access to.

The Black Door, for one.

Christian held tight to my hand as we headed up Fifth Ave, past the Pulitzer Fountain and into the park. I had to admit the place was gorgeous in the fall, overflowing with vibrant orange and yellow leaves that drifted from the treetops and blanketed the ground. He squeezed my hand and grinned up at me, eyes wide as he took everything in.

"Do you have any place like this back home?" I asked.

While Christian and I had talked about a fair number of things, there was still so much I didn't know about him or about his life back home. I knew he was a prince and I knew everyone in his life, except his best friend, tried to control him, but beyond that...

"No," he said, chuckling as one of the fairytale carriages rolled past us. "Nothing this big, and not this many people."

"Tell me about what it's like."

Christian let out a long breath, mouth twisted down at the corner. "Can we eat first?"

I pulled my hand out of my pocket to check my watch, frowning at the time. "You'll ruin dinner."

"Thanks, Dad."

"We can eat," I said.

"You'll just have to keep me up late so I can have dinner at ten," Christian suggested, tugging me toward one of the gyro stands. He bounced up and down on the balls of his feet while we waited our turn. After we got some food, he beelined it for a bench. I sat down beside him, happy to see him dig into his meal with the same speed and vigor he seemed to approach everything else in his life.

"What did you want to know?" he asked, mouth full of meat.

"Pardon?"

He had sauce on the corner of his mouth, and I wiped some away with my thumb, which I sucked into my mouth to clean off.

"Before we got food, you asked what it was like at home," he said, taking another bite. "What did you want to know?"

"Anything," I told him. "Everything."

"There are underground tunnels that connect to the palace," Christian said. "They come out by the river inlet at the far edge of town."

"Did you used to sneak out that way?" I asked.

"Used to sneak boys in," he said, face flushing. "Parrish was a bad influence."

"How long have you known him?"

"My whole life." Christian nibbled at the last bite of his gyro before balling up the wrapper and setting it on the bench beside him. "His father is my father's lead advisor. We grew up together."

His nose twitched at the last comment, and I could tell there was more to the story, but I wasn't sure if it was safe to push him for more. It turned out I didn't have to because, after a short pause, Christian started talking again on his own.

"Parrish always had it easier, though," he went on. "All the perks of growing up in the palace without all the restrictions."

"He got to go home at night," I said.

Christian nodded, then gave me a lopsided shrug. "I would have lost my mind if it wasn't for him. He's kept me grounded for years, made sure my head stayed on whenever I got down about things."

"And he facilitated your kidnapping," I reminded.

Christian grinned, tilting his head to the side and looking up at me. There was something in his eyes, a flash of youthfulness he didn't normally wear, and it felt like I was getting a glimpse of a secret version of Christian that most people didn't have access to. I wrapped my arm around him, pulling him against my side. He rested his head on my shoulder with a soft and happy sigh.

"That he did," Christian murmured.

"What else?"

"I don't know. I spend a lot of time wondering what the future looks like for me there," he said.

"Explain."

"I'll never sit on the throne. Not that I would want to, because I don't. But..."

"You're held to the same standard," I guessed.

He didn't answer because both of us already knew it was true. For Christian, I represented a break from the monotony of his life. I was an escape. I swallowed, drawing up the memory of the times he'd said he loved me, of the moments where the emotion had been telegraphed clearly across his features, so I could try to see if there was any fault or lie in it. Did he truly *love* me, or just the idea of me? The things I represented? New York was a world away and I offered him a reprieve from the life that had beaten him into the kind of submission he didn't need.

"Is there really a castle here?" he asked me.

I cleared my throat. "And some ponds. A carousel. Did you want to go see anything?"

"Maybe the carousel," he said. "I've had my fill of castles and palaces."

"The carousel it is, then." I stood and held my hand out for him, and we headed toward the red brick gazebo that housed the ride. As we walked closer, peals of laughter bounced off the open walls, and Christian leaned into me happily.

"Do you want a go on it?" I asked.

"Will you ride too?"

I watched the horses rise and fall around the ride as it slowly crept to a stop, trying to remember if Boston and I had ever been on the carousel as children. We'd, of course, been to New York to visit our grandparents before making the move as teenagers, but I couldn't find a memory that involved anything beyond the formality of my grandparents' house or their social clubs.

"I don't think I ever have before," I said.

This earned another of those secret smiles that I'd decided I wanted to start collecting.

"Then we have to," he said.

"Then we have to."

I let Christian take the lead, hauling us through the line. I paid for our tickets which earned me a lingering and savory kiss on the mouth, and then Christian found his horse and found one for me too. At one point on the ride, he tipped his head back and closed his eyes, fingers wrapped loosely around the spiraled brass bar that impaled the neck of the black horse he'd picked to ride. He looked just about as peaceful as he did when he was on the brink of an orgasm, and suddenly the idea of sending him home the day after tomorrow felt like the cruelest thing I could do to him.

If I was truly trying to be a partner for him, in whatever way worked best for us...if I was the thoughtful and dominant man I'd always imagined myself to be, how could I send him back to the place and the people who'd caused him so much distress? Because on top of being all those things, I was also a man of my word and it was my word I'd given to Niko, and to Phillip.

The decision seemed impossible.

"That was ridiculous," Christian said as the ride came to a halt. He climbed off the horse and jumped from the carousel. I was much slower at joining him, but once I came to stand beside him, he looped his arm around the crook of my elbow and shoved his hand into the pocket of my coat. "I loved it."

I feigned a laugh. "What do you want to do now?"

"You tell me. What do the tourists like?"

"I've never been a tourist here," I told him. "Boston and I moved here as teenagers and we were in boarding school almost immediately. My grandparents are lovely, but they're not the sightseeing type."

"But you're an adult now," he reasoned. "You could have gone and done all of these things on your own."

"I don't like people," I admitted, scratching the side of my neck. "I mean, I like *my* people, not all people."

"Trust issues, is it?"

"Yes and no, but...I've just never seen the city like that," I said. "It's just...home."

"Well, I hear the Empire State Building is pretty tall," Christian said with a grin.

"Do you have tall buildings back home?"

"Not that tall."

I couldn't tell him no. Didn't want to tell him no. I grabbed his face between my hands and yanked him into me, slanting our mouths together and licking my way past his lips. Christian let out a little whimper that tasted like candy, and I had to shove him away before I got an erection hard enough to count for public indecency.

After I pushed him away, Christian pressed his fingertips against his lips, cheeks flushed.

"Mr. Sheffield," he murmured, lashes fluttering. "You make it hard to be decent."

"I think that's half the fun of this," I said, "but I'd hardly call what's happening between my legs decent."

His stare flickered down to the growing bulge between my legs.

"Tallest tower in the city, indeed."

Christian's tease evolved into a laugh, and I shook my head, turning on the ball of my foot and heading toward Columbus Circle without him.

"You're a brat," I called over my shoulder at him.

He laughed again, running to catch up to me. Then his hand was in mine and his breath was warm against my skin as he pressed a kiss against my cheek.

"I'm your brat," he said.

I swallowed. "My brat."

"And you love me."

I dragged us both to a stop, spinning to face him so abruptly the toes of our shoes scuffed together. He was still smiling and his eyes still sparkled, but there was a hint of concern that I very nearly missed. Maybe he'd heard my brain turning earlier, as I'd worked through all the internal doubt about the truth of his feelings for me. Though I'd never doubted my own for him. Maybe he'd been running through the same one-sided conversation.

"And I love you," I confirmed.

Just like that, the worry was gone from his face and the

feelings that had taken up residence in my chest doubled in size.

"I *love* you," I said again, dropping a kiss against the corner of his lips. His mouth was still salty from the gyro, swollen from all the kissing in the morning. The perfect pink pout that I wanted to lick and suck and defile for the rest of my days.

"I know," he whispered, dipping his chin to his chest. "I know, Mr. Sheffield."

"Not just that part of me," I said, shaking my head. "I love those things, those pieces..."

I trailed off, flattening my hand against his chest until it was over his heart, which battered violently against his sternum.

"The whole deal," I went on, flexing my fingers against the thick wool of his coat. "I'm all in with you, princess."

He covered my hand with his, an almost sad smile flickering on his face, because no matter what I said, we both knew that things were going to change the day after tomorrow whether we liked it or not. There was part of me that wanted Christian to go home and tell his whole family off, back his bags, and be back in my bed before sunrise, but I knew that was too much, too soon. There was also a part of me that wanted him to go home, stand up for himself, and then maybe when all was said and done, find his way back to me. The scenarios were opposing forces in my head, the pros and cons of each running a mile long. In that moment, I worried that what was best for me was not best for him, and I didn't know what it would look like to meet in the middle.

I also didn't think I wanted to meet in the middle.

I wanted everything.

CHAPTER 26

CHRISTIAN

After we left Central Park, we took a slow walk toward the Empire State Building. I wasn't a man who was particularly afraid of heights, but the 86th floor was staggering. The wind whipped around the open air balcony with an unmatched force, and I kept myself pressed close to Kale as we made our way toward the grating at the far edge of the balcony. In my ear, he made a low and happy sound.

"Do you like New York?" I asked.

"I love it here."

I loved it back home, but I didn't think there was any sight or place that drew the feelings out of me that I found myself grappling with in New York. That might have been on account of Kale, but I didn't think it was entirely him. America was massive. New York on its own was a huge city with so many people packed into such a small space, they'd been forced to build up into the clouds to make room.

"What about you?" he asked me.

"It's amazing," I said.

The wool of his coat scratched my cheek, but not in a way I

wanted to get away from. I rubbed my face over his shoulder, looking out at the sprawling expanse of the city ahead of us. The balcony was packed with people bustling around us, taking selfies and laughing, but Kale and I were in our own, quiet little castle at the top of the world.

"Did you want to go up to the 102nd floor?" he asked. "It's not outside like this, but less people."

"Why not?"

With his arm around my waist, we headed back into the elevator lobby, paid for the extra tickets and rode an express elevator up to the narrower—and much less busy—viewing floor. There was less room, less people, and in lieu of walls, there were floor-to-ceiling plate glass windows to enjoy the view through. We walked around to the far side of the building and pressed our way toward the glass. Kale shifted behind me, wrapping both arms around my waist and resting his chin on my shoulder. When he exhaled, I felt it in my bones, and I leaned back against him with a sad sigh.

"Are we boyfriends?" I blurted out, embarrassment immediately burning my cheeks.

"Did you want to be?"

"That's not what I asked."

He tilted his head to the side, resting his temple against mine. "I love you," he said. "Boyfriends feels..."

I swallowed. "Trivial."

"Trivial," he agreed, a soft rasp.

"But I'm not trying to get engaged or anything," I said quickly, turning in his arms so we were more face to face, my back to the city. "That feels rushed."

"Does it?"

"*Doesn't* it?" I countered.

My heart slammed against my ribs, beating harder than it ever had. There was no adrenaline rush I'd ever felt that topped the feelings churning in my gut as we stood tangled together above the clouds. I cursed the fall weather and the layers of clothes that kept Kale's skin from being within easy reach of my fingers.

"I don't think the title means anything," he said after some thought. "It's what you do with it. What it means."

"Elaborate on that one, Mr. Sheffield."

His exhale sounded like a growl, a heady reminder that for as in charge as Kale was about everything in his life, me included, I still held a very powerful sense of control over him.

"You're a prince," he explained, "that doesn't count for much, does it?"

I smacked his chest, rolling my eyes and trying to pull away from him. He tightened his hold and hauled our chests back together, turning us sideways so I could see him and the city at the same time.

"That's rude," I grumbled.

"You know how I meant it."

I did know exactly what he'd meant. I was a prince in title only, none of the benefits afforded my brother or even his children. Though, that felt unfair to say. I'd lived a life of unmitigated privilege, but after meeting Kale, I wondered if it was worth the cost. Parrish would have been free to fly around the world every week if that was what he wanted to do. No one would have protested on account of any social standing back home. He was free to live his life as he pleased, even though we'd practically grown up neck and neck with each other.

"The point is," he went on, giving my hips a wiggle. "I will treat you the same whether you're my boyfriend, my husband, or the man I bury my cock in every night. I'll *think* of you the same. I'll *love* you the same."

I inhaled a sharp breath, pressing my forehead against his chest and closing my eyes. "I don't want to leave."

"I know." His arms came tighter around me, stroking strong and assuring lines up and down the breadth of my back. "But it's not forever. Just...time to decide what's next."

"What's next is I want to be here with you," I said.

Kale pressed his cheek against the top of my head, his breath puffing out over my hair. "I want you here with me, too," he said...carefully.

"But?"

"There's no but. I want you here with me, *and* I want you to be sure you're comfortable with all the things that means."

He swallowed and I dug my fingers into the thick wool of his pea coat. I knew exactly what he meant. I wasn't in a situation where I could just decide I wanted to move to America to be with a man who hadn't been vetted and approved by my father. I didn't have the luxuries of a commoner, and when I decided I wanted to be with Kale for real and forever, there were other parts of my life that were going to fall away.

"You're here another day," he said. "Two more nights with me and then you can regroup and we can go from there. But I promise that you leaving isn't going to change the way I feel about you."

"Are you sure?" I asked. "Not just hormones?"

He snorted, knocking his shoulder into mine. "I have plenty of those, but no."

I turned my attention to the skyline and the view on the other side of the glass. There was a whole city here, a whole world to explore. I had no interest in being chained by my title any longer; I only wanted to be bound by Kale and his whims. That life was what I wanted to explore. More than the sight-seeing and the adventures, I wanted to learn myself by giving control over to him.

"Can we go back to your club tonight after dinner?"

"What are you after?"

"I just want to watch," I admitted, another rush of heat burning my cheeks and my throat.

He ghosted his lips across my ear, dropping his voice to a low whisper. "I didn't know I had a little voyeur on my hands?"

The promise of his tone sent blood rushing south and the altitude already had me dizzy. Or maybe that was just Kale and proximity of his skin and his smell that was doing me in. I swayed, leaning into him.

"What do you want, princess? Tell me what you need tonight."

"I want to go back," I murmured. "I liked the last time we were there. I...I like all the things we do. I want to see what other people do, though."

Kale chuckled, mouth shaping up into a knowing grin. "You want to see if there's anything else that's going to get you off."

I managed a nod, closing my eyes.

"Sometimes I wonder how you're real." He took my face into his hand, stroking his thumb across my cheek. His palm was cool against my burning hot skin. "Always pliant and ready, and fucking perfect. My perfect little princess."

"Not here," I whimpered, pushing my hips toward him.

"Not here and not yet." Kale took my hand and led me

back toward the elevators in the center of the floor. "Is there anything else you wanted to do today?"

I barked out a laugh. "You."

"That's a given, I think. But I meant before then."

I shook my head.

The elevator arrived and we rode back down to the 86th floor, and then down to the ground. On the sidewalk, I stepped back from the building and looked up. The height of the tower made me dizzy, all the blood in my body confused as to whether it should be between my legs or in my head. There was a low layer of clouds that obscured the upper floors of the building, and I wasn't sure the entire trip up to the top hadn't been a dream.

"Dinner at some point," I suggested, which earned me a pleased-looking nod of approval. "What do *you* want to do?"

Kale squinted, scrunching up his nose and answering with a shrug that made him look half his age. "You."

"You said not here and not yet," I reminded him.

"That was five minutes ago." He laughed. "Maybe I've changed my mind."

I slid my arms around his waist and looked up at him, the lights of the skyscrapers glowing from behind him like a halo. My dick ached, pushing against his hip, but I closed my eyes and inhaled a shaking breath before pressing myself against his front. Kale wrapped his arms around my shoulders and held us together, nose buried in my hair.

The moment felt fragile and forever at the same time, like if I breathed the wrong way the puzzle would crumble, but also somehow not...

My relationship with Kale was a series of unknowns, one after another after another, and me going back home in less than forth-eight hours wasn't making that any easier. But in his arms with my eyes closed, the sounds of the city around us, and the smell of him fresh in my nose, I could see the future play out before me in near-perfect time.

I would go home. My father and Phillip would be beyond angry. They'd yell and we'd argue, and I'd concede. I'd scale the wall or take the tunnels, sneak out and go stay with Parrish for a day or so to get my head on straight. Only enough time to build up the courage to do what needed to be done so I could come back to New York.

Come back to Kale.

"Take me to dinner," I whispered. "Order my wine. Order my food."

Kale's pupils dilated, his nostrils flaring.

"Tell me what to eat. Tell me when to stop," I said.

"Never stop." He gave a small shake of his head, and I knew he wasn't talking about food.

"Take me to your club and make me watch everyone get each other off," I went on. Kale's cock was hard too, thumping against my leg in time with his heartbeat. "Ask me what I like the most."

He arched a brow. "And then what?"

"I don't know." I huffed a quiet laugh. "I thought you were the one in charge."

He pinched my ribs, and instead of squirming away, pressed into him. The pain flickered up my side like a caress. Nostrils flaring, I tilted my head back to look up at him. I was so gone for this man, desperate and mindless for him in all of the best—and worst—ways.

"I'll take you to dinner, princess" he said, kissing the tip of my nose. "How do you feel about a little role play?"

"How so?"

My dick jerked against my leg, liking the idea of it very much even though it had no idea what it was getting us into.

"We talked earlier about submission, how it's different for everyone. Different places, different times." He didn't need to finish the thought for me to know where he was going. I licked my lips, grinning at him like he'd just offered me the answer to every prayer I'd ever whispered in the dark. But I realized I wanted him to say it, just the same. I wanted, no...I needed Kale to give voice to it. For both of us.

"Yes."

"I want you to submit outside of the sex," he said, angling his head to the side. "I think you already do, if I'm being honest. But I really want you to think on it tonight. I want you in it."

With every word that left his lips, my head grew fuzzy and light. He was asking me to pretend I was well and truly his, which...felt more like a dream than a demand.

"If you argue or pout, you get punished," he said, carefully tracing my hairline over my ear with the tip of his finger. The gentle touch sent a shiver all the way down to my toes. "You listen and you do as you're told."

"Yes, Mr. Sheffield," I rasped, mind replaying some of the things he said to me the night I met him on the street outside the ballet, the things he made me feel for the very first time.

"If you hate it, tell me to stop and we stop."

"I never want to stop," I said.

"I know." He swallowed, corner of his mouth twitching. Clearing his throat, Kale straightened his shoulders and took my hand into his, setting off down the street, away from the

Empire State Building and back toward where we'd started off. "Christian, there's only two rules for tonight."

"Listen and do what I'm told," I repeated.

He shook his head, squeezing my hand, the smile on his face twisting into something that dripped with pain and promise all at the same time. "Do what you're told, yes. And under no circumstances, princess, are you allowed to come without permission. Do we understand each other?"

My cock leaked, ready as ever to rebel.

"Yes," I managed the confirmation, even though my body was not on board with the plan. "Yes, Mr. Sheffield."

I ordered Christian a steak, of which he ate half. I ordered us a bottle of Chateau Lafite Rothschild, which he also had half of. He didn't even need the alcohol. He'd been flying since he'd signed off on our little game for the night, and I knew there was not going to be any chance of bringing him back down. Not that I wanted to.

Christian, when he didn't care about anything besides himself, was the purest and most joyful version of himself. And I didn't mean that to say he was selfish when we played, far from it. It was the only time he was able to truly focus on himself, and if he did that by turning his attention to me, all the better.

After a short cab ride to The Black Door, I promptly walked Christian to the elevators and took him to the upper level. He was already vibrating, and while I knew he wanted to be in public to observe, I figured we'd have a little more privacy upstairs. Since he didn't have a lot of food in his stomach, but a decent amount of wine, I got him a club soda and then found us a comfortable and mostly secluded loveseat near the door to the balcony.

There was a decent enough view of the floor, some corners obscured by the trademark frosted glass partitions and pillars, but overall it was a good spot. I debated where I wanted Christian once we arrived—on the floor, beside me, or on my lap—and I decided to let him kneel by the outside of my right leg. In that position, it was easy to stroke my fingers through his hair and down the slope of his neck. His entire body had a slight tremor to it, and he leaned gently against me while he surveyed the scene in front of us.

"Fancy running into you here," a familiar voice from the side drew both of our attentions, and I found Alex with a martini in hand. He wasn't drunk, but he didn't look like himself either.

"Did you want to join us?" I asked.

"Is this your little prince?" Alex asked, taking the seat that would have been Christian's if I'd decided that was where I wanted him.

"His name is Christian, and he's taking in the sights of the city," I explained. "Christian, this is my friend, Alex."

"Christian," Alex murmured, raising his glass in toast.

"He doesn't have anything to say right now," I said before Christian was able to open his mouth. He huffed a breath that didn't quite feel like frustration...more like arousal at the reduction to inanimate object again. "Do you, Christian?"

He shook his head quickly. "No, Mr. Sheffield."

Alex chuckled, taking another sip of his drink and turning his attention back to me.

"How have you been?" I asked. "Haven't seen much of you since Beamer moved to L.A."

Alex and Beamer had started up some kind of play relationship with each other right before Beamer's magically forgotten husband had shown back up in the picture. I'd never gotten the impression things were serious between the two of them, but Alex had been a hard man to find since Beamer left for the West Coast.

"I don't know why everyone keeps asking me that," he grumbled.

"Because you disappeared after Dalton Fox showed up," I said.

At my feet, Christian let out a low whimper, his stare focused across the room toward one of the far walls where a man wore nipple clamps with the chain pulled taut between his teeth. Spit dribbled down his chin while his hips bucked madly, cum leaking from his bare cock. The man's partner was fully dressed, hand wrapped around his throat like a necklace. His shoulders were squared and his eyes sparkled when he looked at his partner. Every time the one against the wall gasped for air, the movement yanked on the nipple clamps and his dick leaked a little more.

I leaned down, resting one of my hands on Christian's shoulder and asked him, "What part of that is getting you the most riled up?"

He opened his mouth and snapped it closed like a fish, and Alex laughed at him.

"You found a good one, Kale," he said to me, pushing up from his seat and taking his drink with him. "I won't keep you from him."

"You're not keeping me," I assured him.

Sadness flashed across his face, and he didn't need to say anything else for me to realize the problem. He'd started to develop feelings for Beamer and then...well. Everything went the way it had.

"We'll catch up soon," Alex said, tipping back his glass and finishing off the rest of his martini. "Good to meet you, Christian."

Christian didn't acknowledge Alex's departure because I didn't tell him to, and that sent a wholly unexpected surge of arousal right between my legs. But as soon as Alex left, Christian found the answer to my question.

"It hurts him," he said. "But look how..."

Christian trailed off, swallowing.

"I'm listening."

"He's bearing it because it makes his partner happy," Christian went on softly. "It makes him proud."

"Which one is proud?" I asked, studying the scene across the room for the tells Christian had just called out.

"Both of them. The dominant man is looking at him like he's precious, like he's important. And he's taking on this pain so he can bring that look to his partner's face, and..."

"It's necessary for them both," I finished.

"I think that's what love looks like," he murmured, resting his head against the side of my knee.

"Love looks like this, princess." I kicked the side of his calf with the toe of my shoe until he slid away from me, catching the hint that I wanted him to move. He had that glassy look in his eyes that I knew wasn't from the wine, and I'd never been more drunk on power than I was when Christian found himself careening toward subspace from the most basic aspects of service and submission.

"Yes, Mr. Sheffield," he whispered, chin lolling toward his chest. "This is."

"There's something on my shoe, Christian." I gave a little twist of my shoe like I was putting out an invisible cigarette beneath it. "Maybe you can get it."

He frowned, looking down at the impeccably shined leather of my black oxfords, dusting his thumb across the stitching in case there was a blemish that escaped him.

"You misunderstand me, princess," I warned, threading my fingers through the hair on the back of his head and suggesting he take a closer look. He loosed a surprisingly low growl that vibrated through both of us, feeling a lot more like need than anything else, and then he was prostrate on the ground, his mouth pressed reverently against the toe of my right shoe.

Christian kissed and licked the leather, his back arched like the most perfectly proportioned sculpture I'd ever seen before. The feeling he'd described seeing on that other man's face swelled in my chest, pushing me to tighten my fingers in his hair for a breath before letting go completely and resting my hand on his knee. Christian kept his lips against my shoe until he shifted, pressing his cheek against the spit-slicked leather and letting out a contented little whimper. I bent forward, coming as close to his level as I could manage from my position.

"You're so attentive, princess," I praised him, his hips twitching downward. "You knew exactly what I needed just then, didn't you?"

He kissed my shoe again and looked up at me from the floor, pupils shot into dark black pools that eclipsed the color of his irises entirely.

"Yes, Mr. Sheffield."

I knew the scenario wasn't the same, but I knew the sentiment would carry over. Whatever he'd watched in the scene across the room had spoken to one of the things I loved the very most about power exchange. It was a generally indescribable sense of necessity that existed between two people during any given scene. Of course, anyone could get on their knees and kiss my shoes, but no one would do it as perfectly as Christian did. There were a thousand other people that man could hold against the wall, but their pain wouldn't mean anything compared to the gift his partner gave him.

Christian had given me far more than I'd ever thought a partner could give. He'd done it all without intending to, without even trying. There were always people who talked about others to whom submission or dominance came naturally, and Christian was an example of that in the flesh. Everything about his upbringing would have predisposed him to lean into dominance in an attempt to regain some control of his life, but he was submissive down to the marrow of his bones. He'd shown me new parts of my own dominance, and I knew what he and I had was truly a once in a lifetime kind of love.

"Pull your pants down, Christian," I said, and his hands were between his legs in a flash. I was so hard for him, I couldn't think straight, and I made quick enough work of my own belt and fly. I freed my erection and held it out to him. "Come put it in your mouth how you did earlier today. I want it in the back of your throat the whole time. Do you understand me?"

I didn't have clamps and I wasn't going to get him all the way naked, so I had no choice but to work with the tools I had available. He shuffled between my legs with his pants undone, then buried his face between my legs. It took him a couple of bobs up and down my length to get the whole thing in, but I had no complaints about the work. Christian's mouth was wet and hot and eager, and he was close to getting my entire shaft into his mouth when I folded myself over his back and brought my hand down hard against his exposed ass cheek.

Christian cried out, the opening of his throat giving me the chance to push the rest of my cock into his throat. I petted my fingertips over the place I'd just spanked him, shivering when I traced my way over the gooseflesh in the shape of my palm. He moaned against me, sputtering as he tried to catch a breath around the intrusion in his mouth.

"You know how to do this," I reminded him, giving him a softer spank than the first one. "No one warms my cock as good as you do, princess. Show me how good you take my dick in your throat. That's it. There's my good boy."

At the alternate endearment, Christian whimpered, finally relaxing his throat around my shaft. I hadn't asked him to suck me off and he wasn't trying to. I could tell by the tension in his arms and the rigidity of his spine, he was only focused on trying not to throw up all over my lap. That was well and good, but I wanted more from him. I wanted that arch back. I wanted him to crave the taste of my precum against the back of his tongue as much as I was desperate to leave it there.

I spanked him again and the arch rippled through his spine before going straight again. He clearly needed some more instruction, which I had no issue providing. I knew that if he did a good job with whatever task I gave him, he'd fly headfirst into the feelings he'd been chasing after since the very first time I gave him a command.

"Right here, Christian," I said gently, rubbing my hand across the small of his back, up and down his spine. "You can do both. You can put my cock in your mouth and your ass in the air."

He mumbled some kind of protest around my dick, which I'd punish him for later, but after minimal argument, his spine curved and his breath huffed hot against the trimmed hairs at the base of my cock.

"Just like that, princess. Fuck yes. God, I love you so fucking much like this, Christian. You're a dream come true."

He hummed, the low noise jostling straight down to my balls, already heavy with the need to release.

Getting myself off at the club hadn't been on my agenda for the night. I'd wanted to take Christian out like he asked, let him watch some scenes, and then take him home. I figured we'd both leave with a hard-on and I'd take him home and fuck him until the last thing he wanted to do was have another erection. But like with most things that involved him, best laid plans and all of that.

"Make me come," I demanded.

Christian spread my thighs as wide as my pants would allow, then he swallowed around the head of my cock. His throat muscles milked my crown, the hot press of his tongue drawing shapes on the underside of my shaft until my orgasm slammed into me like a hurricane. I grunted through my release, both hands held tight on the back of his head while I shot my load past his tongue and right into his throat. He didn't choke, didn't gag, didn't sputter. He fucking swallowed and kept his puffy pink lips wrapped securely around my dick until I gave his hair a tug and pulled him off.

Tears shone in his eyes and he blinked quickly, swaying back and forth on his knees. My hand still threaded through his hair was the only thing holding him up and his stare finally focused on me. With a long blink, a slow smile spread across Christian's lips, spit shining on his chin.

"Thank you," he whispered, lashes fluttering as his eyes fell closed. "Thank you, Mr. Sheffield."

"Christian."

He kept his eyes closed, sucking in a slow and deep breath through his nose. I released his hair, cradling his face in my hand. He leaned his weight into me, looking like he was the one who'd just gotten off, not me. Christian licked his lips and nodded, not saying a word.

There were a lot of things I'd understood about the kind of man, the kind of submissive Christian was. But one thing I hadn't taken into account was all the ways his submission was going to call into direct focus the kind of dominant man I was. Or more than that, the kind of man I *wanted* to be.

I wanted to be the kind of man who deserved a man like him.

And that was why I knew sending him away in two days was going to be the hardest thing I'd ever do.

CHAPTER 28

CHRISTIAN

I didn't remember much about the club after swallowing Kale's cum down my throat, but as soon as we stepped back into the heated comfort and familiarity of his house, everything narrowed back into a sharp and singular focus. I knew where I was, who I was with, and above all else, I knew I was safe. The promise of that ran straight into the marrow of my bones, and I leaned against the closed door with a content moan as Kale went to his knees in front of me.

He stripped me out of my shoes and socks, my pants, underwear, coat, scarf and shirt. I was naked and he was fully dressed, a call back to the scene I'd watched at The Black Door that had started the night on its current course. A shiver raced up my spine as Kale rose back to his full height, collaring my throat with the wide stretch of his palm. With his fingers wrapped around my throat, he gave me a push back against the door and my breath left my lungs with a quiet puff.

Kale didn't constrict my throat or hinder my breathing, but his proximity was enough to steal my breath just the same. I gasped as he leaned close, tracing my cheekbone with the tip of his nose. His breath burned hot against my skin and the fingers around my throat flexed when he kissed my ear.

"You'd let me do it, wouldn't you?" he asked.

I would let him do anything to me, and we both knew it. "Yes, Mr. Sheffield."

"Why?"

"I want to make you happy," I whispered.

His nose retraced its path across my face until our lips were less than an inch apart. My mouth parted and my lashes fluttered, pinned against the door like a spread-apart butterfly.

"You do," he said, ghosting his lips over mine. "Go upstairs to the third floor. First door on the left. Get on your knees and wait for me."

With one more flex of his hand against mu throat, Kale released me and stepped back. Even with the floaty haze in my head, I could see the arousal painted across his face and the thick bulge that had once again shown up between his legs. I was able to give him a nod of understanding before setting off to the top of his home.

I'd known from seeing it on the outside that Kale's home had three floors, but his bedroom was on the second and the living area was on the first. I'd never bothered to ask what was up the other flight of stairs, but apparently it was time for me to now find out. The wood creaked beneath my bare feet on the third floor landing, and I twisted the antique knob on the door with a tense breath.

The room looked much like the rest of the house, with wide-planked wood floors and tall windows on the wall that faced the street. Like his bedroom, there were mismatched rugs scattered across the narrow room, a small marble fireplace against one wall, and a giant wooden X against the other. There were leather cuffs dangling from each corner of the device, and a small shelf on the wall beside it that held things like lube and condoms, rope, and riding crops. Under the window was a small velvet couch with matching throw pillows against either arm and a blanket thrown haphazardly over the back.

This was Kale's play space.

I wanted to explore it when I was more in my head, but the pressing urgency of Kale's instruction rang loud in the back of mind and I moved toward the couch, falling to my knees in front of the crushed green velvet. I had no idea how long it took for him to join me, but it was long enough for my breathing to pick up, long enough for that haze to settle back over me and lull me toward that perfect state of arousal that I so often found myself in when Kale was near.

What could have been as long as an hour or short as a minute later, the distinct echo of Kale's shoes against the wood floor came into the room. Instead of tensing, the sound relaxed me, and my entire body lolled forward, shoulders sagging under the relief of his arrival. He didn't say anything, but I could hear him busying himself at the shelf behind me and then he came closer.

"Stand up," he said simply. "Bend over the couch so I can get into your ass easier."

A tremor ripped through me as I climbed to my feet and bent forward, bracing myself on the back of the couch. I hadn't had a lot of time to think about why the things Kale asked me to do made me so hard, and I worried if I spent too much time wondering why being reduced to an object with a hole to fuck turned me on more than anything else in my life, it would lose the appeal. So I shut off that part of my mind, shivering like a needy whore when his lube-slicked fingers brushed across my hole.

Without another word, he pushed one finger into me, up to the knuckle. I moaned, head falling forward as he fucked the single digit in and out of me with a torturously slow speed that wasn't going to do anything besides drive me mad. Sweat beaded against my temples, cold and unwelcome compared to the warmth of his hand, and finally the stretch of a second finger, and then more of that same slow pace. Kale didn't say anything to me, no words of praise or criticism. There was no concern at all, just the preemptive attention that came with this kind of preparation, and then a third finger. A third finger that stretched and burned, drawing a low rumble out of my chest. My back arched at the penetration, and Kale let out a sadistic-sounding chuckle.

"Three fingers to get a sound out of you," he murmured, stretching his fingers apart inside of me as he withdrew his hand. "My greedy little princess."

I hadn't meant to be quiet with the first two fingers, but I'd been so focused on the way he handled me I must have kept all the noises to myself. It was impossible to remain quiet with the third finger, though, even if the sounds that came out of me were beyond my control.

After a time, he pulled all three fingers out completely and I wondered if he was going to add a fourth...and then a fifth. The idea of taking Kale's entire hand inside of my body should have been terrifying. The human body just wasn't designed for that kind of thing, but I knew if he wanted his hand there, I would have found a way to allow it. I whimpered at the loss of his touch, and the need for more, and he rested his palm against the small of my back to steady me.

"I'm here," he soothed, "you're safe."

"Yes," I whispered, screwing my eyes closed, "I know, Mr. Sheffield."

Every nerve in my body was a live wire and this was the complete opposite of what normally happened to me when we played these games together. Not to say I wasn't present, but my head always turned floaty in the most perfect kinds of ways, but this time I was so grounded in my body, I didn't know if I'd be able to bear the rest of the night. He'd worked me up into a state where I was nothing more than my need for him, my entire being attuned to his presence, his demands.

A cold and hard object pressed against my slick hole, and I found myself sad that he wasn't returning to give me more of his hand. The plug he pushed into me was thick *and* long, stretching my hole to an almost incomprehensible circumference. Taking his hand would have been less, and he had to stop the insertion more than once to give me time to get used to the thickness of the toy. By the time he got the entire thing inside of me, I was a crying and gasping mess, even though I had no recollection of when the tears had started to fall.

"Up you go," he said, helping me unfold myself from the couch and stand straight. My legs trembled violently, but Kale didn't say a thing about it as he helped me toward the giant wooden X. He aligned my back against it, tracing his fingers over the goosebumps that had broken out over every exposed inch of my skin. And then he touched my face, and I blinked him into focus, my heart skipping a beat when he smiled at me.

"There you are," Kale said softly, brushing my hair back from my face. "Are you still with me? Still good?"

My eyes rolled back, muscles grasping against the massive plug he'd put inside of me.

"I feel everything," I rasped.

"Good."

He was careful when he stretched my arms above my head, looping the cool leather cuffs around each wrist before attaching me to the corners. Then he went to my ankles, putting the cuffs on, and latching me in. It was reflex to test my range of motion, dick leaking copiously against my stomach when I realized I had nowhere to go.

Kale reached around to the shelf for something, which he dangled in front of my face. It took a few blinks, but I realized quickly what they were. Nipple clamps, just like from the club.

"You're going to feel this too," he promised, leaning down and taking one of my nipples into his mouth. His tongue was hot and rough, laving over the delicate and tender nub of flesh. I fought against the restraints, not because I wanted to, but because my body demanded a reprieve. Kale didn't let up, nipping my nipple with his teeth before moving quickly and replacing his mouth with the rubber-covered clamp.

I shouted, a shocked gasp that trailed off into a needy whimper. My hips bucking for friction, Kale paid comparable attention to my other nipple before attaching the clamp. My sense of focus went wide and narrowed down, ping-ponging from the matching aches in my chest to the glaring stretch and burn in my ass.

"I love you like this," Kale whispered, taking a step back.

I tried to say thank you, but the sound that came out of me

didn't even sound like words. Kale smiled, rubbing his hands together.

"Can I blindfold you, Christian?" he asked.

In any other place, any other world, the answer would have been no. Blindfolds weren't safe, but I was with Kale and *he* was safe.

"Yes, Mr. Sheff..." I trailed off, words still beyond my comprehension.

Kale reached back around me for the shelf, and then very gently he slid a black leather blindfold over my eyes. It was heavy and cool, just like the cuffs, a sharp contrast to the warm glide of his fingers over the places where the leather met my skin.

"Don't worry about what's happening next, princess," Kale whispered against my mouth. "Just feel it, okay?"

I nodded.

"I'm going to touch your cock," he explained, reaching down and doing just that. "I'm going to get you so close and so close and...So. Close. Christian. And then I'm going to take that plug out of you and replace it with *my* cock. I'm going to fuck you right here against this cross until I come, and then I'm going to touch your cock some more, and some more, and maybe after that, I'll decide it's time for you to come too. Do you hear me, princess?"

I was ready to come from his words alone.

Behind the blindfold, I squeezed my eyes shut, fighting back tears. I wasn't upset and I wasn't scared. I was horny and desperate, and I needed him to do all of the things he promised to me. I needed him to hurt me and use my body for his pleasure because it was my body, not someone else's. It was me bringing him off; it was me making him creative and hard and taking his breath away.

That was the feeling, I realized. The heightened sensation racing through every nerve and muscle in my body was control. Even with restraints around my limbs and a cover over my eyes, even with the thickest and longest tool shoved up my ass, I was in control of the man who'd put them all there. He was doing it for me because seeing me like this made him happy and me being that way made me feel the same. The cycle that weaved its way in the space between us was reciprocal and never-ending, and I didn't see any way of coming back from it now that I fully understood how it worked.

Managing a nod and the barest whisper of a confirmation that I heard everything he'd said and that I wanted all of it and more, I said, "Yes, Mr. Sheffield, I hear you."

TEARS SLICKED DOWN CHRISTIAN'S CHEEKS, AND I KNEW IF I WERE TO remove the blindfold, more would spill. He was a masterpiece on the cross, hard and trembling and so very submissive. I squirted lube all over my hand before reaching down and taking his erection into my fist. He was beyond hard, the skin around his shaft stretched taut and burning hot against my palm. His knees wavered when I made a fist around his dick and the clips on his cuffs rattled against the wood. It was one of my favorite sounds in the world, and paired with Christian's perfect little whimpers, I wondered if I was going to be able to keep my word and get to fucking him before I came all over myself.

I hoped that by keeping my clothes on, keeping my own cock tucked behind the uncomfortable confines of my underwear, it would buy me more time, but every cry and groan that fell out of Christian's mouth tested my determination.

His balls were so tight against his body, it took work for me to get my fingers around them. With a slow tug, I yanked them down and his entire body jerked, fighting against the cross and the restraints. Christian thrashed his head side to side, nonsense mumbles landing against my ears when I tightened my fist around his cock.

"You're so close," I said to him, an observation, not permission.

He nodded quickly, fingers scrabbling around the chains at the tops of his wrist cuffs. I released his balls and let go of his cock, which slapped against his stomach with a wet *splat*. Precum mixed with the lube I'd covered him with, making his engorged member look even more pained than I imagined it felt. My cock ached, and I had to give in, unzipping my pants and shoving my hand behind the waistband of my underwear in search of relief.

I was close.

Too close.

I moaned, giving my shaft a long stroke, and Christian's body pulled off the cross, instinctively leaning toward me.

"You've made me so fucking hard, princess. Your body and your mouth. The sounds you make..." I took a beat to appreciate the man on the cross in front of me.

Christian was handsome by anyone's standards, but naked and covered in sweat and tears, he was perfection. I wanted the world to see this side of him, but I also wanted to keep it all to myself. Let them continue to abuse him and underestimate him, because it was that treatment and misjudgment that had brought him right to me....to his place at my feet.

And what the hell was I doing, anyway? Getting more and more involved with a man who could never truly belong to me. At least, not in the ways I wanted. I loved Christian and I didn't doubt him when he said he loved me back, but I could never ask him to give up his life for me. I refused to do it, and if he made that decision on his own, I would fight him.

I was a good man, a deserving man...but I wasn't sure I was deserving of *that* level of sacrifice. No matter how much I wanted it, how much I'd told him I'd take it from him. I had no idea what was going to happen after our time was up and Christian returned home. After he left, all I would have were these memories and my dreams. I supposed I would have to make them count.

With one hand still tight around the base of my cock, I took his erection back into my other hand and gave him a slow stroke from root to tip. His cry vibrated down to my bones, dripping with desperation and arousal in a way I'd never heard before. I stroked him until he was right on the edge again, then let go.

He shouted at me, muscles going tense and locking up before he went limp and pliant against his restraints. God, he was perfect. He was perfect for *me*. And maybe it was no wonder that I'd been fine with casual things and fleeting flings up until I'd met him, because this was what I'd spent my whole life waiting for. This kind of blind submission and trusting commitment was like a drug, and I was in urgent search of my next hit.

Releasing my cock, I curled the chain on the nipple clamps around my finger and gave it a tug. I'd expected another cry or a scream, but Christian moaned with pleasure, still leaning weakly against the cross. I twisted the chain and pulled, watching the way the black rubber-covered clamps stretched his nipples away from his chest.

"Gonna," he murmured, chin angled down toward his chest.

His hair was sweaty and matted against the top of his head. Fisting my fingers through his hair, I yanked his head up, needing to see him, needing more.

"Hold this," I said, tucking the balled-up chain into his mouth. He tried to lift his chin back toward his chest to release some of the tension on his nipples, but I made a quiet and disapproving noise in the back of my throat. He righted his head, and I rewarded him with a quiet, "Good boy."

A tremor wracked through his entire body, and I made quick work unclasping the cuffs around his ankles and finding a condom and rolling it down my length. I studied the tension in his jaw, the chain snug between his teeth while I slathered my cock in lube. I was still dressed, and there was no way I was going to stop course to strip out of my clothes. As much as I wanted to feel all of his trembling and sweaty skin against mine, the biggest regret of my life was that I wouldn't be able to fuck him bare before the end of his trip. The mere thought of shooting my load into his hot and hungry asshole was enough to shove me even closer to the brink of my own release, and I clenched my jaw to fight past it.

I should have been easy with the plug, but I wanted him gaping and stretched when I pushed my cock into him. With a gentle enough twist of my wrist, I reached between his legs and pulled the toy out of him. That earned me a shocked cry that turned into a wail when I replaced the plastic plug with my latex-covered cock. I slid into him with no resistance, shivering when the muscles of his channel tightened and closed down around my shaft.

"Put your legs around me," I said, reaching back and helping him hitch his thighs over my waist. I was so deep inside of him, and the shift in his position helped me push even deeper into him. He fought against the chains, and I imagined it was because he wanted to wrap his arms around me. Because he was as desperate to be close to me as I was to him.

"Don't come, Christian," I warned him, pushing the blindfold up and off his eyes. It slipped off his forehead, tangling in his hair as he squeezed his eyes closed against the light.

"Need," he mumbled, giving his head a gentle shake. Each twist yanked on the clamps and he dropped his head forward to ease some of the pain in his chest, but there was no way I could allow that.

I pressed the side of my finger against the underside of his chin, tipping his head back until the chains were stretched and his nipples were once again pulled away from his body.

"I know it hurts, princess," I whispered, waiting for him to open his eyes. "But keep your eyes on me."

Slowly, Christian blinked me into focus and I found myself overwhelmed at the look in his eyes. His irises were nearly obscured by the blown black pools of his pupils, and just like I'd expected, his eyes shone with a wall of unshed tears that immediately spilled out and over his lashes.

"I see you," I told him, bracing one hand under his left thigh and stroking the other back through his hair. I was grateful to the cross for leverage, and I gave a short pump of my hips to fuck into him.

Christian blinked, more tears spilling, and he nodded at me, pulling the chain tight without a care in the world. Between our bodies, his erection burned hot as a fire poker against my stomach, even through my shirt. Fisting the hair at the back of his head, I gave a rough tug and pulled his head up even further than he'd shifted when I told him to look at me.

He was gone.

I knew I didn't have much longer, so I made quick enough work of fucking him against the cross, crashing our mouths together and fighting past the chain with my tongue. He didn't close his eyes as I kissed him, blinking slowly at me and letting out quiet and needy noises into my mouth.

I slammed into him once more, cock thickening as I shot my release into the waiting tip of the condom. Breaking the kiss, I pressed my forehead against his so I could breathe, and he used his teeth to pull the chain deeper into his mouth.

He was so perfect.

He was so...

"I want you to come while I'm inside of you," I said, reaching between our bodies and making a fist around his dick again.

His legs tightened around me, one of them slipping over my hip as he came almost immediately. The orgasm rippled up through his body, from his feet to the top of his head, rattling against me as it washed over him. I knew the cross would support both of our weights, and I went for the clamps, letting them off of his nipples in quick succession. After a beat, he opened his mouth, jaw quivering but no sound coming out. Hot spurts of cum splattered across my hand, and I yanked the chain out of his mouth so he didn't choke on it.

The clamps fell at my feet and Christian kept coming. Without sound and with as little movement as I'd ever seen, save for the tight clamp of his ass that milked even more cum out of my shaft. And then he was crying, well and truly crying. His forehead dropped against my shoulder and his chest heaved with a sob.

"It's okay," I promised him, managing to get one wrist

unclipped from the cross and then the other. "It's okay, princess. I've got you."

I took us both down to the floor, cradling him against my chest. Scooting us both until I could prop myself against the couch, I smoothed sweat and tears off his face, brushing his hair back and leaving soft kisses against every part of him I could reach.

"You're okay," I assured. "You're better than okay. You're safe and you're mine, Christian. Do you hear me?"

I'd spent my entire life being selfish, and apparently I wasn't going to stop now. I knew that no matter how much I loved him, if Christian tried to continue a relationship with me, it was going to hurt and it was going to be hard. I wanted him as much as my next breath, but I'd always known in the back of my head that I would have to let him go. No matter what I felt, no matter what I said, I'd *known* that I would hurt myself to make it easier for him...at least, in the long run.

But with him naked and wet in my lap, trembling and flying, that piece of resistance I'd been clinging to vanished into thin air. Christian was mine. He was mine, and I was going to fight for him. I knew it would hurt, whatever would come of the arguments he'd have after returning home, and I knew he was going to have to choose.

It didn't matter if I knew I didn't deserve him.

I wanted him, and that was enough.

I would send him home because I'd promised his brother I would, but as soon as the wheels on that jet were up, I'd find a way to get him back to me. Consequences be damned. And I was going to tell Christian as much after I cleaned him up and tucked him into bed.

"Christian," I said again, wrapping my arms around him, "answer me."

He muttered something into my chest that sounded like an affirmative, but the words were slurred. I knew he still wasn't back in his head, flying off in some new and unexplored depth of subspace, and it would take a while for him to come around. I stretched my legs out, doing my best to ignore the cold stickiness of the used condom still on my cock, and adjusted him on my lap. Another unintelligible series of sounds stuttered out of him and I stroked my hands down his back, soothing and shushing him in one motion.

"I've got you," I told him again. "I've got you, princess, and I'm not going to let you go. You are perfect, and you are valued, and you deserve this. You deserve it, Christian. Do you believe me?"

To my own ears, my voice sounded desperate, and I bit the inside of my cheek, blinking back tears of my own for how much I wanted him to believe the words I said, and also for how much *I* wanted to believe them for myself too.

Words were still lost to him, but he untangled one of his arms from my lap and reached up, pressing his hand flat against my heart, and it was as much of a yes as he'd ever given me.

CHAPTER 30

CHRISTIAN

I DIDN'T REMEMBER FALLING ASLEEP, AND I DIDN'T THINK I MOVED the entire night. When I finally woke up the next morning, aching in all of the best ways, I was curled into a ball with my face buried in Kale's pillow. His side of the bed was cold and empty, but the house smelled like breakfast and coffee so I knew he couldn't be far. Stretching out, I kicked down the sheets and climbed out of bed. I grabbed a pair of clean underwear from my bag and hesitated, standing in front of the window and looking down at the street.

New York was so different from anywhere I'd been before. Kale was so different from anyone I'd ever known. Meeting him was like waking up from a dream so realistic, I never even realized I'd been sleeping. With my underwear in place around my waist, I let my hand trail down my crack, fingertips exploring the still tender pucker of my ass. We didn't fuck for long last night, but he fucked me with everything he had, and I was wearing the memories of that still.

I hoped it would carry me through...all the way back home.

Even though the Chance Islands sounded more like a foreign place to me than this house did, than this room, that man in the kitchen making me coffee and breakfast.

Fighting back a wave of nausea, I shuffled downstairs, finding Kale at the small breakfast table in the kitchen, a plate of steaming eggs in front of him and two mugs of coffee on either side. He had the newspaper spread out in front of him, his cell phone in hand, eyes darting back and forth between whatever he was reading in each place.

"Good morning," I mumbled, carefully arranging myself in the seat across from him.

He smiled, turning his phone face down and pushing the fuller mug of coffee toward me with one long finger.

"How did you sleep?" he asked.

"All night." I swallowed, knowing we only had one night left together. "Thank you for that."

Kale's mouth quirked up in the corner and he looked down at the newspaper. "I wasn't even trying."

"I believe you."

He straightened up, catching my stare. His eyes telegraphed an unexpected sense of urgency and he reached across the table until I slid my hand into his.

"The things I said last night…" he trailed off, brows knit together.

I braced myself for him to take them all back. To tell me they were just words said in a scene, in the heat of the moment. I'd been out of my mind with want by the time he got us both off, but I'd remember the words he said to me until my very last breath. I couldn't bear the thought of them not being real.

"Don't," I pleaded.

"I meant them," he said at the same time, letting go of my hand and leaning back. "I'm sorry."

"You meant them?"

"Of course I did." Kale's leg started to bounce nervously beneath the table. "I'm not in the habit of saying things I don't mean."

"Not even in the heat of the moment?"

"Especially not then."

I reached across the table for him, mimicking the move he'd done earlier to take my hand. With some reluctance, he slid his hand into mine and turned them over so mine was on top, his knuckles bearing our weight against the weathered wood.

"I thought you were going to take them back," I said.

"Never." His response came quickly, sounding like it had been torn out of his throat.

I believed him.

"Never," he repeated. "I meant it all, but…things between us present some difficulties and we've talked about it, but we've never *really* talked about it."

Another wave of nausea rolled over me, and the eggs between us might as well have been a plate of vomit for how appetizing they looked. With my free hand, I took a drink of the strong coffee, hoping it would settle my stomach. "Did you want to do that now?"

"I haven't known you for very long, Christian, but it feels very trivial to call you a boyfriend. I want to get that out of the way."

Kale's face was smooth with concentration, and I wondered if he'd been rehearsing this monologue over coffee while he waited for me to wake up. Something about that was endearing in a way I didn't have words for. That he cared enough to try and get it right, to make sure I understood the message he wanted me to hear.

"Okay," I said, waiting for the rest of it.

"But I want everything that comes with that word," he said softly.

"So do I."

"I don't know what that looks like for us...after you leave."

"I can stay," I offered.

He shook his head with a frown, leaning over the table and raising our joined hands. He dragged a kiss across the top of my knuckles before giving me a squeeze and untangling his fingers.

"I don't think long distance is going to work forever," I said to him, and he answered that with a nod.

"I don't think so either, but I'm trying to not think that far ahead."

"Do you think that I wouldn't come back to you?" I asked.

"I know you want to." He leaned back again in his seat, tapping a short article in the middle of the newspaper page he'd been reading when I came into the kitchen. "I don't know if you'll be allowed."

I yanked the newspaper to my side of the table, eyes scanning over the throwaway article about the political unrest in the Chance Islands with calls for Father to abdicate in favor of Phillip, who was widely considered to be younger and more in tune with the expectations of a twenty-first century monarchy. Nothing in the paper sounded new. If anything, it read like insider information.

The ports of the island were integral for shipping routes in the region and neighboring countries had been encroaching on the water for years. My father had always been more war-forward, for lack of a better term, about the whole thing. I'd listened to him and Phillip arguing for hours about how to handle the conflict without turning the people against the crown. The abdication piece felt extremely on point because, while there had always been rumblings about the antiquated way my father chose to rule, his actions over the past year or two had only accelerated the rumors. Unfortunately, I didn't think my brother would be a better choice as head of state, at least not for me.

"Phillip's first act as monarch would be to deport me from the country," I said with a weak laugh.

Kale raised a brow, head inclined toward his shoulder with a disbelieving look on his face. I sighed, reading the article a second time. My father had never given any indication he wanted to walk away from his position, but if he did, the implications would be much farther reaching than Kale even realized. Phillip couldn't stand Parrish's father. He'd always found father's council to be too old guard, too conservative in their ways of thinking. It wouldn't just change my life if Phillip ascended to the throne. Everything would be in a state of upheaval for God knew how long.

"But you're right," I agreed, folding the newspaper closed and throwing it over my shoulder. It fanned out and fluttered to the floor. "There will be things at home that need my attention."

"I can't survive on emails, Christian." Kale tapped his fingers against the back case of his phone and my entire chest constricted at the softness of his confession.

I'd been such a selfish prick the whole time since I met him, worried about what I needed and what I wanted, always taking whatever he'd given me. At no point had I really, truly stopped to think about the implications of what a long-distance relationship with me would be like. And that was assuming I managed to keep him a secret. If word of our relationship were to get out...I couldn't even fathom the changes that would bring to his life.

I wanted to tell Kale I would go home with some false sense of bravado, empowered by the support and strength of his love and tell my father I'd met someone I wanted to be with. I would demand a change to the way I'd been treated and the access I'd been allowed. But if the article in the paper was true, there were far more important things at home that needed to be handled before my unexpected love affair. Even if I wanted to walk away from the crown— and my life— respect for the institution and everything it represented had been ingrained in me for my whole life.

Being with Kale had given me a chance to be selfish, but I couldn't live my whole life like that. And more importantly, I didn't want to. I wanted to be better about taking the things he needed into consideration before acting, because that was part of having a boyfriend. Wasn't it?

"You deserve more than emails," I said. "But..."

He nodded, eyes darting over my shoulder to the discarded newspaper. "I know, Christian. And I understand."

"So, boyfriends who aren't boyfriends. More than emails, situation considered." I gave him a weak smile. "What else?"

Kale bit his lips together between his teeth, working his jaw back and forth like he was trying to saw through the skin I loved so much to kiss.

"I'm out of my depth," he admitted, taking a drink of his coffee and closing his eyes. I wondered if he was as sick to his stomach over the whole thing as I was. "But we can't play pretend forever."

"This isn't pretend," I croaked.

"That's not what I meant. We can't…" He finished off his drink and gestured into the nothingness around us. "We can't pretend the world isn't real anymore. It's not fair to either of us."

"I don't know what you want me to say."

"I want you to say that you're as committed to me as I am to you," he said, and I shoved my chair back so hard it clattered onto the floor, covering the offending news article. I walked around the table and climbed onto his lap, straddling him and taking his face into my hands.

Kale's eyes searched my face, and I flexed my fingers into his cheekbones.

"I'm all in with you, Kale Sheffield," I said, slamming our mouths together before he could ask for something I *couldn't* give him.

Kale groaned into my mouth, lips parting to make room for my tongue. He wrapped his arms around me, fingers splayed out across my back as I kissed him harder, deeper. My cock got hard and his got hard, and then the kiss turned more frantic, and his hand was between our bodies, fishing both of our erections out of our pants. He broke the kiss long enough for me to spit into his palm and then I was back on him, exploring the backs of his teeth with my tongue while he curled his slick fist around us both.

I trembled as he stroked, gasping into his mouth until he worked a near simultaneous orgasm out of us both. I never stopped kissing him, never stopped using my mouth to make sure he knew how honest I'd been with my words to him. I didn't know what the future looked like for either of us, but I knew for certain we would be together in it. Somehow.

Finally, the speed and intensity of our kiss slowed, and he once again brought his hand up to my mouth. Pressing two of his fingers against my tongue, he slid them toward the back of my throat, leaving a trail of our mixed cum as he went. Then he added a third, depressing my tongue and stretching so far into my mouth, I had to fight off choking.

When I didn't sputter around his fingers, he rewarded me with a wicked smile, memories of the way he'd trained me to suck his cock flashing across the backs of my eyelids when I blinked slowly to settle into having his hand in my mouth.

"I still want to put my whole fist inside of you." He twirled his fingers, spreading them out against my tongue. I swirled my tongue around the digits, licking him clean of the sticky and salty cum.

Even after coming, my cock hadn't gone soft, something about his mouth against mine, now the taste of him in my mouth...it had me fired up and beyond control.

"There's the whole day left for us," I reminded him, the words garbled around his fingers.

Kale gave me a quick smile, pulling his hand out of my mouth. He traced my lips with his freshly cleaned fingers, then grabbed my face from the underside of my chin. He tilted my head back, and I stared down my nose at him while he shifted my head from side to side, inspecting me...regarding me.

"I'm going to save that for later." He said it with a sense of finality that brokered no argument. "For when we're on the other side of whatever's coming next."

His hand fell into his lap and I collapsed forward, resting

my forehead against his shoulder. Kale's arms came around me again, and he kissed my ear with a heavy breath.

"Come on, princess." He patted the top of my ass with both of his hands, encouraging me to untangle myself and stand, which sounded like the last thing in the world I wanted to do. "It's time to get the day started."

When I huffed and nestled closer to him, Kale chuckled and grabbed my ass, standing and taking me with him. Heat flooded my cheeks and I buried my face into the crook of his neck as he carried me out of the kitchen and toward the stairs. He stopped with one foot raised onto the first riser, one hand on the banister.

"I'll kill his both if you make me try to carry you up these," he said.

I reluctantly unwound my legs from around his waist and slid to the floor. At this angle, I was taller than him by at least a handful of inches. I stared down at him, appreciating that he gave me the time to admire him fully before I took a backward step up the stairs. He matched me, step for step, until we were safe on the landing, then he picked me back up, slanted our mouths together and pressed my back against the wall.

Kale rutted into me, thrusting up with one hand gripped around the underside of my thigh, the other flat against the wall beside my head. He kissed me like it was the last time we were ever going to kiss, tearing himself away from my mouth to lick and suck his way down my chin and my jaw to my throat. He moved like a man possessed, and I threw my head back, closing my eyes and letting the intensity of *him* swallow us both.

CHAPTER 31
KALE

THE REST OF THE DAY AND NIGHT PASSED IN A BLUR OF SWEAT AND tears and bruised skin. Before either of us knew it, the sun was up and Christian buried his face into my armpit, legs tangled through mine. I stroked my fingertips down the curve of his spine to the swell of his battered ass and back up again.

"Princess." I kissed the top of his head. "Let's get you in the shower."

"No." He shook his head, sucking in a long inhale, nose still buried in my pit. His cock surged in response, jutting hard and wet against the outside of my thigh.

I'd lost myself in him, lost all sense of time and propriety, and it was only the annoying alarm on my phone that broke through the haze to let me know our time had run out.

"I promised you'd go home," I said softly.

"I knew I heard that asshole's voice." Christian rolled onto his back, our legs still half twined together. "I can't believe he came all the way here to bring me home."

"The sooner we get it over with, the sooner we can see each other again."

I told him that, hoping it wasn't a lie. I didn't know anything about his life back home besides the little he'd said, but I'd watched the news my entire life. I'd seen more than one royal walk away from their duties in the name of love or boredom. I knew anything was possible, but the one thing I didn't know was the cost.

"I don't want to shower," he grumbled, fully twisting his legs away from mine and sitting up in bed. His hair was a disaster, mussed and matted from all the tugging on it I'd been doing no doubt.

"You smell like sex."

"Good." Christian bent his legs at the knee and dropped his forehead on top of them. "I want them to know."

I scooted toward him, kissing the visible knobs at the top of his spine until some of the tension leaked away and his arms fell down toward the sheets.

"This is hard for me too," I said, watching as he flung his legs out of bed and onto the floor. Another pause with his bent back and defeated shoulders. "This isn't what I want."

He muttered something under his breath that I didn't hear, and I didn't ask him to clarify because I wasn't convinced the message had been meant for me in the first place. Christian finally stood, staring out the window and giving me his back. His thighs and ass were speckled with purple and red bruises from my hand and from a belt, and I knew there was a mark the shape of my mouth on the inside of his thigh where I'd sucked a bruise there that I hoped would outlast the rest.

"Why don't you go make some coffee," I suggested, crawling out of bed and steering him toward the doorway. "I'll get you packed up."

He drew his teeth between his lips and nodded, shuffling out of the bedroom...still naked. Gathering Christian's belongings from my bathroom and bedroom proved to be a herculean task, one I was glad I'd taken on for myself instead of delegating to him. I took my time carefully folding his shirts and his pants, tracing my fingers over the starched cuffs and collars as I went. He didn't have a lot with him, but with every garment I picked up, my room smelled more like him.

After I made sure I'd collected all of his toiletries from the bathroom and tucked the monogrammed leather case into his bag, I zipped it closed and set it in the hallway. I'd left an outfit out for him, a pair of jeans and a black button up shirt that I'd yet to see him in and no underwear. I wanted the denim to rub against the marks I'd made for him the whole flight home. If I couldn't touch him, it was the best I could do. Swallowing back something that tasted like regret, I dressed in a pair of gray jeans and a black v-neck shirt and headed downstairs to join him in the kitchen.

The coffee was brewed and poured, two mugs sitting on my small breakfast table with the newspaper in front of my usual seat and Christian there in front of the chair on his knees. When I entered the room, even though his back was to me, he sighed out a long breath, chin dipping toward his chest.

"What are you doing down there, princess?" I smoothed a hand through his hair, coming around his kneeling form to sit in my seat. He shuffled closer to me and rested his cheek against my thigh. I knew better than to ask him to join me at the table, so I passed his coffee down to him.

"I like it here," he answered.

I didn't know if he was talking about New York or at my feet. I didn't think it really mattered.

"I like you here too." I took a drink of my coffee, knowing at that point, we were on borrowed time.

We finished our coffee in silence then, with a defeated sigh and without prompting, Christian climbed to his feet and shuffled back to the bedroom. He returned five minutes later in the outfit I'd laid out for him, his hair still pulled every which way. He hadn't even bothered to brush it.

"I stole your cologne," he said.

I arched a brow. "The whole bottle?"

"Yes."

"Alright."

"And your deodorant," he said, folding his arms over his chest.

"Alright." I stood up and opened my arms to him. "Did you take my soap and shampoo too?"

He walked right into my embrace and melted against my chest.

"I left you mine."

Something in the middle of my chest twisted in an unforgiving way and I wrapped my arms around him just as someone knocked softly at my front door.

"I didn't think you'd called a cab already." Christian sounded betrayed, his grip on me tightening.

I'd seen Christian a lot of ways, but never like this. In these moments, he was more a scared little boy than the brave, yet spoiled man I'd fallen in love with. He moved timidly, like he'd broken a neighbor's window and was about to have all of his allowance taken away. Though, I didn't imagine Christian had spent a lot of time playing catch with his parents as a child.

"I didn't."

"Is it my brother?" he asked, lips pressed against my chest.

"It's probably Niko," I said.

"Lesser of two evils, then."

Christian stepped back and reached for his bag, and it was reflex that had me smacking his hand away. He worked his jaw side to side, looking up at me with guarded eyes.

"I don't want you to go like this," I said, smoothing my hand down the buttons on his shirt.

"Then I have to stay forever, Kale."

"This little interlude isn't forever. This is a break and then we need to figure it out for the real world. We agreed, didn't we?"

"It's going to be hard," he whispered.

I hooked my finger over the top button of his shirt and pulled him toward me. He came without protest, and there was another knock at the door, which we both ignored.

"You can do hard things," I assured him. "You're going to sit on your ass for the whole flight home, putting your weight on all those bruises I left you. That's not going to be easy."

Christian's cheeks pinked, but his mouth twisted into a tight frown. "Don't send me away with a fresh hard-on that you can't help me with."

"I'll help you with it when you're home. Once you're back in your room and alone, call me and I'll talk you through it."

The knot in my chest twisted tighter, and I tried to swallow past it, even though I felt like choking. Everything in my body was screaming at me to send Niko away, to keep Christian here for me forever, but my brain knew better. Keeping Christian here would only hold off the inevitable for another day at best. He had his life and his responsibilities that he needed to take care of before either of us could figure out what a future would look like for us. Of course we'd talked about wanting to be together; we'd agreed that was the end goal. The undecided factor of the whole equation was the how, with neither of us sure of how we'd get there, only trusting in the end that we would. Christian trusted me in the role of a dominant—*his* dominant—and he was holding me to my word that we would figure out a way through. The only thing left was for me to have as much trust in myself so I could prove him right.

Christian rubbed his nose with the knuckle of his pointer finger, blinking quickly and turning away from me. He grabbed his suitcase and dragged it toward the front door. I understood how hard it was for him to walk away, because letting him go was just as hard for me, but if he for a second thought he was going to go without giving me a proper good-bye, he had another thing coming entirely.

"Christian." My voice cracked and I cleared my throat. "Stop."

He was three feet from the door, and he came to a stop, his back to me. I closed the space between us, reaching out with tentative fingers and curling them around his hip. A shiver tore through him, and he shook his head.

"Please don't make me go," he whispered, the plea sounding watery with unshed tears.

"I don't want to be an escape, princess."

He turned, our toes so close together he stumbled as he spun. Of course, I was there to catch and steady him, a fact which seemed to send him right over the edge. Tears leaked from both corners of his eyes, and I saw a flash of that petulant and troublemaking man I'd met on the street outside the ballet what felt like so many weeks before.

"If you make me go, I won't come back," he lied.

"Don't say that."

His lower lip quivered, and I gently wiped tears from his cheeks. His eyes scanned my face, even though I didn't know what he was searching for. I imagined he wanted to see me being as affected by his pending departure as he was, but what he couldn't see was how it took every ounce of willpower I'd ever possessed to stop myself from reaching around him, opening the door, and telling Niko to kick rocks and not come back.

"What if they won't let me come back?" he asked next, cheek hollowing as he chewed it.

Another knock at the door, this one more insistent.

"Then I'll come get you."

"Why then and not now?" he asked. "Why do I have to even go if you'll just chase me in the end?"

"Christian, we talked about this." I took his cheeks into my hands, and his entire expression faltered and fell apart. He tried to shake his head no, but I held him still so I could keep looking at him, even if this was far from the last impression I wanted to have of him.

"You're going to go face your responsibilities like a man," I said. No, I demanded. He worked his jaw, swallowing back a small sliver of his frustration. "Because that's what we agreed. It's what I told you to do, right?"

"Yes," he whispered.

I gripped his face tighter and he screwed his eyes shut.

"Yes, Mr. Sheffield," he corrected, and then it *was* my turn to fight back the wave of a thousand kinds of emotions I had no capacity to process in that moment.

"I love you," I promised, giving his face a shake until he opened his eyes and looked at me. "I love you, and you are mine."

"Your what?" The corner of his mouth twitched, even though he was still crying.

"My good boy." I kissed the tip of his nose. "My princess."

He tried to smile through the tears, lifting onto his toes and slanting our mouths together. The kiss wasn't long and it wasn't deep. It was his tear-slicked lips against mine, and he tasted of sleep and coffee, and before I could ask for more, he tore himself away.

Another knock at the door, and Niko's voice calling out his name.

"Hold on! You insufferable fucking hired man!" Christian shouted over his shoulder.

The change in tone was enough to break the smallest amount of tension in the moment, and when he turned back to me, he had half a smile on his face. I leaned in and kissed him again, as soft and chaste as he'd done for me. I didn't want it to feel like a goodbye kiss for either of us because that's not what it was meant to be. This break wasn't anything more than a layover.

"I love you more than I thought I could ever love another person." I sniffed, moisture welling up in my eyes as I wiped the never-ending tracks of tears away from Christian's face.

I slid my arm around him and walked us backward until the doorknob was in my hand.

"And I know that this hurts, princess."

"Don't you fucking dare," he warned, a fresh batch of tears falling down his cheeks.

I managed enough of a grip on the knob that the door opened, and even though I registered Niko's frame on the porch, I didn't give him so much as a second glance. I kept my eyes focused on Christian, giving him the same thing I demanded in return.

"Keep your eyes on me," I rasped, walking him back until his heels hit the threshold of the door.

He shook his head, and Niko took his suitcase.

"Kale," he whimpered.

Another step and he was out of my house, on the stoop with Niko right behind him.

"Christian." I gave him a weak smile, lips stretched into a tight line. "Eyes on me."

He gave me a jerky nod, then took a step down the stairs backward, with his gorgeous and trusting stare still locked on me. I shifted my weight, leaning onto the door to hold me up, and then he and Niko were through the front garden and at the gate on the sidewalk. There was a black town car idling against the curb, and Niko left him there to stow his suitcase in the trunk. It wasn't enough time—it wouldn't ever be enough time.

I wanted to hold him again, kiss him again, because I didn't know how long it would be until I got to do either of those things again, but if Christian were back in my arms, I wasn't sure I had the strength to let him go again. And for as much as we both wanted him to stay, leaving was what he needed. He had the opportunity to assert control of his life for what might be the very first time, and that would only make the power exchange between *us* even sweeter in the end.

Niko dragged Christian across the sidewalk, a hand on his head to lower him down and tuck him into the back seat of the car. Christian tucked his feet inside and blinked, doing his best to offer me some bravery in his expression.

I wondered if I was that transparent, if my struggles to remain strong were as evident on my face as his were.

"I've got him from here," Niko assured me, closing the door to the town car, stealing the image of Christian from my vision.

The comment sounded so idiotic, I couldn't even stop the flash of a smile that I felt building around my mouth.

"No, you don't," I said to Niko, even as I stared through the pitch black tint of the back window, knowing Christian was still following orders, keeping his eyes on me. "But he has himself now, and that's enough until I can have him again."

Niko didn't even bother locking the door to my apartments after we returned home. He hadn't spoken a word to me since he tucked me into the back seat of the town car in front of Kale's house. Short of offering me a tissue after I well and truly broke down about the road ahead, he didn't acknowledge me at all.

"Will you let Parrish know I made it back?" I asked while Niko was still in the doorway.

"Yes, sir." He hesitated, then asked, "Anyone else?"

I had a very dead cell phone in my suitcase with a burner email account that was my only real way to get in touch with Kale. I knew I needed to get my act together, go to my father and demand some basic liberties, like a cell phone with an actual phone number and a data plan. Let them read my text messages—I didn't care. I couldn't keep living the way I had been, but before that...

"No," I muttered, throwing myself face-first onto my bed.

I wanted to wallow awhile.

Parrish was already in cahoots with Kale, so I knew he'd

hear through the grapevine I'd made it home all right. And even though we'd tearfully talked about me calling him for a wank upon my return, I didn't have it in me to touch my dick or hear his voice just yet.

"Very good," Niko said, sounding like it wasn't very good at all.

He closed the door and the room lapsed into a silence as miserable and overwhelming as the feelings unfurling in my stomach. Flopping onto my back, I kicked off my shoes and covered my eyes with my forearm. My skin still smelled like Kale's soap, his sweat. I wondered if I licked the backs of my teeth, could I taste him there? I didn't bother to try, tired of crying and content enough to save that little sliver of anguish for later in the day. Instead, after what felt like a lifetime of staring at my ceiling, I fell asleep.

I woke later to the creaking of my mattress and a weight settling somewhere near my hip. My brain was foggy with love and sadness and sleep, and I stretched my fingers out, reaching for Kale to drag him back to bed.

"You're here," I murmured, eyes still heavy from my unplanned nap. I didn't know what time it was, what day it was. Didn't even know which way was up, but Phillip's quiet voice was as shocking as a bucket of ice water on my face.

"Of course I'm here," he said, prim as ever. "Unlike you, I enjoy living here."

I rolled over, scooting up and resting my back against the headboard and folding my arms protectively in front of my chest. I'd been dreaming about Kale. Bits and pieces of the fantasy still floated in the front of my head, even now that I was awake. His skin and his mouth and the things he said to me, the way he sounded when he called me princess. Shifting away from my brother and crossing my legs, my jeans abraded the very real bruises on the backs of my thighs, and I winced.

"There's the reaction I love when people see me come into a room," Phillip said, rolling his eyes.

"What do you want?" I grumbled. "Here to tell me to fall back into line and pull my weight?"

The argument was old and tired, and I wasn't sure I had it in me to hear it one more time.

"Yes, but—"

I cut him off, lifting a hand. "I know it by heart, Pip."

My brother's mouth contorted into something sad at the use of his old childhood nickname.

"You don't need to tell me again."

"I think I do."

"It's not going to stick," I told him, climbing off the bed and walking a few steps toward the window to try and shake off some of the sleep and jetlag that was weighing me down. I wasn't going to roll over and take his and my father's control anymore. I wanted to find a way back to Kale, and for that to happen, things needed to change. "But I'm glad you're here because there is something I need to talk to you about."

Phillip watched me with an amused expression, but didn't interrupt me. I'd expected further protest and every nerve in my body was ready to fight and argue. Conflict, I could do. Civil conversation, not as much. But he wasn't going to give me an inch, only adjusting his position on my bed so he could still see me as I paced around the room.

"I don't want to live like this anymore," I said.

He raised a brow. "Your life is of your own doing, Christian."

I barked out a sharp laugh, running a trembling hand

through my hair. "My life is orchestrated how you and father think it should go."

"Father," he said.

"What about him?"

Phillip cocked his head to the side like we were kids again and he'd explained something rudimentary to me and I still wasn't grasping the concept. "How Father thinks it should go."

"And who are you, if not a tiny father?"

"I'm taller than him."

"And twice as insufferable."

Phillip huffed out what sounded like half a laugh, and I turned my stare toward my feet to try and hide the smile that had started to pull at the corners of my mouth. I rested my ass against the windowsill, fingers curled around the wood frame for support. Phillip rotated around my bed, sitting cross-legged at the foot and resting his hands primly on the footboard. Something about seeing my brother in that pose was laughable, but all it got out of me was a rough chuckle that tore out of my throat like barbed wire.

How had my life gotten so out of hand? Had my decisions ever truly been my own or had this always been the expectation? Christian Davenport-Spencer, youngest son of King Arnault, perfectly content to be the headline maker and one to watch out for. I had no chance at shaking up the monarchy, so I would just make everyone around me miserable in the process.

"Father's way of ruling is not sustainable," Phillip finally said, which caused my head to snap up. He studied me from across the room with a cool and unflappable expression on his face.

"Then why do you go along with it?"

"Because it's my job, Christian." The answer earned me another eye roll, which looked so much more than out of place on his face. "Because he's far more stubborn and stuck in his ways than either of us will ever be, but unlike you, I have the slightest sense of self-preservation."

"What do you think my entire life has been, Phillip?" I shoved off the window and stalked toward him, coming to a stop on the other side of my footboard. It was the first time in as long as I could remember when I looked down at my brother, because he *was* taller than my father, taller than all of us. "Everything I do is just me trying to hold on to the smallest shred of my sanity. Of myself."

Tears burned in the back of my throat, and I swung away from him, swiping madly at my eyes like I could preemptively stop them from falling if my fingers worked fast enough. Behind me, the bed creaked and Phillip came to stand beside me.

"I don't think I can imagine what life for you has been like, Christian, nor do I want to, but my days are overflowing with duty and responsibility and tactical decision-making."

I cut him off with a snort, but the scathing look he shot me silenced any further protest or sass.

"I cannot get him to ease up on you if you insist on continuing to act like a child who needs constant supervision," he said softly.

I scoffed. "Like you've even tried."

"Christian." He sounded tired, beaten down, and I glanced at him from the corner of my eye, maybe seeing him for the very first time as the man he was, not the man he'd been in my head.

Phillip was my oldest brother, but he was also a husband, a father, and next in line to the throne. That came with more burdens that I'd ever understand, but he'd also been groomed for that from the second he was born. While our names were the same, our upbringings couldn't have been more different.

"Pip."

"Do you think you would have made it to America last week without some sort of intervention?" he asked carefully, like he was picking every word with the utmost care and consideration. "Do you think that you would have been able to stay?"

I swallowed.

"You sent Niko after me," I reminded him.

"I *brought* Niko," Phillip corrected. "Or, rather, he offered, but..."

"I don't understand what you're saying," I said.

"What I'm saying is we are on the same team, and I need you to start acting like it," he snapped. Phillip's hands flexed and relaxed, and then the cool and composed mask was back on his face like he was ready to engage with Parrish's father about some foreign conflict or whatever they did behind closed doors.

"I'm going to need you to explain this to me like I'm five," I said.

"I'm heir to the goddamn throne, Christian. I don't need to explain myself to anyone." Phillip tugged on the cuffs of his shirt and shook his head, sidestepping away from me to take his leave.

There wasn't any air in the room and I still didn't have a phone that worked, and I should have told Niko to get in touch with Kale and let him know I was dying back home without him. It didn't matter what we'd talked about before I left because I couldn't do any of it without him. My brother and father terrified me, they always had, and I worried one day I would push too far and lose it all.

Maybe today was that day.

Without warning, my legs gave out and I slid down to the floor with a disgruntled and very un-royal noise. It was enough to catch Phillip's attention, and he stopped, turning back to glare at me over his shoulder. But when he saw me on the floor, something in his face softened, if just for a second, and then he approached me and dropped down into a squat.

"Come on, Pisstian." He pressed the side of his finger against the underside of my chin, thinking that use of his childhood nickname for me was going to somehow be enough to soften me to the reality of what I'd walked back into.

"That's not as cute as you think it is," I grumbled, letting him coax my stare up to meet his.

"It's perfect for you."

"It's cruel," I said, jerking my chin against his finger, but he held steady. "Pip is adorable and culturally recognized."

"Pip is appropriate for an heir to the throne," he agreed, "Pisstian is better suited for a man who's going to do so much more than his older brother ever could."

"Like running off to America for a booty call?"

"That man is far more than a booty call," he said, sliding down onto the rug and again crossing his legs. He let his hands fall loose into his lap, and in unison, we both sighed under the weight of it all.

"I love him," I whispered. "I want to be with him."

"Then you should."

Snorting at the absurdity, I gestured around the room. "I tried. You brought me back."

"Your American sent you back," he corrected, "because he promised me that he would. Because he understands that love isn't everything, Christian."

"I think I liked Pisstian better."

"Duty comes first for me," he said, ignoring me.

"I know."

"So I have to maintain tradition until I don't have to maintain tradition. Do you hear what I'm saying to you?"

Phillip tilted his chin until I looked at him, finding a sudden and unexpected truth on his face that I'd never seen before. I replayed the conversation we'd just shared, even though I'd tried my best to ignore most of it while it was happening. I'd tuned my brother out so long ago, that I never even noticed when the words coming out of his mouth had shifted away from being a mimicry of our father's and into being something of his own.

"Phillip."

"Do you hear me?" He pushed himself into a standing position, knee cracking as he righted himself. Phillip adjusted all his cuffs and his hems, then smoothed his hair back as if it had dared to come out of place during our little emotionally stunted heart to heart.

"Why didn't you just tell me that before?" I asked, mouth falling slack as realization dawned.

"I thought we covered this already. I'm heir to the throne. I don't need to explain myself to anyone." He spun on his heel and strode toward the door, back straight and shoulders squared.

"I want a cell phone, Pip!" I shouted after him.

He stopped, hand on the doorknob. Years of repetition had conditioned me to expect a biting denial to my demand, but instead he answered me with one quick nod of his head. Phillip let himself out without another word.

We'd never been an *I love you* kind of family, but I'd seen as much of the confession in his concession than I ever had before. With the door closed between us, the air finally returned to the room and I sucked in a breath so deep it made me dizzy. My spine crumbled and my arms went tingly, and I fell onto my back, spreading out like a starfish on the floor. Staring up at the ceiling, I breathed easily because, for the first time in years, I felt like I had the tiniest semblance of control over my own life and that meant everything was going to turn out okay in the end.

Even if it turned out to not be true, I had no choice but to believe it.

I slept like shit and washed myself with Christian's soap to convince myself he was closer to me than he was. Parrish had texted to let me know Christian was safe at home, back under the rule of his father, but Christian had yet to reach out to me on his own. I don't know what I expected, but...

Silence hadn't been it.

I emailed him once, then threw myself into work with more focus than anyone who worked with me or for me would have liked. When Stefan's glaring absence became too much to bear, I finally gave in and called my brother.

"Do you still want a job?" I asked.

"Yes!"

"Your first job is to do something with those rotting pumpkins from Mom and Dad, then get your ass down here and help me get my schedule back in order."

"Thank you, Kale." My brother sounded more excited than I'd ever heard him. "You won't regret this."

That was yet to be seen, but at least I knew Ford wasn't going to fuck Boston for two reasons—one, my brother was straight, and two, he was my *brother*. Either way, for better or worse, I'd given him the job he wanted which felt to me a lot like Boston's first step out of the city and back to the farm. I'd deal with the ramifications of that later, though. My schedule was a mess, my brain was a disaster, and I stared out the window while I waited for my brother to show up and dig me out.

"This isn't like you," Boston observed...three hours later, after we'd gotten everything in my life back on track. "You're one of the most diligent and stringent people I've ever met."

"Right, well, I went and fell in love with a prince who isn't answering my emails now, so my head isn't quite as in the game as it normally is."

Boston stared at me, brows knit in confusion, then he blinked and laughed.

"That's a good one," he said. But when my expression didn't change, his was quick to. "Wait. Were you serious?"

I dropped my forehead down onto my desk at the same time someone knocked on my door.

"Ignore it," I told my brother, but he was already on his feet and across the room.

"Is Prince Charming back in the real world?" I heard Ford ask from the doorway.

Rolling my head over so my cheek pressed against the cool wood of my desk, I sighed in his direction. "Am I the prince in this scenario or are you talking about Christian?"

"Holy shit." Boston stepped aside to let Ford into my office. "You really are dating a prince?"

"I don't think you're the damsel in distress here." Ford threw himself down in the guest seat that had just been occupied by my brother. "Glad to see you back amongst the living with your cock in your pants."

"Can you watch your mouth?" I forced myself to sit up, adjusting my tie. "My brother is here."

"Your brother is the same age as you, and not that I've personally checked, but..." Ford raked a devilish look up my brother's body. "I'm sure he has a cock."

"Don't," I warned.

"Uhm..." Boston cleared his throat, fidgeting with his tie, which wasn't nearly as well-knotted as it had been before Ford's arrival. "I can go."

"You're on the clock." I pointed to him and then the second guest chair. "Sit down."

Ford quirked a brow. "On the clock?"

"Ford Carlisle." I turned my finger toward my insidiously horny best friend. "Don't you dare."

He held up his hands, a calculating smirk playing across his mouth while he leaned back in his chair and stretched out, clearly making himself at home. Boston settled into the second seat, reaching across my desk to pull his laptop closer.

"There's just one last thing on your list we haven't gotten to," Boston said.

Even though I'd let my calendar get unruly since I met Christian, I knew—in painstaking detail—what every item there entailed, and I knew which had been left behind during my brother's impressive scheduling overhaul.

"I'll do it later," I said.

"Call Beamer," Boston said at the same time.

Ford made an amused sound in the back of his throat, and I had half a mind to crawl over my desk and strangle the man with my bare hands.

"What's so preposterous about that?" I asked him instead.

"Is that man of his even going to let him answer your calls?"

"If he doesn't, he's going to have a bigger problem than he already does," I countered, squaring my shoulders. "I'm sure he'd rather manage me on the phone than on his porch."

"They have a doorman," Ford said conversationally. "You wouldn't even get to the elevator without his approval."

"How do you know that?"

"Because I talk to Beamer once a week," he said.

I snapped my mouth closed, biting my lips together until it hurt. I truly had been the biggest piece of shit to Beamer when he introduced us to Dalton. I'd made peace enough before Beamer left New York for Los Angeles, but there was still a lot left unsaid. The conversation I had with Alex at The Black Door echoed around my head as a reminder.

"Of course you do."

Ford feigned confusion. "He's my friend, Sheffield. That's what friends do."

"I think it's time for a lunch break." I stood abruptly, shoving my chair back so hard it almost crashed into the wall. I was well aware of the fact I was being unfair to both of them, more overbearing than I had any right to be, but the silence from the other end of my phone had already started to wear me down. Knowing it was hypocritical of me, I wondered if Beamer felt the same way when my name never flashed on his caller ID. Especially knowing that Ford, of all people, had gone out of his way to maintain contact...

I felt like the asshole I'd always told people I was.

"That's why I'm here," Ford said, standing and giving a quick adjustment to his suit jacket. "I know it's your first day back out of the sex bubble, and I wanted to make sure you were taking care of yourself."

"I'm a whole adult, Ford. I can manage a meal on my own."

"Probably so, but not today." Ford squinted at Boston. "Did you want to join us?"

"No," I answered, shooting my brother an apologetic look. "He's my brother, but he's still an employee."

"Right." Ford gave a conciliatory shrug to both of us. "And you have that pesky no fraternization rule."

"I have that you don't fu—you know what. Never mind." I turned to Boston. "Are you good on your own today? We can get dinner later and level set the day."

"I'm fine, Kale," he assured me, snapping his laptop closed and tucking it under his arm. "I'm also a whole adult capable of managing a meal on my own."

At that, Ford laughed and knocked his elbow so hard into my ribs I thought I was going to keel over on the spot.

"I forgot how much I like you, Boston."

My brother shot my best friend an endearing grin, and I rolled my eyes at both of them.

"Lunch is fine," I said to Ford, "but can you give me five minutes? I'll meet you in the lobby."

"Sure thing." Ford gave me a mock salute and then ushered Boston out the door, closing it behind him with a quiet click.

Carefully—and slowly—as if I could drag out the inevitable, I wheeled my chair closer to my desk and sat back down. There were still no messages on my phone from Christian, and I did my best to ignore the way that made my heart crack a little bit. It was basically what I'd asked for. Before he returned home, I'd been clear that he needed to face his responsibilities there like a man, but I'd foolishly assumed that was something he would do with me by his side, at least in spirit. That was clearly not the way things had gone, and I tried my best to swallow back any impending panic I felt about all the *other* things his silence could mean.

In my gut, I knew if something was wrong, Parrish would tell me. I also knew that, absolute worst case scenario, I could reach out to him and check up on Christian. But if the separation was how Christian chose to get his next steps in order, I wanted to respect that and give him the control to make those choices on his own.

I swiped through my contacts and mentally marked off the last unscheduled item on my always overflowing agenda.

"Hello?" Beamer sounded confused when he answered the phone, and I would have rather thrown myself out the window than listened to that tone come out of his mouth again. He had been—he was—one of my closest friends since college, and I'd ruined better than fifteen years of friendship over a childish pissing match because I didn't like his new husband. The worst part was, I had no reason not to like Dalton Fox. The man was head over heels for Beamer and as committed as any man ever had been. He was exactly the kind of man I should have wanted for my friend, and yet...

I was jealous because he stole my best friend from me.

"Hey." My voice cracked, and I cleared my throat. "Hey, Beamer."

"Kale." I could almost hear him smiling. "I didn't expect to hear from you."

"I know. I'm sorry."

"What for?" he asked.

The list of things I had to apologize for was nearly as long as the agenda it had taken Boston and me half the day to sort through.

"Can I say everything?"

He was quiet for a moment. "You could."

I could, but that would be the easy way out.

"I'm sorry for not calling sooner." It was the least of the things I had to apologize for, but that somehow made it the easiest place to start. "And I'm sorry for...for how I treated Dalton."

"How did you treat him, Kale?"

I closed my eyes and sucked in a breath that felt a lot like razor blades.

"I thought being gone, some of that dominance would wear itself out of your attitude," I mumbled.

"My husband is more dominant than you give him credit for."

"I saw you on your fucking knees for him, Beamer. I know how dominant the man is," I snapped, scrubbing a hand down my face.

"And that's the problem."

"I'm sorry that I'm possessive and that I'm jealous," I grumbled. "Sorry that I was mean to him."

"Anything else?"

"I'm sorry that...sorry that I treated you like you were lesser for—" The words caught in my throat, wrapped around that jagged breath I was still struggling to get into my lungs. "For being submissive to him."

I'd been a dominant in the bedroom for as long as I'd been having sex. The roles and the responsibility came naturally to me, and the thought of giving up any of that had previously been enough to make my skin crawl. I appreciated the bravery and power that came from submission, as I'd been witness to it on plenty of occasions, but it wasn't until Christian that I well and truly understood the strength it took to go to your knees for another man.

"Apology accepted," Beamer said quietly. "Now tell me about your prince."

A startled laugh broke free of the tangled mess in my throat, and I leaned back, pressing my phone against my ear. "It's that simple, then?" I asked.

"You're my best friend, Kale. Of course it's that simple."

Relief washed over me, plastering me down to the chair, and I was happy to let it roll back toward the wall as my weight settled deeper into the seat.

"Thank you," I said.

"It's nothing."

If I closed my eyes, I could see him waving me off, his blond hair coiffed back like nothing in the world had ever dared to bother him. That was what I wanted for Christian, as well. To be under my care, my watch, so that he could feel as carefree as Beamer sounded now that he had Dalton's ring on his finger.

"Ford says you're really in deep with this prince you met," he said, picking up a conversation like I wasn't the worst friend in the world, freshly forgiven of my sins.

"I love him," I admitted, and Beamer responded with a content little sigh.

He always had been a lovesick fool. And now with Christian on the brain, I wasn't any better.

"I'll tell you everything you want to know, but I have Ford in the lobby and I'm worried he's going to try and sleep with my brother if I don't get out there soon, so can we catch up later tonight?"

"Isn't Boston straight?"

"As an arrow, but you know how Ford can be with his fingers when he sets his mind to something."

"You don't really think he would try to sleep with your brother, do you?"

I turned off my computer screen, then grabbed my wallet and keys, tucking them into my pockets and heading toward the door.

"I don't think so, but he wouldn't be where he is today if he didn't seize an opportunity when he saw one."

Beamer laughed, and I promised I'd call him later that night, then I headed out to make sure my best friend kept his hands off of my brother.

CHAPTER 34

CHRISTIAN

I jerked off every day, thinking about Kale telling me how to jerk off. With my eyes screwed shut, holding back what felt like an endless supply of tears, I shot load after unsatisfying load across my chest and then went about my day. Phillip had gotten me a proper cell phone, but the temptation to call Kale and beg him to come steal me away was too strong. I needed to deal with the disaster of my life and my legacy before I could go to him and, worst case, I knew Parrish was letting him know I was alive.

I spent a lot of time thinking about not just the games we'd played together in the bedroom, but also what all of it meant. There were more than a few sleepless nights when I stared out the window at the familiar crisscross of the garden trellis, wondering why it was okay for him to tell me what to do and not anyone else. Why I *wanted* him to tell me what to do. Why it made me hard.

The only conclusions I'd reached were that he was right—it was because I made the choice to give him that power, when in the other parts of my life that option had been taken from me. It didn't hurt that Kale was one of the sexiest people I'd ever met in my life, and I didn't just mean that in regard to his looks. It was his personality and his heart, the way he carried himself and moved around the world too. I loved all of it, wanted all of it.

A soft rap at my door reminded me it wasn't time to daydream about Kale, though.

"Coming," I hollered toward the door and to Niko on the other side of it.

My brother hadn't been back to see me since my first day home, except to give me the phone. He used Niko as a guard—and as a messenger. It was finally time for the monthly council meeting, and my brother had strongly encouraged my attendance. With one last check of myself in the floor-length mirror tucked into the corner, I adjusted the cuffs of my blazer and twisted tight the knot on my tie, then joined Niko in the hallway.

"You don't have to walk me there." I rolled my eyes at him and set off down the hallway. "I know my way around here better than you do."

"If you think I don't know about the tunnels, you're mistaken, sir." Niko's face remained unflappable, and he pressed his finger against the black monitor in his ear, walking behind me toward the council rooms without another word.

I had no idea how or when Niko learned about the tunnels. It wasn't like I was staging extravagant escapes these days or anything, but it was still an interesting piece of information to have. Maybe I hadn't been as clever with my escapades as I'd imagined. Knowing now that Phillip had all but condoned my jaunt to America, I wondered how many other adventures he'd had oversight on. The thought of it put my nerves on high alert. Another choice I thought was mine, having been taken away from me without my consent.

By the time I reached the chambers, the meeting was already in session. They didn't wait for me, and why should they have? It wasn't my place to attend, but it was my right. When I pushed the door open, a dozen heads swiveled in my direction, none of them looking pleased to see me, save for Phillip, whose mouth only twitched up from a frown for the blink of an eye before turning downward again.

"We'll be with you when we're done, Christian," my father said dismissively, "this doesn't concern you."

To his right, Parrish's father stood, one hand pressed flat against the buttons on his blazer like his fingers were the only thing holding him together. He glanced down at Phillip, then back at my father. The only thing that betrayed his loyalties were a slight shift of his weight toward my older brother. It appeared Phillip really had been busy behind the scenes.

"I just need a minute, Daddy," I said, striding toward the table and yanking out the chair farthest away from where all of them sat. Phillip gave me a tired look. This wasn't the script we'd talked about, but I'd had too much time to myself over the past two weeks to think, and even though his plan was a good one, it was his.

Not mine.

"Mind your manners," Phillip warned me, shooting daggers down the length of the table.

"Quite right," I agreed. "My manners have always been an issue, haven't they?"

After meeting Kale, something inside me had shifted. It was a subtle thing at first, but now sitting in this room where I used to play hide and seek, I'd never felt more rooted in the truth that this life wasn't for me. Phillip had hatched a plan that would effectively force my father into an early retirement, and with my brother's ascension to the throne came a whole wealth of freedom for me, but...I'd go from being under my father's thumb to my brother's. And while Phillip was the lesser of two evils by far, he was still...

Not Kale.

Not me.

"Christian."

"I know we've talked, but—" I gave my brother an apologetic look at the same time my father sent him a scathing one.

"Have you now?" my father said, directing the question to my brother and not me. "You had your orders."

More of the same.

More of the same.

People talking about me like I wasn't even in the room.

"Christian needs more allowance than you've given him," Phillip said to my father. Bless him, for going to bat for me even though I'd walked into the room and ruined his grand plan. All I was supposed to have done was come in and pretend I was interested in whatever was happening, take the lashing from my father, tuck my tail between my legs, and retreat. Rinse and retreat until my father believed I'd really decided to fall in line... and then Phillip was going to make his move.

I was tired of waiting. It was time for me to make my own moves.

"I need more than you'd offer me too, Pip," I said, barely loud enough for them to hear at the other end of the massive wooden table. Flattening my palms against the wood, I yearned for the small and unfinished table in Kale's kitchen where we'd spent so much of our time. I missed his coffee, the way his brow furrowed when he read the newspaper. I missed how important I felt when he was next to me.

"Just wait."

"I've waited my whole life."

Behind me, Niko moved closer, like I was a flight risk. In a way, I was. They just didn't know that the next time I flew would be the last.

"Christian." My father rubbed the bridge of his nose, shoulders sagging under the weight of how bored my abstinence made him. "Now really isn't the time. There are important matters on the table."

I didn't know what came over me, but before I could talk myself out of it, I climbed up onto the table and folded my legs together. Sitting on my ass and facing them both with my head cocked to the side, I begged the question, "Then what's one more?"

"Christian, get off the table," my brother said, voice low.

"Christian, get off the table. Christian, go away. Christian, this doesn't involve you. Christian, Christian, Christian." I snapped my fingers against my thumb, making mocking hand puppets of them every time I repeated my name. "There's nothing here for me, and I'm ready to make that official."

Phillip stood up so quickly, his chair almost fell over. "We talked about this," he reminded me.

"You talked and I agreed," I countered. "My whole life that's what it's been. Other people saying how it's going to go, and me agreeing because I didn't know any other way. But now I do."

Kale had taught me I could say no.

That it was my right to say no.

"Pip." I swiveled toward my brother, using the childhood nickname because I hoped it would soften the blow. I knew my abdication wouldn't ruin any of this plans. If anything, it would throw our father far enough off-balance that it would be easier for Phillip to make his move. "I appreciate everything you've done for me, everything you were going to do, but it's still..."

He pursed his mouth, a long and slow exhale deflating his chest, and then he nodded. He was conceding his place to me, but even without his approval, I would have carried on the same course.

"I want to move to America," I said, before correcting myself. "I'm *going* to move to America."

"I can carve a role out, Christian," my brother hedged.

I shook my head, smile tight. "I know you could."

"Like hell you could," our father interjected.

"I'll deal with you later," Phillip warned him. Parrish's father took one more step closer to my brother, so slight I didn't think either of them noticed.

"Please, just let me cut these ties and go. It'll be easier for you and it's the only thing I've ever asked for."

"It sounds like you're demanding."

"I want to go," I said. "I don't want to lose my brothers and my nephews in the process."

"You won't, Christian," my brother promised.

"This isn't a life someone can just walk away from." My father's face was red as a beet. If we were cartoons, steam would be shooting out of his ears.

"You sure?" I stood up, heels clacking against the wood of the table before I jumped down onto the floor. My landing echoed around the room, and I gave everyone on the other end of the table a haphazard shrug. "Because I'm about to."

"Are you certain?" My brother stood, which caused me to stop.

"I am."

"Alright," he said with a solemn nod. "Take Niko with you, though."

"I don't need security. There's not even room for him."

"Take him, and we'll figure out a long-term solution before the end of the month."

"Phillip." My father shot him another horrible look, but Parrish's father was already behind the right side of my brother's chair, and just like that, the alliance had shifted.

"We'll talk soon, Christian. This isn't cut and dried."

"I know."

Phillip nodded, then turned his stare down toward my father. "Now that *that* is out of the way, we can move on to those pressing matters you alluded to earlier, starting with the duration of your time on the throne."

"Is he staging a coup?" I whispered to Niko, suddenly very interested in whatever the politics and the arguments were about to devolve into.

"Let's take our leave, sir." Niko placed his hand against the small of my back and ushered me out of the council room, closing the door behind us with a heavy thud.

"It was never fun before." I pressed my ear against the door, trying to listen in. "I'm not in such a rush if it's entertaining."

Niko had been tired of me since the first day he was hired and put on my detail, and it showed in the lines around his eyes and the way he had to work to fight from smiling at me.

"Sir." He gestured toward the hallway ahead of us.

"I don't think you have to call me that for much longer." Reluctantly, I peeled myself away from the door and set off after him, back toward my apartments. "I'm pretty sure I just told them I didn't want to be a prince anymore."

"Well, until then."

I pulled the cell phone from my brother out of my pocket and dialed the only number saved in the contacts. Kale answered on the first ring, his voice full of confusion and also the most beautiful sound I'd ever heard—hope.

"Christian?"

Hearing my name come out of his mouth after so much quiet between us was enough to take me out at the knees. I stumbled and pressed my back against the wall, clutching the phone against the side of my face and humming like a lovesick teenager for how excited I was to talk to him again.

"Princess," he purred into my ear, and I swallowed, closing my eyes and diving in head first.

"It's done," I whispered, tears thick in my throat, even though I wasn't sad. In fact, I'd never been happier. "I'm coming home."

It was seventeen days between when Christian called me to let me know he was ready to come home and when the wheels of his jet touched down on the tarmac. Time moved slower than molasses as the plane taxied in, and it must have taken another seventeen days until the plane door was opened and Christian's familiar silhouette came into view.

I pushed off the trunk of my hired black town car and strode toward the stairs with more purpose than I'd ever felt in all the years of my life. Christian all but ran down the stairs, and heat exploded in the center of my chest when his body crashed into mine. Wrapping my arms around him, we stumbled back a step before I was able to regain our balance. I buried my face in his hair, not surprised in the slightest when I inhaled a nose full of my own scent instead of his. Christian rubbed his face against my shoulder like a cat and let out a relieved-sounding sigh as he melted deeper into my arms.

"Welcome home, princess." I kissed the top of his head and he tightened his arms around my waist.

"I missed you," he murmured.

Movement at the top of the stairs pulled my attention away from the man currently clinging to me, and I watched as Niko stepped onto the stairs, adjusting the dark black sunglasses on his nose.

In the end, there was no way around taking Christian and Niko as a package deal. Phillip was insistent, and there was no amount of bartering Christian could manage to get out of it. It felt like a fair enough concession because it brought Christian home to me, which was all we'd wanted in the first place. The palace was still managing Niko's pay—and his lodging—which was an apartment they'd found three blocks from mine. Christian had fought against his brother tooth and nail, but I wasn't sure how Niko felt about the move. The man was a vault and extremely dedicated to his job.

I knew Niko's employment was not going to last in the long term. The hours and rules that Christian's brother had set out were not sustainable for either of them, and Christian had spent his entire life evading the rules set by his family. His rejection of his role as prince should have been the final nail in that coffin, but I appreciated Phillip's love for Christian winning out in the end. To Phillip, New York wasn't anything like their home, and I did believe he only wanted the best for his brother.

I walked Christian back to the car and opened the back door for him to climb in. He didn't give Niko a passing glance as he did, but Niko knew his place, climbing into the front seat without a word. I'd already rolled the privacy partition up, so as soon as Christian and I were alone in the back seat, I was on him. He moved at the same instant, our mouths crashing together with all the desperation and need I'd been horrible at internalizing.

Christian scrambled onto my lap, taking my face into his hands and spearing his tongue into the back of my mouth. He was already hard, his body primed and hot against mine, even through all the layers of our clothes. I steadied my hands on the swell of his hips, pressing my head against the headrest as I let Christian steer and deepen the kiss.

"I missed you too," I whispered against the corner of his mouth when he gave me a second to catch my breath.

He grunted, ready to dive back in, but I dug my nails into his waist to stop him. All it got me was a grimace and a slower incline back toward my mouth, which I was able to avoid.

"Settle down, princess," I said, leaving a closed-mouth kiss against his upper lip. "We have all night."

"It's been weeks."

I let my hands drift up his sides and down his arms, curling my fingers around his wrists for a quick squeeze. Christian shivered, his weight twisting against my cock, which was as excited to see him as the rest of me. He whined out a moan, head falling back as he realized the movement of his hips made enough friction for both of us to feel better than we had in far too long.

"I know."

Releasing his wrists, I returned one hand to his waist and collared his throat with the other. Tipping his head back, I bent closer and dragged my nose up the long angle of his neck to his ear, kissing and nipping as I went.

"Kale, please," he whimpered, trying to turn his head to catch my mouth.

I tightened my fingers, keeping him where I wanted him.

"Seventeen days and you've already forgotten who you are when I'm around."

The time we'd spent apart hadn't been spent solely on moping over the separation. I'd caught up on work that I'd neglected during his stay, I'd gotten Boston settled in his new role as my assistant, and I'd paid enough attention to Ford that I was confident he wasn't going to try anything funny with my brother. Boston had gotten rid of the pumpkins in time for ten pounds of carrots to show up, which we donated to a local soup kitchen.

I'd also made a trip to Los Angeles to see Beamer.

I wasn't keen on the idea, and I didn't think Dalton was either, but Beamer was so excited to show me around town and introduce me to all of his new friends. I had a good time, in spite of myself, and left feeling safe in the knowledge that one of my oldest friends was as well taken care of as I'd ever wanted him to be. Dalton and I reached as much of a truce as we ever would, and all was well again in my world. The only thing missing was Christian, and now...here he was.

"I haven't forgotten," he grumbled. "I'm just waiting for you to show me."

Seventeen days and the attitude and arrogance from the first night we met were back in full force. The glint in his eye let me know the biting comment was intentional, and when I shoved him to his knees in the back seat of the car, it didn't shock me when his eyes immediately started to glaze over.

"Is this what you wanted, Christian? What you were asking me for?"

He licked his lips, pressing his throat against the palm of my hand where I still held him. God, he was a gorgeous man.

Inside and out. And I loved him. I loved him beyond reason and beyond measure. Beyond sanity sometimes.

He blinked slowly, tracing his tongue over the swell of his bottom lip. "Mr. Sheffield," he whispered.

"Insatiable little thing." With my free hand, I wrestled out of my belt, tugging down my fly and freeing my cock. It sprang free in front of his face and he swayed, entranced. "You don't remember how to act, but do you remember how to suck my cock?"

"Yes, Mr. Sheffield."

I released his throat and hooked my finger around the base of my shaft, pointing it toward his waiting mouth. "Show me."

Christian swallowed my cock down to the back of his throat on the first go, fighting past the inevitable gag and wave of spit that built in his mouth. He sealed his lips around the base of my dick, right above my fingers, then he hollowed his cheeks and sucked. His mouth was hot and tight, and I lifted off the seat to chase after another inch of his throat. Christian groaned as I fucked his mouth, and I knew there wasn't long left for me. I wasn't ready for the pleasure to end, and I didn't think he was either, so I forced myself to look out the window instead of down at the perfect tousle of his dark hair or the glazed pleasure on his face. He bobbed up and down my thick cock, his hands splayed out over my thighs for balance, then he swallowed, the muscles of his throat gripping at the head of my cock with the practiced level of precision I'd spent the last three weeks missing.

"Just like that, princess," I soothed, threading my fingers into his hair and holding his face down in my lap as I came. He didn't even sputter as I shot jet after jet of hot cum straight into the back of his throat, the orgasm tearing through me like a tsunami. My vision flashed white, his teeth grazing against my shaft as he readjusted my length in the cavernous heat of his mouth, and then the car rolled to a stop on the curb in front of my house.

I was nowhere near ready to take my dick out of his mouth, and I wasn't sure if either of us possessed functioning legs, so I locked the doors and let my eyes fall closed. Christian hummed, seemingly content to hold my cum in his stomach and my cock in his mouth until I went soft and started to slip out. He rested his cheek against the inside of my thigh, and I finally loosened my grip on his hair, stroking the strands back into place as much as I could manage.

"They're going to know what you did back here," I murmured, and in response Christian closed his eyes and smiled.

"Let them."

Christian kissed the sticky tip of my cock and tucked me back into my pants, adjusting himself on the floor of the car between my feet.

"I want to go home," he announced, face flushed and lips swollen.

I scrubbed a hand down my face and helped him back onto the seat beside me, then unlocked the doors and busied myself helping him out. Niko was already out of the passenger door, and I didn't shy away from his curious stare. He took in the state of our rumpled clothes, the shine on Christian's lips and the dark pools of his pupils, then cleared his throat and held open the gate to my house.

I'd never shied away from having sex in public, and I wasn't going to start now, but Niko was different from the patrons at The Black Door, and I needed to set some ground rules.

"Go inside," I said to Christian, kissing the side of his temple and giving his hip a gentle tap. He looked at me like he wanted to protest, his mouth already parted and primed to say something bratty, but I cut him off, shoving my keys into his hand before he could get started, "I just need a minute with Niko."

At the mention of his name, Niko's spine went straight, and Christian looked between us before doing as he'd been told and letting himself into my house.

Into our house.

"I need to know if you're uncomfortable with this," I said to him plainly. I didn't think I needed to elaborate because I knew for a fact, at some point, they'd found out where Christian and I had run off to the night we met, and I knew for certain they knew where we'd gone on his last trip to America.

"I don't know what the rules are, sir," he said, adjusting his sunglasses to keep his eyes hidden from me. It was New York in November, we hadn't seen the sun in days. The sunglasses were far from necessary, but who was I to tell *him* what to do.

"Does it make you uncomfortable to know that I fuck him?"

"I know you fuck him," Niko said.

"Is it a problem if I fuck him when you're around?" I pressed.

"I think it's just part of the job."

"I don't know what you think of me, Niko, but I can keep it in my pants until you're off duty if that's what I need to do."

"You're supposed to pretend like I'm not here, sir," he said.

Closing my eyes, I traced my tongue across the front of my teeth, glancing toward the front door, which Christian had left open.

"I'm not a big fan of unwilling consent here," I told him, "and even though you're not an active participant in this, I don't want to go too far."

"Just." He worked his jaw back and forth. "You can pretend like I'm not here, sir. I don't have an issue with what the two of you do together."

"Do you....enjoy it, Niko?"

"I don't mind watching," he said softly, "or hearing. I'll bring your bags in, Mr. Sheffield, and then I'll take my leave for the day. Just let me know if the two of you plan on going out and I'll come collect you both. Thank you."

Christian's security was actively dismissing me with a whole head full of things to think about. I didn't have an answer to anything he'd said to me, so I headed into the house to find Christian. He was in the last place I expected to find him—the kitchen. Sitting at my breakfast table, he spun my morning paper in a circle with the tip of his finger.

"I think Niko likes to watch," I said, collapsing into my usual seat.

"Watch what?"

"People fucking."

Christian arched a brow. "Did you invite him to watch us?"

"I wouldn't do that without asking you first, but no, not directly. I was trying to be mindful of his proximity to *our* relationship and the things he might see and hear. I wanted to know if I needed to keep my hands off you when he was around," I explained.

He inhaled a deep breath, mouth twisted in thought.

Niko's presence posed an interesting problem for us, because while it was one thing for Christian to suck me off or bend over my lap and get spanked at The Black Door, Niko was more of a captive audience.

"Does it bother you if he hears us sometimes?" I asked. "If we're out at dinner or a movie and I want to touch your cock?"

I leaned around the table and grabbed the seat of his chair, yanking him closer. Our knees bumped together, and I ripped off his belt and tugged his slacks down around his knees. His cock tented his briefs, a quickly spreading dark spot from how wet he'd gotten sucking my cock in the car. I loved how Christian was always primed and ready. Loved how responsive his body was to mine.

"I don't mind," Christian whispered. "Maybe if he hears how hard you make me come, he'll understand why I had to return. Why you were it for me."

He angled his head to the side, expression thoughtful. I pulled down his briefs, tucking the elastic waistband behind his balls so his whole package was on display for me.

"I'm it for you?"

Christian blinked slowly and nodded even slower. "I thought that was obvious."

From the other end of the house, the front door closed quietly, and I stood up, holding out a hand for Christian.

"We're alone," I said, pulling him toward me. His pants fell around his ankles and his hard cock dragged a drop of precum across my thigh. He groaned at the pressure, and I reached behind him to knead his half-covered ass in my hands.

"Disappointing."

"My little princess is an exhibitionist," I murmured,

kissing the shell of his ear. "I'll take you to the club later so you can show off, but for now, it's time to take off your clothes. I need to show you how happy I am to have you home."

Christian scrambled out of his clothes while I undid my fly, freeing my erection. I loved having him naked while I was still dressed, feeling the heat of his skin through the soft fabric of my clothing.

"Bend over the table," I rasped, stroking my cock and rubbing precum down the length of my shaft. "I want to fuck you bare."

"You better," he pleaded, already half over the table with his ass on display.

I knew there was a way this was meant to happen, and I'd deal with all of that later. I was too excited to have him home, too ready for the rest of our lives together to begin to worry about what was proper and what was right.

"Get yourself ready," I said. "Put your fingers in your mouth and suck them like you sucked my cock earlier."

Like always, Christian did what he was told, spitting on his fingers before reaching back and shoving them all the way up his ass with the first thrust. He whined, bucking forward as he pulled his fingers out, spreading himself open for my cock. I moved behind him, spitting down onto his fingers to help him along, then I spit on my cock for good measure.

"This is going to hurt, princess," I warned.

"I fucking hope so." He withdrew his fingers for the last time and spread his ass cheeks apart. His hole was pink and slick with spit, the tight muscle puckering into a small gape as he pulled himself open.

"This is going to be quick."

"I fucking hope so," he said again, throwing me a near desperate look over his shoulder. "I missed you so fucking much, please don't make me wait any longer."

I couldn't tell him no, not anymore.

Even with our mixed spit, the slide into his body was tight and dry. I had to hold him down against the table to get all the way inside, but once I was fully seated, he settled and shivered, that familiar peace washing over his body as his brain flickered toward subspace. He whispered something under his breath that I didn't think was meant for my ears, and then he clamped his muscles down around my shaft like a vise grip. Gritting my teeth against the pain, I gathered as much spit in my mouth as I could, slid my cock out of him to the tip and spit on my shaft before fucking back into him. The way he writhed underneath me, alternating between moaning and screaming my name, paired with the tight and unobstructed heat of his body, was enough to bring me toward an orgasm in record time.

"I'm going to come."

"Please. Oh God, *please.*"

Two more snaps of my hips were all it took, the friction of our bodies an aphrodisiac meant to drive me mad with lust. I pulled out at the last minute, ropes of cum flying out of my tip and painting stripes against his ass and the small of his back. My knees trembled, and I used the head of my cock to smear cum around his asshole before pushing just the tip back in. A shiver tore through his entire body, table legs skittering across the floor beneath the weight of our bodies.

"Did you come on the table, Christian?" I asked, clearing my throat and blinking the room back into focus.

"Probably. Maybe." He reached an arm down between his legs. "Yes."

I popped the head of my cock out of his body and took a step back, smacking his ass and rubbing more of my cum into his skin.

"You're gonna pay for that one, princess. Get your ass upstairs right now so I can collect my punishment."

KALE TOOK ME TO THE BALLET.

When he proposed the idea, I was quick to balk, suffering traumatic flashbacks from the last time I had to pay off a bathroom attendant so I could escape through the employee hallway. But it was that romp through the back alleys of the Upper East Side that had brought me to him, and honestly, he didn't give me much of a choice in the matter anyway.

Our relationship was equal, in the way that I was happy to let Kale drive most of the time because I knew his choices would always put my own best interests above his. It didn't feel anything like what my growing up had been, with everyone making decisions about me and for me in the ways that benefited *them* the most. So Kale hadn't asked if I wanted to go to the ballet. He'd told me we were *going* to the ballet. When I frowned at the idea, he took me over his knee and spanked me until I was begging him to go.

He'd assured me he would make it worth my while, but the last thing I'd expected was a thick, vibrating plug getting shoved up my ass while I was trying to take my tux off the hanger. Kale had pressed his hand against the small of my back, then went to his knees, shoving his tongue so far up my ass I saw stars. With spit and cum leaking down my balls and the backs of my thighs, he filled me right back up with that massive toy, then resumed fussing with his bowtie in the mirror.

By intermission, I was losing my mind, the unpredictable vibration pattern enough to push me to the edge only to drag me back away again, over and over and over. I reached over the arm of the chair and grabbed Kale's thigh, throwing my head back and hoping my arousal wasn't as clear on my face as it felt through the rest of my body.

"Are you okay, princess?" he asked, threading our fingers together and dragging his thumb across my knuckles. Even that chaste and simple touch was electric, sparking through my fingers and up my arms, straight to my brain and then everywhere else.

"I'm about to come in my pants," I warned through grit teeth.

"I doubt that." Kale kissed the top of my hand, and reached into the interior pocket of his coat. The buzzing started again.

"Please at least get me a drink," I pleaded.

"I need you sober for what I have planned later."

"I'll be dead by later if you don't let me take some of this fucking edge off."

I wasn't done sassing, but he moved quick, grabbing my chin between this thumb and finger, giving my whole head a yank to the right so I faced him head on.

"You'll survive this," he said, leaning in and dusting a tease of a kiss across my mouth. I leaned closer to him on instinct, my body magnetized and attuned to his in a way I'd never thought possible. "But there's no telling if you'll make it to the morning."

With that, he released me and stood, cutting off the buzzing inside my channel with a disappointed huff of a breath.

"I'll go get you some wine," he said, stepping around me without so much as a parting glance.

I waited until he was in the aisle to shift my weight off my legs, pulling my cell phone out of my pocket to find a series of messages from Parrish.

Parrish: What's the best hotel out there? There's so many
Parrish: Can you answer me please.
Parrish: It's not even ten there. Where are you?
Parrish: Are you having sex?? Oh God.

I sighed, tapping out a reply.

Me: We're at the ballet and I've been busy. Why do you need to know about hotels?
Parrish: For when I come visit you in the new year.
Me: You're visiting?
Parrish: Of course I am.
Parrish: Don't worry about the hotel. Niko already gave me a list.
Me: We'll talk about this later.

Kale was back with a little plastic cup of wine in hand, and he sat down just as I returned my cell phone to my pocket.

"Everything all right?" he asked, settling in with a smirk

that I wanted to lick off his face. He was always hot, but when he was *on*, the attraction I felt for the man was next level.

I took a healthy swallow of the wine, but my body was already on fire. "Please promise me I can come again as soon as we get home," I begged.

He leaned in close, pressing his mouth against my ear, then he whispered, "I promise you can come as soon as I let you come."

By the time the ballet was over, I couldn't even hold Kale's hand. Every inch of my body was primed and I'd been hovering somewhere on the precipice of an orgasm since I finished the intermission wine. When he ordered the car to an address that wasn't home, it took every ounce of strength in my body to not burst into tears on the spot and beg him to reconsider. The car eventually pulled up at the curb alongside The Plaza, and I carefully followed Kale to the elevators and up to a suite on the twelfth floor. There was a voice in my head that said *this is the same room*, but words didn't make much sense by the time the door closed behind us.

Before he could get his shoes off, I was on my knees, palms turned up on the tops of my thighs with my head dropped back and my eyes barely open. I focused on breathing, but everything felt so good, it hurt.

"Impatient little thing," he murmured, kicking the inside of my knee with the shiny toe of his shoe. "I can't do much with you until we're stripped down, though, princess."

He pressed his shoe against me again and I managed to pluck the laces undone and get his feet out before collapsing forward onto my hands and knees with my face pressed against the carpet. I mumbled something, but I didn't know what I had tried to say. Kale pulled his belt through the loops of his pants and dropped his hand down, letting the tip of the leather dust the floor right in front of my nose.

"You really are gone, aren't you?" He joined me on the floor. Trailing his hand down my back, he rucked up the tails of my tuxedo jacket before yanking my shirt from behind the waistband of my slacks. He reached around me with one hand and fussed with my belt until it came free, then he tugged down, exposing my bare ass and the vibrating plug that had been stretching my hole for the past four hours.

"Yes, Mr. Sheffield," I whimpered, rolling my face against the carpet.

"I had so many plans for you." He petted his fingers over the flared base of the plug and moved behind me. The expensive wool of his slacks brushed against the back of my legs, the entire position awkward because my pants were still around my knees, keeping my legs pinned together.

"Sorry," I whispered.

"Never apologize for being a slut for me, princess." Kale twisted the plug and gave it a tentative pull. The flared base teased against my rim and my cock jerked, precum already leaking from the slit like a faucet. "I'm a smart man. I can think on my feet."

Before I could respond, Kale took the plug out of me, turning my hole into a slick and needy gape, which he filled in one thrust with his lube-slicked cock. My arms quivered and gave out, chest slamming into the floor, and then he had my shirt and my tux in his fist, his cock hammering in and out of me with a punishing pace that shoved my body across the room with every snap of his hips.

"Fuck, Christian."

As much as I loved when Kale called me his princess, the

times he slipped and used my name felt just as special. And then his arm was around my chest and he hauled me up. With my back pressed against his front, he kept fucking up into me, his other hand fisting my achingly erect dick. It didn't even take a full stroke before I came, cum jetting out of my tip like a geyser. Everything went white, then black, and my face was back in the carpet, Kale's hands tight around my waist and his own hot load was filling my asshole.

Kale grunted as he came, the only sound I could make sense of over the deafening slam of my heartbeat in my ears. And then it was his breathing, my breathing...his mouth against my ear whispering things that sounded like words, even though my brain couldn't assemble them together. He rolled me onto my back, his cock sliding out of me with a wet pop, and I whined at the loss of him.

Everything felt good and everything hurt, and I didn't dare open my eyes, even as I felt Kale get up and walk away. It wasn't long until he was back, wrapping a warm and wet cloth around my cock, which he stroked clean with a little more force than I would have thought necessary. But if I'd learned anything, it was he knew what I needed better than I did.

And that was the real magic I'd found with Kale.

My attitude and my rank in life had never meant anything to me. Kale wanted me for me, and it was through being on my knees for him that we both learned who *I* was meant to be. I sometimes wondered what Niko thought of me, of the things he had to know Kale and I did together behind closed doors, but he'd never given any real indication he judged either of us at all. Maybe it wasn't so outlandish, self-exploration through sex. All this love and understanding that I'd found with the most wonderful man by my side.

"I love you," I murmured, rolling onto my side.

Kale sat beside me, his belt discarded in his lap alongside a bright flash of blue I hadn't even thought about in what felt like an entire lifetime. I reached out and trailed my fingers over the chevron cut edges of my royal order.

"Where did you get this?" I asked. It should have been left behind, part of the deal I'd cut with Phillip when I stepped away from the family.

"I've had it the whole time," he said softly, weaving the length of ribbon through his fingers. "I never gave it back to you."

I huffed, closing my eyes and pressing my forehead against his knee. "That's property of the crown."

"Hmmn." Kale wrapped the ribbon around both of my wrists, tightening it into a knot. "And now it's property of mine. Just like you."

Shivering, I pried my eyes back open, blinking up at him in absolute awe. He must have felt the same, because he smiled down at me before pushing onto his knees and then his feet. He hooked a finger around the knot in the order and pulled me to my feet beside him. Though, my legs were far less coopera-tive and I barely made it to my knees. Kale didn't seem to mind, leading me into the bedroom and helping me half onto the bed without another word.

With my arms stretched across the mattress and my waist bent forward, I scrambled to keep my feet beneath me. My pants had slid down to my ankles, but until Kale helped me out of my shoes there wasn't much to be done about it. With rough hands, he helped situate me so my back was arched and my ass was on display then he stepped back and made an approving sound.

"Bear down, princess. Let me see you try and push my cum out of your hole." He snapped the belt, and my muscles clenched and relaxed on their own. Hot cum bubbled out of me, sliding slow and sticky toward my balls and my thighs, and the approving sound Kale made was enough to send more chasing after.

I didn't know if I'd ever get enough of the way he made me feel, the absolute out-of-this-world sensations of bliss and pleasure that he always managed to bring me through. Even if we weren't having sex, the mere act of submitting to Kale was enough to make me hard and horny for him. I didn't know much about the things we did, beyond how they made me feel, but he assured me that wasn't usual. He told me I was perfect, that I was special, that I'd given him the most precious gift every time I kneeled for him.

I believed him.

"Do you know what I want?" he asked, snapping the belt again.

"Tell me, please."

"I want to spank you until you come, just like the first time we were in this room," he said.

So, I was right. It was the same room.

That was oddly romantic and sentimental in a way I would have to process and pick apart when I had more of my wits about me.

"Yes, please. Thank you, Mr. Sheffield."

The leather cracked cold and sharp against my ass, and I scrabbled against the bedding with my fingers, trying to hold on for dear life. Kale didn't wait to swing the belt again and again, raining down a firestorm of leather against my ass and the backs of my thighs.

It hurt.

It hurt.

It *hurt*.

And then it was heaven.

I relaxed my fingers, my body, my mouth. Leaning into the pain, it transformed into bliss, and my cock pulsed, flattened between my stomach and the sheets, leaking another orgasm into the expensive cotton. The belt continued to come down against the tender flesh of my backside, even as I jerked and writhed through another orgasm so rough it almost sent me unconscious. I screamed, desperate to get away from the onslaught, but not willing to go. Kale would stop when I'd had enough, and even though it hurt and burned, I knew I could take more. I knew in my bones that another strike of his belt or three and I would be in an absolute perfect freefall of pleasure.

He gave me that many and then some, crawling onto the bed with one knee beside my waist. Then he bent over, hand flat against my back and his mouth hot against my ear. I wanted to thank him, to promise him my devotion and love for the rest of our days, but the only thing that came out of my mouth was drool, leaving another puddle of wetness on the very expensive hotel sheets.

"Princess," he whispered, licking against my ear, my cheek. "Christian, are you with me?"

I hummed, pressing my body against his.

"Use your words," he coaxed.

I swallowed, my throat sore and parched, but I croaked an affirmative reply, which earned a smile against my temple.

"Come back a little, Christian. I need you to hear what's coming next."

"I'm here," I rasped, "I'm here."

"Good. You know I love you, right?" Another kiss, another lick, his hot tongue erasing the tears and spit from my cheek and my chin.

I shivered, cock smearing through the quickly cooling evidence of my second release. "I love you too, Mr. Sheffield."

"Don't forget that, because you're in a lot of trouble, princess."

I should have been alarmed. If I had any sense about me, my muscles would have tensed and fear would have snaked its way up my spine. But I was so happy, so in love, so aroused and cared for, that I didn't even know what it meant to be afraid anymore. Instead of all those reactions, I blinked slowly, half a frown pulling at the corner of my mouth because, while I wasn't afraid of the outcome, I couldn't pick out what I'd done wrong.

"Why?" I asked, the ribbon of the order biting into my wrists in a way that only made me more aroused than I'd been when he first tied it.

"You've had two orgasms so far and I never even gave you permission for one." Kale made a pleased sound, righting himself and plucking at the buttons of his shirt before shrugging out of it and leaving him on the bed, half dressed and fully hard. I closed my eyes, burying my face—and my apology—in the sheets. "Now dig in, because we're both going to have a long fucking night. I hope you're up for it."

A soft smile fell across my mouth and I nodded slowly, ready for whatever the night—and the rest of our lives—was going to bring.

"I'm all in, Mr. Sheffield."

ALSO BY KATE HAWTHORNE

—

Trophy Doms New York

All In

Tied Down

Cried Out

Roughed Up

Trophy Doms Social Club

Humbled

Edged

Praised

Bound

Shared

Giving Consent

Worth the Risk

Worth the Wait

Worth the Fight

Worth the Chance

All in Good Time

Necessary Space

Necessary Time

Duality

Dual Destruction

Dual Surrender

Dual Defiance

Two Truths and a Lie

A Real Good Lie

A Cold Hard Truth

A Matter of Fact

Room for Love

Reckless

Heartless

Faultless

Fearless

Limitless

A Very Messy Motel Brothers Wedding

Relentless

Secrets in Edgewood

A Taste of Sin

The Cost of Desire

A Love Made Whole

Secrets in Edgewood: The Complete Series

The Lonely Hearts Stories

His Kind of Love

The Colors Between Us

Love Comes After

Until You Say Otherwise

<u>STANDALONES</u>

Rebound

One for the Road

Daybreak - Vino & Veritas

Unfettered

Dreams

A Thousand Lifetimes

<u>COLLABORATIONS</u>

With E.M. Denning

Irreplaceable

Future Fake Husband

Future Gay Boyfriend

Future Ex Enemy

With J.R. Gray

May the Best Man Win

ABOUT KATE HAWTHORNE

Kate Hawthorne is an author of character-driven LGBT romance, known for crafting emotionally intense stories with high heat and a kinky twist. Creating worlds where passion and angst collide, Kate's books bring you complex protagonists in fearless pursuit of self-exploration and happy —if not sometimes unconventional—endings for everyone.

Visit her website
http://www.katehawthornebooks.com

Sign up for Kate's newsletter
http://www.katehawthornebooks.com/extra

facebook.com/authorkatehawthorne

x.com/katewriteswords

instagram.com/kate.hawthorne

patreon.com/katehawthorne